To Liz, again. You're my huckleberry.

Her Adventures in Temptation

She was the first to speak. "It is nonsense to think either one of us has to sleep on the floor. We are both reasonable adults, we can sleep together in the bed. It serves no one if we are exhausted tomorrow. I, for one, do not see the point of foregoing a good night's sleep because of this," she said, gesturing vaguely toward the bed. "Besides, we're already guilty in Society's eyes because we've dared to spend time together alone. Why not be comfortable while being scandalous?"

"Fine," he agreed.

They stared at one another, the familiar impulse toward seduction coming over Simeon. This would usually be the moment where he would grasp the lady's shoulder, gently drawing her into his arms for a kiss.

But this was Miss Allen, and she was paying him for his services—and not those services, mind you—and they were about to get into that bed together with no intention of doing anything. He needed to put all thoughts of seduction out of his mind.

Even though she was looking up at him with those soft brown eyes, her lips slightly parted, her remarkable brain likely thinking all sorts of intriguing things.

Those curves being . . . curvy. Reminding him of Rubens's most stunning works, the painter showing just why women were so distinctly different from men.

He was not doing a good job of putting all thoughts of seduction out of his mind.

By Megan Frampton

HER ADVENTURES *in* TEMPTATION

A School for Scoundrels Novel

MEGAN FRAMPTON

AVON

An Imprint of HarperCollinsPublishers

HER ADVENTURES IN TEMPTATION. Copyright © 2024 by Megan Frampton. All rights reserved. Printed in the United States of America. No part of this book may be used or reproduced in any manner whatsoever without written permission except in the case of brief quotations embodied in critical articles and reviews. For information, address HarperCollins Publishers, 195 Broadway, New York, NY 10007.

First Avon Books mass market printing: January 2024

Print Edition ISBN: 978-0-06-322429-2
Digital Edition ISBN: 978-0-06-322425-4

Cover design by Amy Halperin
Cover illustration by Victor Gadino
Cover image © Anna Krivitskaia/Dreamstime.com

FIRST EDITION

24 25 26 27 28 BVGM 10 9 8 7 6 5 4 3 2 1

Chapter One

At least the cake was magnificent.

Myrtle sat splayed out on the ballroom floor, her evening gown billowing around her as she assessed which cake element to try next. She didn't generally approve of adding anything superfluous to cake, but she had to admit that the pieces of candied orange studding the top were delicious.

"Why?" her brother asked, sounding beleaguered. Which he usually did when speaking to her.

It wasn't that she *wanted* to be aggravating; in general, she just wanted to swan around wearing beautiful gowns, eat delicious foods, and indulge her need (some, including her brother, might say *compulsion*) to use her brain for more than just idle conversation and remembering which utensil to use at mealtimes.

They all did the job to varying degrees. She didn't see why there had to be a fuss about it. But apparently it seemed that Society—the world she traveled in, unfortunately, having been born a viscount's daughter—found it unsettling, perturbing, and disgraceful if one used a fish fork to retrieve an errant pea.

But that wasn't what was making her brother Lord Richard Allen, Viscount Leybourne, so irate. So aggravated.

The siblings were alone in the ballroom, the rest of the family and their houseguests having long since retreated to their beds. The party had been a rousing success, at least until Myrtle had spoken her truth. One that her brother apparently objected to.

The ballroom was in the Leybourne country estate, a sumptuous, sprawling house with well over one hundred rooms, situated on over seven hundred acres of land.

The Leybourne holdings—not Myrtle's own charms, she knew quite well—were why she had received so many offers of marriage.

And thus far had accepted none of them.

"I just told him the truth," Myrtle said with a shrug, attacking her current slice of cake with gusto.

It was yellow sponge cake with white icing, the aforementioned candied oranges a tart contrast with the icing and the raspberry jam filling.

"You told him—in front of everyone, mind you—that you could not marry him because he didn't understand Babbage's Table of Logarithms." Richard pinched the bridge of his nose with two fingers. "What do logarithms—whatever they are—have to do with marriage?"

Myrtle held up her hand to indicate that she was still chewing. Richard glowered at her, but she merely smiled—close-mouthed, of course, what with the chewing and all—and he looked away.

"The thing is," she said after she swallowed, "that it isn't just Babbage Mr. Oakes doesn't understand. I didn't want to tell him I would not marry him because he is stupid, that would be just rude." She shrugged again. "So I went with a simple notion, one his brain might be able to comprehend." A pause as she considered. "And understanding logarithms is essential in order to calculate interest on loans or payments, for example. How well an initial investment has done, and so on." She sniffed. "Mr. Oakes—or any man, for that matter—needs to know basic math if he is going to handle my considerable fortune."

A fortune which wasn't hers outright, unfortunately. Its control lay in the hands of her brother, and it seemed he was desperate to hand it over to someone else. Just not her.

It was completely unfair. It was also why she'd resolved to do whatever she could to help other unfairly placed ladies in similar situations. She would not sit by eating cake while others suffered.

She could do a lot more good with her mathematical brain than if she married some lummox who merely required her to have a dowry and then produce a massive amount of children.

Richard would not hear of it, however. Anytime

she'd even hinted at wanting something else he'd gotten that look on his face, and she wondered if he was going to shut her in the cellar until she changed her mind.

"You have refused every offer made to you, and I estimate you have had no fewer than twenty-seven proposals." That nose pinching again.

"If I had accepted at any time that would be the end of the proposals," Myrtle pointed out, not incorrectly. "Like when you say 'Oh, I found the thing I was looking for in the last place I looked!' because of course you would stop looking once you'd found the thing." She frowned. "The number is technically thirty-two, but that includes the Hollister twins and a few of Joseph's schoolmates."

Joseph, Richard and Myrtle's younger brother, was away at school, something Myrtle envied greatly. She'd had a governess, but that lady had given up when it was clear Myrtle knew more about everything than she did. Miss Rogers was currently living her best life, having made several shrewd investments on Myrtle's advice. And was Myrtle's best—and perhaps only—friend, with the exception of Myrtle's niece, Lilah.

"That isn't the point," Richard said. "And haven't you had enough cake?"

Myrtle looked down at the cake in question. "There's still more of it, so no, I'd say I haven't had enough cake. Unless you want some?" She glanced up at her brother, waving her spoon in the air.

"I do not want any cake," he ground out.

"Then why did you ask if I'd had enough?" She gestured toward his face. "You should be careful about getting so enraged," she said. "You've got a vein popping in your forehead. That cannot be healthy for you."

"I would be less enraged," he shot back, "if you would find yourself a husband!"

Myrtle blinked. "I have *found* them. I just don't *want* any of them."

Richard's gaze hardened, and she almost—*almost*—felt bad. But not as bad as she would feel if she were married to an idiot. And all of the gentlemen, and most of the ladies, Myrtle knew were idiots.

She wasn't opposed to marriage per se; it just seemed to her that if the people who were related to her by blood, like her brothers, found her so difficult to deal with that it would be impossible for someone who wasn't obligated to do so to make a go of it. Marriage was certainly good for others; she just didn't think it would be good for *her*.

Thank goodness for cake, she thought, looking down at the once-noble dessert. Her spoon had made inroads that would put cow paths to shame, and one part was teetering as though it was considering a graceless fall onto the plate.

"I cannot continue this," Richard said, though he did, in fact, continue. Myrtle was very pleased she restrained herself from pointing that out. She didn't want to make her brother's head explode. "You have to find a husband or do something because your presence here is disruptive. Regina has Lilah to launch into Society, and she is already anxious that you will do or say something to reflect badly. If Lilah isn't able to make a good match, then—"

"Then gentlemen are idiots. Lilah is wonderful," Myrtle interrupted, speaking in a firm tone. Her niece, Lilah, was beautiful and accomplished, with a lively, engaging disposition that made everyone love her. Myrtle included; she couldn't bear it if she was the reason Lilah's debut was tainted somehow. Lilah, unlike her aunt, actually *wanted* the whole "death till you part" thing. It was all she could talk about, and Myrtle could not, would not, do anything to disrupt that.

It was annoying to hear all of Richard's talk when Regina, her sister-in-law, had herself engaged in some suspect behavior, but because it wasn't brain-related it was somehow less egregious.

Myrtle didn't understand that at all. Something else to add to the list that included utensil use, marriage, and tea without milk.

She picked up her spoon and angrily stuffed another piece into her mouth. She would not be the cause of Lilah's unhappiness.

"And it is not seemly for you to interfere with the running of the estate. A lady should not spend her time balancing ledgers and badgering the estate manager. Farrows was quite upset." He took a breath, clearly trying to compose himself. Myrtle took that moment to retrieve a piece of errant icing at the corner of her mouth. "I have no choice but to give you this ultimatum," he said, his tone gentle. "You have to find a husband or do something to—"

His words were cut off by a scream.

SIMEON JONES HAD a secret.

It wasn't that he was charming. That had been known since he'd been five years old, and persuaded all the other children in the Devenaugh Home for Destitute Boys to join him in an intricate plot to raid the kitchen pantry at midnight. Three-quarters of a cherry pie had been downed by the time the scheme was discovered.

The staff spent two days getting cherry stains out of nightshirts.

It wasn't that he was handsome. Simeon was possessed of a roguish grin, a dimple on the left side of his face, and brown eyes that pierced the soul of anyone he looked at. That he was tall, athletic, and had fine, silky black hair that seemed to invite caresses was enough to place him amongst men deemed remarkably handsome.

And it wasn't that he was talented. He'd begun drawing while serving punishment for the kitchen caper, and had progressed to watercolors by ten. He was adopted into an artist's home, and she taught him everything she knew, plus supplied him with enough oil paints and canvases to fill a museum. The two of them didn't always have enough to eat, but they always had art materials.

No, it was that Simeon Jones—debonair, polished, and suave—was softhearted.

He gave money to anyone who needed it. He

rescued stray kittens, tossed coins at children and beggars, tipped extravagantly, and ended up funding a variety of ventures because he just couldn't say no.

He was therefore, as the saying went, poor as a church mouse.

It was a secret that would mortify him if anyone—even his closest friends, his four fellow orphans—ever discovered it.

It meant he didn't indulge in anything for himself that cost money, which meant his enjoyments were found in pleasures of the flesh, good conversation, and books from the lending library, the fees of which he'd persuaded the woman at the desk that day to forego.

Normally, he could afford everything, and keep his secret safe.

But three weeks ago, he'd received a letter that had skewed his entire life sideways.

Dear Mr. Jones,

I hope this letter finds you well. I am writing on behalf of the late Mrs. Wellsford, the sister of Miss Jones, your adoptive mother. I understand that this might be a shock. Mrs. Wellsford has been taking care of Miss Jones's child, but Mrs. Wellsford has passed, and the child's guardianship is passing to you. It is most urgent we receive instructions for how you wish to proceed.

The Revd William Aglethorpe

Even now, those five words—*how you wish to proceed*—made him want to punch something. *Someone.*

It wasn't the letter writer's fault, of course. But this was a child's life that hung in the balance, and in his hands. Him, whose only responsibility up to now had been to himself and his art. His adoptive mother had made his priorities absolutely clear: nothing should come in the way of his art. Not love, not comfort, and certainly not an unexpected child.

But he would not damn the innocent to the kind of life he had had.

No matter what he decided, it would all cost money. Much more money than he currently had.

His mother had died a few years ago, leaving him nothing but his belief that his art was the most important thing in his life, and that he had to do whatever was necessary to fulfill his artistic promise.

But he also had to eat and clothe himself and now he had to decide how he *wished to proceed*.

Which was why Simeon was stuck in the country, having taken a commission to paint a portrait of Regina, the Viscountess Leybourne, a job that would pay a substantial sum.

And was also why he was frantically trying to shoo the clearly inebriated viscountess out of his rooms at four o'clock in the morning.

"You shed I should creep acrosh the hallway." Lady Allen, clad only in a nightdress and wrapper, her hair undone and trailing down her back, squinted up at Simeon with an accusing stare. "I have crept, but now you're trying to get rid of me?"

The last two words were said in a rising pitch, her tone getting increasingly louder, as Simeon's mind raced. How was one supposed to handle it when a portrait subject arrived in the middle of the night for, he presumed, propositional purposes?

"If you would just return to your room—" he said, only to be interrupted by the now irate viscountess.

Dear lord, what a mess.

"I can't return to my room!" she said, all indignation.

"Uh . . ." Simeon said, taking her arm. "We can talk about this. I am certain we can reach an understanding."

She swatted his arm away, then tilted her face up in an unmistakable invitation. "Or you could just kish me."

Simeon was accustomed to people propositioning him; he'd reached his current height at age fifteen, and had had the face of an angel for a lot longer than that. But he knew full well that there were many reasons not to oblige in this instance, not the least of which was that Lady Allen was well in her cups, and could not be relied upon to make an informed decision.

He didn't know if she had mistaken his room for another's, or if she mistook his politeness for something more, or if she was just prone to spontaneously bursting into gentlemen's rooms, but it didn't matter.

He took her arm again and drew her toward the hallway, muttering indistinct soothing noises.

"No!" she wailed, so loudly it made his ears hurt. "Noooo!" And then she stopped using her words and just screamed.

To his horror, he heard footsteps, and doors opening, and saw people's faces appearing, and he closed his eyes, wishing for once he had less of a rakish reputation.

Nobody would believe that he hadn't intended to dally with the lady of the house. Furthermore, it didn't matter if they actually believed him or not; he was a bastard, a hired artist, not a respectable lady like her. That he had come specifically to paint her portrait would only intensify the belief that it was entirely his doing.

Clearly he could bid his commission farewell, which meant the orphaned child—whose name and gender he didn't even know—would have to wait even longer for how Simeon wished to proceed.

Fuck.

Chapter Two

It was an hour before Simeon sagged against his door, completely exhausted. Everyone had appeared in the hallway, including Lord Allen, who hadn't looked surprised at his wife's behavior, though that didn't matter. Simeon's fate was already sealed.

"You'll leave in the morning," the viscount said sternly, after his wife had been extricated from Simeon's side and returned to bed by her lady's maid. "And obviously you'll return the advance I gave you, since you won't be completing the work."

"Obviously," Simeon echoed.

A few people still stood in the hallway, not even pretending they weren't eavesdropping.

"I won't mention this incident," the viscount continued, "and since I believe you value your reputation, you won't either." He looked uncomfortable, and for a moment Simeon wondered if he was going to indicate he knew the truth of it. If the viscount would acknowledge that Simeon had done nothing wrong, even if it was just between them.

"It is unfortunate," Lord Allen said in a censorious tone, and the moment was gone. "But I cannot allow any scandal to touch my family. My daughter makes her debut soon, and you see—"

"I do see," Simeon said, cutting him off. "I will leave in the morning." He nodded, going into his room and shutting the door, leaning against it with eyes closed.

It wasn't that he minded so much about losing the commission itself; portraits weren't his favorite work to do, and it was always a possibility that the subject of the painting wouldn't like the result. But he did like the money. He'd negotiated a larger than usual sum because the viscount required the work to be done at his country house, and not in Simeon's London studio. Perhaps because he was aware of his wife's nocturnal behavior?

"That poor child," he muttered. How was he going to "proceed" when he didn't have the funds? He shook his head in frustration.

Which then pounded as a knock sent reverberations through his skull, since his head was tipped back against the wood.

He jerked away from the noise, staring at the door in horrified anticipation. Had the viscount ordered his staff to thrash him? Or Lady Allen herself returning, either to proposition him again or perhaps offer an explanation for her behavior?

The knock came again.

He swung the door open, bracing himself for whomever might be there.

And frowned as a strange woman stood there, her face alight with what looked like excitement.

Not again, a voice said in his head, but he only nodded to the woman. "Can I help you?"

"It is my belief, sir, that we can help one another," she said, then brushed past him to stand in the middle of his room. "You might want to close that, I wouldn't want there to be a second round of scandal." She spoke in a no-nonsense tone that dared defiance.

He shut the door automatically, then cursed himself for an idiot. But the woman didn't look as though she was bent on seduction; she wore an evening gown, now somewhat bedraggled, and with what appeared to be some icing on the lace edging the neckline. It was very finely made, of a light pink satin, with tiny sleeves fashioned out of net. She was perhaps in her mid-twenties, too old to be the viscount's daughter, and she was regarding him with an expectant look.

Who was she?

"I'm sorry, have we met?" Simeon asked.

She raised one dark eyebrow, folding her arms over her chest. "We did. Earlier this evening, in fact. I am Miss Myrtle Allen, Richard's sister."

"Oh," Simeon said, still baffled, but now even more on his guard. "Did your brother send—"

"No," she said, sounding impatient. "Do keep up, we don't have long."

"Keep up with what?" he replied, bewildered. "Have long for what?"

"We can help one another," she repeated. "As I said at your door—that one right there," she said, pointing to the item in question, "no more than five minutes ago."

"I'm sorry if I'm not following you," Simeon replied, feeling as though he was being tossed around like a ship on a very stormy sea. "Could you review how you and I can help one another?"

She gave him an exasperated look, then spoke. "You have to leave here. I would like to leave also, only for reasons I don't want to make widely known. I mean both the reasons and the fact that I am going in the first place. I cannot make either of them widely known." As though that explained everything.

"So you want me to . . . ?" Simeon said, feeling as though he was speaking to an inebriated dictionary.

"Yes, I want you to take me to London. Preferably now." She glanced around the room. "It shouldn't take you long to pack, you've only just arrived."

"No, my lady," Simeon said, wondering if he'd accidentally wound up at a madhouse. It felt as though everyone was speaking a language he didn't understand. Perhaps *he* was the madman. "I will not take you to London." And then the reality of it hit him, and he got angry. It had been a very long and trying evening. "But if I *were* to take you, after what just happened tonight, you would be irrevocably compromised, my reputation would be in tatters, and I could never find work again." He drew a deep breath. "I do not understand what might have led you to make the suggestion, but I assure you, I am a gentleman, despite what occurred earlier."

And despite my illegitimacy.

Simeon found it chafing, to say the least, that he was treated as lesser simply because his parents weren't married. Or simply because he didn't even know who they were in the first place. How could any of that be held against him, when it had literally happened long before he was born? Nine months before, in fact.

Which was why he was so determined to help Decision Child, the child he had to make decisions about "how to proceed." Simeon had had a relatively good childhood, but it had been tainted by the realities of his birth. If he could spare another human that—or at least ameliorate it by throwing a wad of cash at it—he would.

"I know you are a gentleman," she said, still impatient. "Everyone knows my sister-in-law likes to wander at night, especially after a few too many Madeiras. I am not asking you because I have designs on your person or anything." She spoke in a scoffing tone, and he nearly went and looked in a mirror to be certain he hadn't turned into an ogre in the past hour. "I need to get to London, and I know I cannot just go on my own. That is, I could go on my own, but it would be less safe. I need to *safely* go. Not to mention I'd have to walk, and they would find me within a few hours. And you are my best option." Her tone made it clear the best option was far from the actual best, but was the best she could do at the moment.

"No," he said in a firm tone. "Do keep up."

Her eyes widened in surprise. "Oh! Excellent retort. I had not expected that of you."

Why did he feel proud for having impressed her with his wit?

He reached for the doorknob as he spoke. "You need to leave before anyone discovers you here."

She uncrossed her arms to grab his wrist. This close he could see her face, which was quite pretty; she had curly, dark brown hair, brown eyes, an upturned nose, and full lips that looked as though they might burst into laughter at any time. Her eyebrows were straight, dark slashes, giving her an intense appearance.

She was substantially shorter than he, and lushly curved, the evening gown cut so as to display her lovely bosom.

"Stop staring," she snapped, and he shook his head to clear it. "My proportions are admittedly extreme, and I've calculated if I continue my current course I will only become more so."

"You've calculated?"

"Yes," she said, and he could hear a hint of pride in her voice. "I am a mathematician." She huffed out a breath. "A mathematician who loves cake."

"When you're not attempting abduction of strange gentlemen," Simeon said in a dry tone.

She still had hold of his wrist. "Seriously, you have to leave."

She only tightened her hold. "How much?"

"Pardon?"

"How much money will it require for you to give me a ride to a place you're going to anyway? I know Richard just told you to go, and I know he'd agreed to pay you a substantial amount—I heard him grumbling about it last week. How much?"

Simeon opened his mouth to refuse, to tell her nothing was worth risking his reputation and future earnings. But the amount of money he needed for the child, for the Home, and for his own survival, was an enormous pound-and-pence-shaped object in his head.

"Twice what your brother was going to pay me," he said instead.

She gave him a piercing look. "Very good. I will make it triple. I have calculated the risks, and I want to anticipate any setback." Her face brightened. "My first business negotiation! I am making an excellent start," she said, clearly talking to herself.

Simeon's chest tightened. "Any setback" would mean anything that would expose what he and this oddly cheerful woman were doing to the world at large—or, more precisely, the world that governed how he led his life. A life he quite liked, when he wasn't concerned with rescuing stray orphans. Or fending off unexpected female visitors to his bedroom.

"Agreed," he said.

She released her hold on him. "Excellent. You're not as stupid as you look."

He frowned, wanting to ask how stupid he looked, but realized it was beside the point. Even though it chafed his vanity.

"Meet me at the stables in an hour. I'll go there now and tell them to prepare your carriage."

She didn't wait for his reply, just gave a firm nod and exited, shutting the door behind her.

Leaving Simeon feeling as though he'd just encountered something he couldn't handle. A feeling he'd never had before.

MYRTLE GRINNED AS she made her way down the hall to her room. She was always able to adapt, but this was a remarkable pivot even by her standards. Once she'd seen the ruckus Regina had caused, and heard Richard grousing about portraits and money, she'd realized she could take destiny into her own hands. She could create her own future.

After all, Richard had said, *You have to find a husband or do something*; she was choosing the "do something" option.

Not that Richard likely thought she had any choice but the "find a husband" option, but that was the whole issue, wasn't it? Not being able to decide for oneself what one's future would be.

She would go to London and use her mathematical skills to assist ladies with their monies, hopefully helping them become more financially secure. The first step—the heading to London one—was clearly the most important, and she was on her way.

She would be *doing something* without saying "I do." She smiled at her own wit, relieved she could find humor in these most dire of circumstances.

Once she'd demonstrated her business acumen, and garnered support and trust from her clients, Richard would be less inclined to force her to marry.

If she was able to *do something* that would get her out of the house and have her more than earn her keep, there would be no reason to force her into something she didn't wish to do. Marriage topmost among that, of course, but also going out and about in Society—she knew she could be awkward, though it generally didn't bother her.

But if she could skip that nonsense it would make her life even better. Better than cake, better than lovely gowns, and better than math, even.

And perhaps what she did with her brain would be valued more than what she did with her utensils.

Her solution was so logical she knew Richard would never agree to it. So she had to make an independent decision. One she knew, she just *knew*, Richard would be fine with later. Much later.

"Good morning, John," she said in a soft voice to the sleeping stableman. He started awake, and she gave him a reassuring pat on the shoulder.

He'd been concerned about one of Richard's horses, so he'd taken to sleeping in the stables, which she'd known when she proposed the escape to Mr. Jones.

"Good morning, my lady," he replied. "Is there somethin' I can help ye with?"

"Yes, and I need you to be quiet about it all."

His face grew pale. Most of the staff had experienced enough of Myrtle's adventures to have natural trepidation when she required discretion.

"It's nothing, truly," she said in a light tone of voice. "Just a dispute at the house, and one of our guests—Mr. Jones—needs to leave quickly."

His face cleared. "Aye, I heard about that. He wants me to prepare his carriage?" He frowned in confusion. "Then why isn't he here himself?"

"My brother is still somewhat irate," Myrtle explained, "so he asked me to come see about it. He'll slip out later." Even though that was a total lie.

"I see. Of course, my lady. Carriage'll be ready in fifteen minutes." He paused. "I'll get the coachman up as well. He's sleeping in the stables."

"Thank you, John," Myrtle replied, giving him a coin. "That's from Mr. Jones."

"Tell the gentleman I'm grateful," John said.

Myrtle nodded, then rushed back to her room, glad that that part of the escape plan had gone so well.

The only variable in all of it was Mr. Jones.

Mr. Jones was naturally reluctant to assist, but she'd accurately assessed his situation and knew he needed funds. She was aware of his reputation as an artist, and knew that his taking this commission was below his talent, so there must have been some compelling reason. When she'd heard Richard discussing the negotiations, she'd figured out Mr. Jones's motivation. It was simple to dangle enough money in front of Mr. Jones's face to persuade him.

And what a face. Myrtle wasn't usually all that interested in people's faces if their brains weren't also attractive, but Mr. Jones's beauty rose above that standard. He was tall, with an elegant build, ink-black hair, a gorgeously sculpted visage, and an ability to make it seem as though he was focused only on the person he was speaking to at the time.

It was lowering to know he didn't recall meeting her earlier, but she was accustomed to that—the only times she got noticed by attractive gentlemen were when they'd heard about her attractive fortune and thought they had a chance of obtaining it.

"Plus," she reasoned to herself as she entered her bedroom, "this will make it much less complicated. He won't bother about me, since all I represent is money, and I won't bother about him, because he is not my future."

She busied herself stuffing a few items of clothing into her bag, regretfully removing her icing-tinged evening gown and putting on something much plainer. Lilah's lady's maid generally assisted her, but it wasn't too hard to remove the gown, though a few buttons scattered on the floor.

She wouldn't need anything fancy to wear in London since she was just going to be working. If and when Richard caught up with her—which she doubted he would do quickly, considering he had a full house party and a desperate need to avoid scandal—she'd have proven herself, and could set herself up in her own household.

Her own household. Independence.

The thought of it, the possibility of it, made her stagger a little as she packed her books: a few of Cauchy's works, even though her French wasn't up to reading them, Fibonacci's *Liber Abaci*, Boole's *Mathematical Analysis of Logic*, and Peacock's *A Treatise on Algebra*. Then she took all her money—thankfully she kept a large sum at hand, Richard was generous with her allowance. She'd have more than enough to get to London and begin her work.

If she succeeded—which she had a 37 1/2 percent chance of, she'd calculated the odds already—she could choose her own future. Richard wasn't unreasonable, he was just exasperated. Eventually, once she'd shown him what she was capable of, he would agree to let her have her fortune. By then, Lilah would likely be married.

Lilah.

For a moment, Myrtle considered waking her niece to say goodbye, and to let her know that her aunt was making a wise, logical, and well-thought-out decision in heading to London.

Even though that wasn't quite the truth. And Myrtle found it impossible to lie.

But in a month or so, her falsehood wouldn't matter. She'd have decided her own future and Richard would stop pestering her to do something she didn't wish to. She would have *done something*, and done it well. She just had to.

Lilah would be in London soon enough herself—the Season would begin in a few weeks, which was why it was imperative Myrtle go to London now.

Where Myrtle would be on her own. Forever, perhaps. Was it a lonely future she was contemplating? It might be seen that way, but the alternative—marriage to someone who wasn't nearly as capable as her intellectually—was far, far worse. The very idea of it made her feel as though she were choking.

Packed, she retrieved a cloak from her wardrobe, slipping it on and putting the hood over her head. It was five o'clock in the morning. The servants would start to rise in a half hour or so, so she had to go. Hopefully Mr. Jones understood the urgency and would be waiting for her at the stables. She scribbled a quick note, tucking it under the corner of the glass on her dressing table. Hopefully it wouldn't be noticed for hours.

And now all she had to do was go to London, set up a business and find clients, and prove she could do the work.

All before Richard came to retrieve her.

THIS WAS QUITE possibly the most ludicrous thing Simeon had ever done. And that included the interlude with a baker, the baker's assistant, and three loaves of pound cake.

He wasn't actually contemplating doing this, was he?

Hard to deny, what with hasty packing and a generally frantic feeling. He had to leave anyway; perhaps his host wouldn't know that Simeon had absconded with said host's sister.

Though that he and Miss Allen happened to depart at precisely the same time was something far beyond a coincidence.

But she'd offered him enough to be able to figure out how to humanely proceed with Decision Child. That baby deserved a chance in life, at least a reasonable chance that only money and thoughtful support could give.

"I'm being foolish," he muttered to himself as he closed his valise. He'd brought only a few things with him: his painting tools and a few changes of clothing. He didn't keep a valet—couldn't afford one—and he'd already borrowed his friend Fenton's carriage. He hadn't wanted to owe any more favors than he already did.

Fenton was off gallivanting in Paris, so the carriage was just sitting there. Simeon had made sure to tip Fenton's coachman well, though he knew Fenton paid all his staff good salaries. Fenton, like Miss Allen, was skilled in mathematics, and had worked out the benefits of paying servants well versus not. It just made common sense, he'd explained.

This way Fenton's coachman would be able to return to Fenton's home in London a lot earlier than anticipated. Simeon was actually doing everyone a favor by returning early.

"And that is the most convoluted argument ever," he said, exasperated at himself.

But the truth of it was he had to leave, and he might as well leave with a passenger. If Miss Allen was so bold as to burst into strangers' bedrooms in the middle of the night, there was no telling what she might do if Simeon turned her down. Better to keep an eye on her, at least until they got to London. She had shown herself to be fearless, if not naïve, and was willing to head off at inappropriate hours with a random stranger, it should be him and not someone less honorable than he.

If the viscount confronted him, he could explain. Maybe.

Though he strongly suspected the viscount wouldn't accept any explanation that didn't include Simeon's head on a platter. Or, worse still, him having to marry the inebriated dictionary lady.

But he was already in deep trouble with the viscount, and by extension, the rest of Society, so he might as well make some money by doing what he was going to anyway.

Thus decided, he picked up his belongings and left his room, making sure to walk softly as he made his way downstairs. Nobody was up yet, though he imagined it wouldn't be long—this was a country house, and the family and its guests kept country hours.

He pulled the door open, coming face-to-face with Miss Allen, whose expression brightened at seeing him.

"Good," she said, giving him a satisfied nod, "I was hoping I wouldn't have to drag you out."

"Drag me . . . ?" Simeon said in disbelief. Not because she'd said it—his acquaintance with the lady had already let him know he shouldn't be surprised at anything she said—but because there was no possibility a small scrap of a thing like her could drag him anywhere.

Unless he wanted to be dragged.

And where did that idea come from? he wondered.

"The carriage is here," she continued, pointing to where the carriage indeed was.

Fenton's coachman looked pleased, so at least Simeon was doing right by someone, even if he knew he was doing wrong by Miss Allen. An unmarried young lady, no matter how eccentric she was, should not be traipsing about in closed carriages with unmarried young men, particularly if the unmarried young man was illegitimate and she came from the aristocracy.

But she'd offered, and he needed, and he had to take advantage when his other option—painting the viscountess's portrait—had been rescinded. The Decision Child needed Miss Allen's money.

"Let me take that," she said, trying to grab the satchel that held his paints, brushes, and other supplies. He held the valise with his personal belongings in his other hand.

He held tighter instinctively, glaring at her in the early dawn light. "I can handle this myself," he said.

She rolled her eyes. Clearly he was not keeping up.

"You can, but isn't it easier to let someone help? Honestly, nobody has common sense anymore."

He snorted, but let her take the satchel and place it with what he presumed was her bag, putting his valise next to the other two.

The coachman had leapt down from his seat and held the door open. Miss Allen clambered up, not even looking at the hand Simeon held out for her, and she sat at one end, immediately beckoning him. "Come in already, we have to go!"

Simeon bit back his retort, then got into the carriage beside Miss Allen.

The coachman shut the door and the carriage lurched as he returned to his seat atop the conveyance. Within a few seconds, another lurch as the horses started.

Fenton's carriage wasn't opulent, but it was comfortable. Simeon had enjoyed the novelty of carriage travel, since he so seldom left London, and preferred to walk rather than pay for a hackney.

And on his travels he would invariably run into someone who could use some help, so his walking ended up sometimes costing him more than he would have spent on hackney fare. But that was how he most wished to spend his money, so it felt good.

Even if it meant he had very little to spare.

The cushions of Fenton's carriage were upholstered in a light tan color, while the curtains at each of the two small windows were a darker brown in a swirling pattern. The horses, the coachman had told Simeon proudly, were of good quality, not racehorse fast, but reliable and steady. Fenton had gotten the carriage, its horses, and the coachman from a gentleman who'd had a downturn in his investments. Rather than forcing the man into ruin, Fenton had taken some of his possessions, thereby relieving him of having to pay his coachman and also allowing the man to save face.

Miss Allen waved her hands in the air and chuckled in delight. "We're off! I cannot wait to see what adventures we have!" she exclaimed.

Simeon turned his head slowly to regard her. "What adventures do you anticipate, my lady?" he asked warily. "Because I am only willing to escort you to London. I do not want any adventures."

"Of course you do," she replied, nudging his shoulder with hers. "Everyone does."

He wondered why her words sent a chill down his spine.

Chapter Three

"Since we're to travel together, at least for the next few days—" Myrtle began, then winced. "Oh dear. We'll have to stop to rest, won't we? Hmm. I wonder how we'll manage that."

"You mean," Mr. Jones said in a biting tone, "how we will take accommodations without drawing attention to the fact that we are two unmarried people traveling together with no chaperones?" He paused. "I thought you would have worked out all the details when you came to my bedroom at four in the morning. How disappointing to find you did not."

"I have misjudged you, Mr. Jones," Myrtle replied in a bright voice. "You are quite clever, something that is rare to find in very attractive people. Usually they are able to sail through life just being attractive."

He responded to her compliment by burying his face in his hands. Odd, but she'd been accused of being odd herself, so she couldn't fault him.

"I find that most people assume I am not clever

either," she continued. "But not because I am attractive, mind you. Mostly because of my fortune."

He snapped his face back up. "Are you intimating you're not attractive? You're lovely. Distinctive. You are very definitely you, and that is a good thing." He jerked his chin toward her. "I would paint you as Artemisia leading her ships into battle, or perhaps Grace O'Malley leading her band of pirates."

An unexpected heat came to her cheeks. Another oddity. "Thank you," she said hurriedly, "but that is not the point." She would have to ask about those two women some other time. "People assume I have nothing more in my head than gowns and cake and marriage." She paused, wrinkling her brow as she considered her own words. "I do enjoy two out of three of those things, but the enjoyment of what some people think are frivolous pleasures does not mean one is not capable of deep thought."

"So you're saying not to judge anyone by their appearance because they could turn out to be actually intelligent?" he said in a dry voice.

She turned to stare at him, speechless for possibly the first time in her life. "My goodness," she said, when she could find words, "I am just as bad as those other people! I do apologize, Mr. Jones."

"You might as well call me Simeon." He sounded weary. Not surprising, since both of them had been up all night. "We're going to have to pretend to be a married couple," he continued, startling her, "since you cannot take your own room in any of the inns we might find along the route." His tone of voice made it sound as though he was saying they should pretend they loathed sweets, or worse yet, thought that the Pythagorean theorem was mere nonsense.

"Pretend to be . . . married?" she squeaked, then frowned, annoyed at her own reaction. "I suppose it makes a certain sort of sense," she went on, as though she fluttered about pretending to be married to every man she spent time alone with. Not that there were very many of them; some of the servants, and several of the twenty-seven or thirty-two suitors, and those interludes had been blessedly brief. "I am entrusting you with my safety, after all, and you won't get your money if I am hurt or injured. Which are the same thing, drat it," she said in an irritable tone. "Spending the night together in the same room does sound safer than being separated."

He exhaled, the kind of exasperated sigh she was accustomed to hearing from Richard. "I would want your safety, my lady, more than I want your money."

"Well, either you're lying or you're foolish," she pointed out. "You've just met me, and it's obvious you need the money quite badly, or you would have never come to the estate in the first place. I might have to revise my good opinion of you."

He just stared at her, shaking his head.

"And you should call me Myrtle," she added.

His eyes widened. "Myrtle?"

"Yes, didn't you hear my name the first two

times we were introduced?" she asked sharply. Hmm, interesting that his forgetting her the first time still stung. "Myrtle. My younger brother, Joseph, calls me Turtle, but other than the rhyming bit, I am nothing like." She began to tick items off her fingers. "I do not have a hard shell," she said. "I prefer cake to bugs, and most importantly, I am not a reptile."

"I see." He spoke so seriously she wondered if he was making fun of her. But they had just met, he wouldn't be making fun of her so soon, would he?

Then again, she had burst into his bedroom, as he'd said, and insisted he take her to London, even though if they were discovered it would mean certain ruin for both of them.

So perhaps he was alleviating his anxiety by teasing her.

His version of eating cake, perhaps.

"Myrtle," he repeated.

Her stomach growled just then, so loudly both of them could hear. She started, then glanced over at him. His handsome face looked shocked, but then his mouth curled up into a smile and he began to laugh, and she had no choice but to join him.

SIMEON HADN'T EXPECTED so many different emotions before breakfast. Which, as her stomach reminded them, should be forthcoming soon.

She was fascinating, and chaotic, and he couldn't help but be charmed by her . . . *distinctive* way of approaching the world. As though propositioning men in their bedrooms was a perfectly reasonable thing to do, and if they *couldn't keep up* they weren't worth her time.

She reminded him of his fellow orphan Fenton, one of the Bastard Five, as another member Theo had dubbed them.

But Fenton was a man, so his eccentricity was tolerated far more than this lady's would be. Yes, Fenton was illegitimate, but he'd also parlayed his adoptive parents' modest means into vast wealth, so any oddness was endearing rather than . . . odd. Especially to his four friends.

Simeon was the only one of the five who hadn't been adopted into a family with money. His mother had taken him in because she'd seen his talent, and she'd known she wanted to help him achieve his full potential. They'd lived on her earnings, money she made by painting portraits and landscapes for well-to-do merchants and tradesmen. Some months there was more work than other months, and Simeon had taken to helping his mother with her work as she got older.

She'd loved him, though, and so he never regretted being the lone pauper among his friends. They'd lived a chaotic existence, one that made him appreciate stability and contentment and confidence.

He didn't want Decision Child to have to live that kind of existence. It had been fine for him, it *was* fine for him, but he would do whatever he could if he could prevent it for another human being. And it wasn't as though he could just incorporate Decision Child into his determinedly singular life. Neither his art nor his own personality would tolerate that. He'd need to find somewhere for Decision Child to live, a *home*, where he or she could grow up without having to worry what might come next.

Simeon lived above Mr. Finneas's Fine Establishment, a haberdasher, and he paid rent to Mr. Finneas, whom he'd known since he'd been taken in by Miss Jones.

Mr. Finneas's custom, like Simeon's, waxed and waned, and Simeon had moved in during a waning period, but now the shop was doing a bustling business, thanks in no small part to Simeon and his friends always being handsomely turned out, and other gentlemen wanting to know who dressed them.

"We should stop for food at some point," he said. Normally it wouldn't be polite to mention a lady's growling stomach, but nothing about this situation was polite; it was unprecedented, yes, but not polite.

"I want to push on as much as we can today," she said, looking stubborn. "Richard will have realized I am gone by tonight, and so I want to have as much distance between us as possible."

"Why do you need to go to London anyway?" he asked. He'd told himself he shouldn't involve himself in her affairs, but that ship had sailed nearly as soon as she'd knocked so abruptly on his door.

She gave him an assessing look, as though deciding if he could be trusted.

"I am here with you, promising to protect you. It's only right you tell me what I might be protecting you from," he added. "I know you said you wanted to keep your reasons quiet, but surely you don't mean from the one person who is aiding you in your scheme?" He paused, then spoke again. "After all, we are business partners, of a sort, in this adventure, aren't we? At least, that is what I thought you said."

"I suppose." She didn't sound convinced, but she kept speaking. "Richard said I had to marry or do something, so I am going to *do something*." She gave the last two words a heightened emphasis, as though that made it any clearer. It did not.

Simeon waited, but she didn't say anything else.

"And 'do something' means . . . ?" he said, when they'd sat in silence for five minutes.

"I have some plans," she said vaguely, "and I have calculated the chances of success. I believe I should be able to accomplish them, if things go well."

"Yes, that is the definition of things going well," Simeon said, irked at her evasion. "That you are able to accomplish what you wish. Otherwise it would be a failure."

If she couldn't succeed in her plans, perhaps she could become a politician, since she seemed to be masterful at avoiding saying anything definite.

"Exactly right!" she said, sounding like she was cheering him on. "I was saying to Richard something similar—he said that I'd refused each of my twenty-seven proposals—thirty-two if one is being particular—and I said that if I had accepted any of them that would have been the end of it. Like when you're searching for something and you find it in the last place you look. Because of course—"

"—it's in the last place because you'd stop looking," both of them said.

They regarded one another, then both burst into laughter again. At least this journey wouldn't be boring; it might end up ruining his life and his prospects, but it wouldn't be *boring*.

A FEW HOURS later, and Myrtle's stomach had become noisier than the carriage wheels.

"We should stop," Mr. Jones—*Simeon*—said.

"I suppose," Myrtle said, albeit reluctantly. "I imagine the coachman requires something to eat as well."

Simeon half rose, raising his hand to rap on the roof. They heard an answering tap, and he sat back down. "He'll know to stop at the next inn," he explained.

"Your coachman must've been surprised that you were leaving so soon."

"He's not my coachman."

Myrtle stared at him, eyes wide. "Did you *steal* this carriage?" She moaned and covered her eyes. "I don't know that I have enough to pay for a carriage and horses on top of everything else." Plus she could have just as easily stolen a carriage herself, if that had been the plan; she wouldn't have involved a third party.

Why did she have to have a third party?

This was not at all a good situation.

Mr. Jones gently plucked her fingers away from

her face. His own expression was amused. "No, I didn't steal it. My friend is in Paris, and he isn't using it at the moment." He shrugged. "He lets me use it anytime I wish. Your brother happened to commission my work when Fenton was away, so I took it. It was much more comfortable traveling this way with all my tools."

"Your paints and such?" Myrtle said, giving a vague wave of her hand.

"Yes, my paints and such," he replied. Sounding as though he was annoyed at her casual words.

"Well, thank goodness for friends," Myrtle said, ignoring his tone. "Though I don't have very many—I envy you, having someone like your Fenton. Someone who would lend you a carriage so you didn't have to steal one, that is."

Mr. Jones looked abashed, and she wondered what she'd missed. "Actually, I have four very close friends. All five of us are orphans—I'm certain you've heard of my birth."

Myrtle nodded. "Yes, Richard said you behaved quite properly for a—" And she stopped, feeling her face heat.

"—for a bastard," Mr. Jones completed. "Yes, that is a frequent comment directed toward all five of us. Even Fenton," he added, his tone fond.

"My closest friend is my former governess, Miss Rogers," Myrtle replied. "But she lives several hours from Richard's country house, and she never ventures to London. We correspond regularly, but it's not quite the same as being in person."

And it was a good thing Miss Rogers was no-

where near her now, even though Myrtle missed her dearly; Myrtle knew that Letty would have tried to persuade Myrtle her plan wasn't, in fact, a good one, and would have sat on her if she had refused to change her mind.

Letty was quite tall and bony, and it was unpleasant to be sat on by her. Myrtle knew from personal experience.

"All of us still live in London," Mr. Jones continued. "We make certain to meet at least once a month, all of us, to discuss books."

Myrtle squinted at him. Surely she hadn't heard him correctly. "Discuss . . . books?" She would have thought his time with his friends would have been spent much more raucously, to be honest—Richard had also mentioned, in addition to his illegitimate birth, that Mr. Jones was well-known to be a favorite of many. Which Myrtle understood to mean that he was a rake as well as being an excellent painter.

Which also explained why everyone was so quick to believe that he was guilty of attempted seduction, even though it was patently clear what had actually happened. The truth was usually there, it was just that people didn't want to see it. At least, that was true in Myrtle's experience.

"Yes, we discuss books," Mr. Jones replied, his tone terse. "Is that odd? I presume you discuss things you like with your Miss Rogers."

Myrtle snorted. "No, I don't. Miss Rogers doesn't share my passion for mathematics."

Now it was his turn to snort. "Mathematics? How can that be a passion?"

Myrtle felt her chest tighten, the way it always did when someone challenged her. Why was it so odd that she found it delightful to solve a particularly difficult problem? And yet people always gave her a look, as though she had sprouted another head, when her own one head was more capable than theirs.

Though perhaps it was that type of thinking that made people find her odd in the first place.

"I've upset you," he said after a moment. "I apologize," and he sounded sincere, which surprised her. "I did not mean to be derisive—I think I am sensitive because you are not the first person to find my love of books surprising."

"So we are both surprised by the other's interests," Myrtle said in a thoughtful tone of voice. "And we are able to negotiate that conversation. I have most definitely underestimated you." She cleared her throat. "And I have to apologize about earlier. About sounding so cavalier about your work materials. I can see where that might be overly dismissive, Mr. Jones."

"Simeon," he corrected, just as her stomach gave another loud grumble.

"Simeon," she echoed, refusing to be embarrassed.

"We need to feed you, Myrtle." His mouth lifted in a genuine smile, and she nearly fell over—and forgot her hunger—because of her visceral reaction.

It was not safe to be traveling with someone as beautiful as he. Not because he was a danger to her; she had no conceit that he would find her

tempting, despite his saying she was lovely earlier. No, it was because he was so beautiful she might do something far more embarrassing than have a growling stomach.

She might accidentally fling her lips toward his, or touch his face because she needed to trace the shape of his eyebrows, not realizing her fingers had moved of their own volition. And they would be sharing a bedroom, at least for one night; perhaps she should stay up all night so she wouldn't sleepwalk over to him and drape herself around him like a shawl.

How did other people manage it usually? She had to imagine she wasn't the first person to be struck by how stunning he was. She definitely would not be the last.

There was a simple answer to that. She would just ask.

"Tell me," she began, but the carriage slowed to a stop, and he had flung open the door and was outside, holding a hand out for her before she was able to continue.

Well, since she had been thwarted in her attempt to get information, at least she would be able to get fed.

FENTON'S COACHMAN—SMITH WAS his name, but Simeon always thought of him as Fenton's coachman—had found a small, tidy inn that looked as though it would be a good choice to stay the night. It was still just midday, but they'd been traveling for hours, and the horses needed resting, and Miss Allen needed feeding, or at least her stomach seemed to believe so.

"Good day, sir, madam." An older man, perhaps about fifty years old, approached them, wiping his hands on a towel as he spoke.

The common room of the inn was cozy, with a few long tables where patrons would sit all together, rough wooden chairs pulled up to them.

It was a few hours from when most people would think to go to the local inn, so there were only a few people dotted about the room. Most had tankards of ale in front of them, while a dog lay sleeping in front of the unlit fireplace.

"Good day," Simeon replied. "We are hoping you can serve us some food, and possibly give us a place to sleep this evening?" He gestured toward Miss Allen. "My wife and I are on our way to London, and we are both quite hungry." He accompanied his words with what he deemed his medium smile—not so dazzling as to stun anyone seeing him, but not so mild as to make anyone think it was insincere.

Simeon, born a bastard, with an unusual profession that required a lot of social interaction, had developed the skill of gauging how best to manipulate anyone around him, with the notable exception of the Bastard Five. It was an automatic response now, and he generally wasn't aware he was doing it until it was over.

"I am far hungrier than him," Miss Allen admitted. "He wasn't the one whose stomach has been rumbling for an hour." Her expression grew

Chapter Four

"Oh, this smells marvelous!" Miss Allen enthused as the landlord brought two plates over to them. She offered the man another one of her bright smiles. "I am so glad I can sate my hunger with delicious food. It is terrible, isn't it, when one only has the choice of lumpy oatmeal or a mealy apple? Though," she said, her brows drawing together in puzzlement, "I suppose you could combine the two, if you were clever. Perhaps add some brown sugar." Her eyes had a faraway look, and Simeon almost found himself craving what she was describing. "But since I am not clever about food, I would have to eat the lumpy oatmeal. So never mind."

By this time, the landlord had placed both plates in front of them, as well as linen and cutlery. He stood, his hands clasped in front of him, clearly waiting for Miss Allen to finish speaking. "Is there anything else?" he asked, when she'd picked up a fork and was waving it in the air above the food.

thoughtful. "In fact, I don't suppose it matters if your food is any good, I will eat it, nonetheless. So you need not concern yourself if it is of poor quality," she added with a generous smile.

And apparently there was Miss Allen, who was incapable of any kind of polite obfuscation.

"Yes, well," the man replied, clearly unsettled, "though you need not be concerned, our food is very good, my wife does the cooking. I will bring you something in a moment. Please take a seat."

Miss Allen glanced brightly around, unaware she'd just offended the innkeeper. Simeon hoped the man's lack of paying customers would overcome his being offended.

"Shall we sit there?" she asked, pointing to the table closest to the dog and the fireplace. It had the fortunate benefit of being nowhere close to any of the other patrons, so it was unlikely she would offend anybody else. Unless she shouted.

Please don't let her shout, Simeon silently begged.

He held her chair for her, at which she gave him a startled look. "What?" he blurted, surprised at himself for his reaction.

"I hadn't expected you to be so formal," she replied. She waved her hand in that vague gesture he was already beginning to dislike. She frowned. "Though I suppose you have to be polite always, to compensate for whatever preconceptions people might have about you."

And there she went, defusing his ire before it even began.

"Something to drink, please," she replied, not glancing away from her plate.

"Right away," the man said, then shot Simeon a baffled look, as if to say, *Is this the way she is all the time?* and Simeon had to try to keep a bland expression so he didn't burst into laughter again.

He placed the linen on his lap and picked up his fork. She'd already begun eating, so he did the same. The food was as delicious as it smelled, thank goodness; Simeon had eaten far too many meals that were precisely like the one Miss Allen had described. His mother hadn't always had enough to keep them in painting supplies and well-fed, so she'd often decided to skip good food in service of their art.

It made sense, both now and at the time, but it left him with a lingering resentment of mediocre-tasting food. A good reminder of why he was doing all this—he needed to make certain Decision Child never had to eat mealy oatmeal and lumpy apples. Or the other way around, he couldn't remember.

"Mmm, these carrots are delicious!" she enthused, holding up her fork, which held a stabbed carrot. "Do you ever wonder," she said, taking a bite of one end of the carrot and chewing vigorously, "how it was that someone thought that digging up a long orange thing from the ground would be good to eat? And what about lobster?" She jabbed her fork at him accusatorily. "You'd have to be very hungry indeed to think of eating that."

Simeon opened his mouth to reply, but thought better of it. She wasn't just an inebriated dictionary, she was a chaotic encyclopedia, veering from one subject to the next with no topic sentence in between.

He owed Fenton an apology. His friend, at least, had never delved into the history of eating crustaceans.

"Do you like it?" she asked, gesturing toward him with her now empty fork.

"Yes," he replied, spearing his own carrot and taking a too big bite of it. She was right; the carrots were neither over- nor undercooked, and they were dressed in a sauce of lemon, butter, and parsley, from what he could tell. Though he wasn't much of a cook either.

The landlord returned with tankards of ale, placing one in front of each of them. "I've got the best room in the house for you, sir, ma'am. I can have your bags brought up, if you like."

"Yes," she answered, before Simeon could say a word. "Thank you." Her words were a clear dismissal, and the landlord glanced at Simeon again, then bowed and left.

"If you can, perhaps allow me to answer?" Simeon said, trying not to sound annoyed. "It will go toward persuading people we are actually married."

Her eyebrows rose, and she gave him a quelling look. "You mean if I defer to you rather than answer an obvious question it will let people know we are tied together irrevocably? Good to know."

She bent her head to the plate again, and Simeon felt a surge of frustration. Not just because she was so dismissive, but because she was correct.

His mother had remained single her entire life; not because she didn't have suitors, but because she didn't want anybody getting in the way of her art. Instead, Simeon had had a succession of uncles, men who thought they could convince his mother to marry them if they were kind enough to her unfortunate orphan.

That never worked, however; his mother would invariably tire of the men long before they tired of her, and she would send them off, telling Simeon he was the only permanent gentleman in her life.

He'd followed her pattern, falling in and out of love with remarkable ease, but always knowing that the moment must eventually end. Usually he was the one who broke it off when the other person was seeming to get more serious than Simeon could tolerate.

It wasn't a lonely existence; he had his four friends, and his art, and other people he'd met along the course of his life. Most of his ex-lovers had stayed as friends as well.

His choice of lifestyle made it imperative that he find another solution for Decision Child, though he would not abdicate responsibility. It was what his mother would have done, and he knew how important stability— even stability as tenuous as what he'd had—was crucial in developing a young mind.

"What are you running away from?" he asked.

He might as well be as blunt as she was, at least when it was just the two of them. It wasn't as though his plain speaking would make their absolutely scandalous situation even more scandalous; it had reached peak scandal already.

"I told you," she said curtly. "Twenty-seven suitors or thirty-two, depending on how you count."

"But what is it about that—about marriage—that frightens you? From what I understand, a young lady in your position would have nothing but a pleasant experience." Not that *he* believed that, of course; he'd been approached by many married ladies, several of them having expressed dissatisfaction with their husbands, hoping Simeon could fill in the gaps, so to speak. He'd always declined, not because he was all that honorable, but because if things went wrong—which they always did—it would be more than awkward. It would be dangerous. A bastard dallying with a married woman would mean death to his career, and held the very real possibility of damage to his person.

But marriage was what young ladies were told they had to do with their lives from the day they were born, so he was curious how she came to have a different opinion.

"I am not *frightened*," she said in an affronted tone. "I value myself too highly to be viewed only valuable for the children I can produce or the expenditures I can fund." Her voice softened. "I know marriage is for some—my niece, Lilah, is about to make her debut, and all she can talk about is finding someone to love. But I have never felt that for myself."

"Married women have a certain freedom single ladies are not accorded," Simeon observed, as much to make the point as to get her to speak more about it. How had someone in her position come to have her views, which were radical for a young, unmarried lady? Her brother seemed to be unremarkable, and her niece had traditional expectations. What made her so different?

Though perhaps if more unmarried ladies had her views, marriage wouldn't be the first and only opportunity a lady in her position would be offered, he thought.

She snorted. "Married women trade one sort of tether for another. Yes, they can do some things I cannot. But they are also bound to their husband's will, required to do what he says if there is a disagreement. Forced to pretend the husband's decision is more important. That his actions are more important." Her expression was disingenuous. "Like when he insists he can handle moneys better than she, even if he has no idea who Babbage is."

"That's a cynical view of it," Simeon observed. Not bothering to ask who Babbage was, since he assumed it was someone mathematics related. Miss Allen and his mother would have gotten along—his mother had always maintained she was happier on her own, and she didn't want anyone else's complications when she was already dealing with her own and Simeon's.

"I don't know if I can explain to you how frustrating it can be," she continued. "To know there are funds out there that belong to you, but that you are not given control of because—because of your gender. I think even Richard would agree I am more intelligent than he, but because he is male he can dictate what is to be done with my fortune. Dangled in front of everybody as incentive to take me." She sounded bitter, and he couldn't blame her.

"I see your point," he said at last, clearly surprising her, judging by her expression. "It's not fair, but marriage is what people expect to see." He shrugged. "So until we part ways, we should try to adhere to what people expect. It will cause the least amount of comment."

Her nose wrinkled in distaste, making her look like an angry kitten. "I suppose," she said, reluctance evident in her tone. "Though I do not like to lie," she continued. "I am terrible at it as well."

"Our first fight," he said, accompanying his words with a sly smile. Hoping to get her to laugh after being irritated.

It worked, too. One moment she looked entirely grumpy, and then the next she was smiling back at him, clear delight sparkling in her brown eyes. He wondered if he had ever met anyone whose thoughts were so visible, as though they were written on her skin. It *would* be very difficult for her to lie, he imagined, though that was what they were doing now, wasn't it?

But this was her adventure, so she'd have to own that part of it, or suffer the consequences.

"What is it?" she asked, her expression shifting again. A mercurial encyclopedia, then. Not just chaotic, but reflective of her surroundings, paying attention when it interested her, and not when it didn't, as evidenced by her first interaction with the landlord.

"Nothing," he said. He slid a piece of beef onto his fork, putting the flavorful morsel into his mouth. "If you've finished eating, perhaps you'd like to take a walk around the village? It's too early to go to be—" he said, then felt his face heat and corrected his wording, "too early to go to sleep."

WAS HE BLUSHING? Was that even possible? Myrtle peered at him, her gaze traveling over his face, from those dark brown eyes, to the faint flush on his cheekbones, to his mouth.

His upper lip was curved in, making it look like an irresistible treat. And his lower lip—much fuller, and an enticing red shade that made him look so bitable.

Though she had to both resist and not bite. As though she was a dog being strictly trained not to devour any morsel presented to it.

You are not a dog, Myrtle, she reminded herself. Though she *did* like being praised, and she often found herself wishing she could just lie down wherever she was and take a nap.

"I would love to take a walk," she said. Another

doglike behavior, she thought, feeling gleeful at the realization. She liked walking. It was often the only time she could be alone with her own thoughts, at least when Richard and his entire family were at the estate. "Do you suppose there is any place we could find some cake?" she added.

Not that she needed any cake, but it would make the journey far more enjoyable. Though she'd have to make certain she didn't get any on her clothing; she didn't have a maid and an entire household staff at her disposal, at least not for some time, until she could establish herself in her own household. How long that could take, she had no idea—she couldn't even begin to make that calculation.

"On second thought, no cake," she said in a firm tone of voice.

"Did we have our second fight and I didn't notice?" he asked mildly, but she saw the glint of humor in his gaze.

"No, it's not that," she said. She rose abruptly, placing her linen on her chair. "Shall we go?"

He got up nearly as quickly, sliding his chair out with an elegant gesture. If there was more time, she would ask him how he was able to make everything he did look so effortlessly graceful. Though he might not know, it might just come along with being so handsome and charming. Like when you ordered a lamb chop and it automatically came with mashed potatoes and peas. The lamb chop wouldn't think to question why it was always accompanied by potatoes and peas; it just *was*.

"Do we need to check in with not-your-coachman?" she asked over her shoulder as they made their way to the door. The dog by the fireplace—a regal-looking fellow, all floppy, golden limbs and ears—picked his head up and watched as they walked. She nearly went back to pet him, but decided against it. Mr. Jones would have to wait for her, and she wouldn't be that rude, even though the dog was undoubtedly deserving of pets.

"My not coachman—Smith, as it happens—will be fine," he replied, sounding amused. Why? Was it because she was concerned about a servant? Though she didn't think he had that kind of attitude, given his own antecedents.

"I just wondered if we should ask him if he needs anything," she said with a sniff.

"Let's walk and then check in with Smith, dear," he replied, speaking in a louder tone than he might have used normally. Perhaps to convince the landlord and the other customers that they were actually married?

She appreciated his commitment to the ruse, though she didn't think it was necessary. No one was paying attention to them, except for the occasional admiring glance cast Simeon's way.

The village was small, but picturesque, with shops lining either side of what was clearly the main street. After confirming that the coachman was comfortably settled, he'd taken her arm. It felt different and odd, but not entirely unpleasant. In fact, if she were being honest—which she always was, at least to herself—it was entirely pleasant.

It felt as though she was in his care, and it was surprising to her that that didn't chafe, as she might have expected.

Perhaps there was something to this whole "until death do you part" thing.

But that would mean being with someone all the time, and suffering their inability to think as quickly as she, and having to tolerate it when they suddenly decided that all books should be turned the other way on shelves, or some other idiotic decision a man might be liable to make. So that was a firm no on marriage.

"Are you all right?" he asked, glancing down at her. He was so very tall. She felt like one of Jonathan Swift's Lilliputians, and he was Gulliver. If they were to dance together, or to do anything together, in fact, it would be an exercise in angles and degrees worthy of anything Pythagoras had ever thought of. Perhaps she should try to work out the calculations to see the best positi—

No. Stop that, she told herself sternly. *Remember what you just said? A firm no.*

"I am fine," she said, forcing herself out of her own thoughts. It was just that he was so remarkably good-looking, and it didn't seem as though he was stupid.

Of course it didn't miss her notice that he was someone she would have absolutely no business marrying, given who he was, and who she was, and that he was the only gentleman she'd even considered that would be tolerable out of the thirty-three suitors.

But, she reasoned, she'd had very little experience in the world. Perhaps she would meet thirty-three more gentlemen, and there would be one amongst that group who would be more acceptable.

Though why was she even thinking about marriage when she'd already decided? Wasn't she determined not to, given that her husband—whoever it was—would have total control over her? Over her body, her actions, her fortune? Who she saw, how she dressed, what she ate?

Who she was?

"IS THERE ANYTHING else you'd like to look at?" he asked, when they had reached the last shop on the street. The road stretched out ahead, but it was clearly changing into a residential area.

She nodded toward the other side. "I'd like to go there. Just to see." And to walk on his arm for just a bit longer. It felt wrong, to be soaking up the feeling of being with such an attractive man when she had no intentions toward him, but wasn't that the point of very attractive people? To appreciate their attractiveness?

"Why are you staring at me like that?" he asked suddenly, making her start.

"Oh dear, I am—that is, I do apologize," she said. Now she was the one blushing. "I was just admiring your face. You're quite handsome, you know."

"You're disconcertingly blunt, Miss Allen. Myrtle," he corrected, before she could speak.

"Is that bad?" she asked, frowning.

He snorted in laughter, so loudly that a few

of the other pedestrians turned to look at them. "Proving my observation by asking that," he said. "I don't know that any other person would be so effusive about another's appearance—"

"*You* haven't been proposed to thirty-two times," she murmured, making him laugh harder.

He held his hand out in an apologetic gesture. "I am sorry, I mean I don't know that any other person would be so *sincerely* effusive about another's appearance. You sounded as though you truly believed what you were saying."

"Of course I do," she shot back. "Have you not used a mirror? My God, man, just look at yourself!" She flung her hand up toward his face, barely missing his chin.

He caught her hand, his eyes gazing intently at her, and she felt her breath catch.

"Thank you," he replied, his voice low and rumbly. It did interesting things to her insides. But it would be a tremendous mistake to let those interesting things dictate her actions, no matter how irresistible and bitable he was.

Why did he have to be so irresistible and bitable? Why couldn't the artist who was going to paint her sister-in-law be an old man with yellow teeth and a limp?

Because then that same sister-in-law wouldn't have taken her tipsy self to his rooms and propositioned him, forcing Richard to kick him out of the house, giving Myrtle an opportunity to escape.

"Fine," she said, aggrieved at how she'd just proven he had to be that attractive.

"Fine?" he echoed. He still held her hand. "Are you offended by my saying thank you?"

"No, of course not. I was just having a conversation with myself," she said hastily, snatching her hand away.

"Of course you were," he said, that amused tone back in his voice again. "I have to say, I never expected my return journey to be so enjoyable."

She felt a warmth of pleasure in her belly. Not entirely due to the meal she'd just eaten.

"It almost makes the risk worth it," he continued, making her frown.

"The risk? You mean traveling alone with me?"

He gave her a scornful look. Though it didn't feel as though he was scorning her, just the whole situation. "Yes, that. Directly after, the gossips would say, asking a married lady to visit my bedchambers at night while her husband sleeps down the hall." He glanced away, frustration coloring his expression. "It's that people assume the worst of you if your birth is suspect. As though someone whose parents were not married are inherently less than others, when actually it's been hard work to do as well as I have."

"Goodness, do you think people will talk about what happened with Regina? I mean, nothing happened," she added hastily, "just that there was a ruckus."

Now his scornful look was directed at her. "Have you ever known people to pass the opportunity to speculate about someone else's behavior? Surely you're not that naïve."

She bristled at his words. "No, of course not, but I presume—at least I hope—that Richard did something to explain it all away. It's not the first time Regina has—"

"Has wandered the hallways at night?" he put in, and she nodded.

"Will that truly affect your reputation?" she asked.

He shrugged. "It might enhance it, though I am not sure I want that type of enhancement. It's difficult enough to navigate your world when you don't have a title. To add this to that is harder."

"That is so unfair," she said, scowling.

He gave her an amused glance. "Unfair, yes, but it's the world."

"My world, you mean."

He kept her gaze for a moment. "Yes, I suppose. *Your* world. Where my reputation is critically important, and was also tarnished as soon as I was born." He twisted his lips. "Hopefully no one will find out about this particular escapade."

"They won't," she promised, though she didn't know how she was to keep that promise. Just that she would do whatever was necessary to make certain he didn't suffer because of her.

Chapter Five

The sky had darkened some time ago. They'd spent an hour or so in the common area downstairs, sipping their ale as Miss Allen petted the dog that lay on the floor.

The dog's name was Bow Wow, she gleefully informed him. He was fond of cheese and long walks, she added, making it sound as though she was very fond of those things as well.

And now it was time for bed.

The room was clean, and well-appointed, but it was also small. With, Simeon could not help but notice, only one bed.

Though it would have been odd for there to be two beds, so he didn't know why he had to remark on it, even in his mind.

There was one bed. There were two people.

"I can sleep on the floor," he said. Just as she said, "I'll be entirely comfortable down there."

They stood side by side in the room, both facing the bed that seemed, in Simeon's imagination, to be expanding as they regarded it. Perhaps it would grow so huge that they could both sleep in it with no awareness of the other.

She was the first to speak after that. "It is nonsense to think either one of us has to sleep on the floor. We are both reasonable adults, we can sleep together in the bed. It serves no one if we are exhausted tomorrow. I, for one, do not see the point of foregoing a good night's sleep because of this," she said, gesturing vaguely toward the bed. "Besides, we're already guilty in Society's eyes because we've dared to spend time together alone. Why not be comfortable while being scandalous?"

She said it in such a reasonable tone, as though she was working through a complex equation, that he couldn't help but laugh. He'd done that a lot since meeting her not even twenty-four hours ago—he didn't think, when he agreed to escort her to London, that there would be so much laughter.

He was actually enjoying himself, he realized.

"Fine," he agreed. She turned to him, an expression of surprise on her face. "What, did you think I was going to argue?" He nodded toward the floor. There was a throw rug placed at the bottom of the bed, but other than that, the floor was bare. "I have no desire to subject myself to more discomfort than necessary, and as you say, the damage is done already." He shrugged, then met her gaze. "Why not be comfortable while being scandalous?"

Her mouth curled up into a smile, and then she reached out to poke his shoulder. "You are very clever," she said.

He waggled his eyebrows at her. "Clever and handsome."

They stared at one another, the familiar impulse toward seduction coming over Simeon. This would usually be the moment where he would grasp the lady's shoulder, gently drawing her into his arms for a kiss.

But this was Miss Allen, and she was paying him for his services—and not *those* services, mind you—*and* they were about to get into that bed together with no intention of doing anything. He needed to put all thoughts of seduction out of his mind.

Even though she was looking up at him with those soft brown eyes, her lips slightly parted, her remarkable brain likely thinking all sorts of intriguing things.

Those curves being . . . curvy. Reminding him of Rubens's most stunning works, the painter showing just why women were so distinctly different from men.

He was not doing a good job of putting all thoughts of seduction out of his mind.

"I'll need help with this," she said at last. She was gesturing toward her gown, and he felt—well . . . he felt things. He shouldn't be feeling things. Things were not to be felt, not here. Not when they were business partners.

"Turn around, then," he said, his voice gruffer than usual.

He undid the buttons of her gown, then spun away from her as soon as it was clear she could remove it by herself.

"I'll wait until you are safely in bed to join you." This was actively difficult, and Simeon wasn't accustomed to any kind of difficulty when it came to attraction. The opposite, in fact. He had never denied himself, nor anyone else, when it came to sexual indulgence.

And even though he knew she felt it—not because he was any kind of psychic, but because she'd said it, aloud, to him—he wouldn't take advantage of this situation.

Not when she was depending on him for her safety. Not when she was paying him, for God's sake.

And her saying he was attractive was merely fact. It didn't mean she wished for anything more, and it would be presumptive of him to think so.

So instead he counted backward from one hundred in Latin, then did it again, but forward this time.

"I'm in," she said at last, her voice high-pitched and strained.

He exhaled sharply through his nose, then bent to remove his boots, assessing what articles of clothing he should sleep in to maintain some semblance of propriety.

Eventually, he arrived at removing his coat, shirt, and cravat, because he only had one other shirt packed, and he didn't want this one to be so wrinkled or stained he couldn't wear it.

The trip shouldn't take much longer, but his mother had always told him to hope for the best and expect the worst. It had saved him in the past, and he presumed it would save him again.

Which meant he was bare-chested when he laid

down on the cool sheets, immediately uttering a groan of satisfaction. She gave a yelp of surprise, and he winced.

"I'd forgotten we didn't get any sleep last night," he said by way of explanation. Or more accurately, by way of trying to pretend he wasn't in absolutely sensual pleasure, lying on the cool sheets, a warm set of curves just there within arm's reach.

"Good night, Mr.—Simeon," she said at last.

"Good night, Myrtle," he replied.

MYRTLE'S FIRST THOUGHT, upon awakening, was to wonder just where she was. The view she saw from the window was unfamiliar, as was the window itself; it wasn't her bedroom window, that was for certain. Her bedroom window was on her left, and this window was on her right.

But all of that was forgotten when she realized there was an additional hand resting on her stomach.

She scrambled up, flinging the hand off her as she squeaked in surprise.

And then remembered where she was, who she was, and most importantly, who she was with.

She closed her mouth, squeezing her eyes shut as she twisted to the side. Then opened them just barely enough to see him.

"Good morning." His voice was gruff with sleep.

"Good morning."

That was the correct response, wasn't it? Any etiquette training she'd had hadn't accounted for sleeping next to a gentleman to whom you were not married and how to greet him when you were both awake. "I didn't mean to scream like that, I was just startled."

"It's understandable," he replied, still in that low, ragged voice.

He rolled over and got out of bed, his back to her. She hadn't gotten a good look before, but goodness—his upper body, at least his back, was spectacular. She suspected that the front was equally glorious, but she'd have to have proof before she could confirm it as fact. But no, she would not be asking him to turn around so she could inspect him. The back was plenty view enough, as it happened.

His shoulders were broad, the muscles in his back well-defined as he reached for his shirt, which was folded on a chair. He shook it out, making other muscles appear, and then he stretched his arms up, the fabric sliding onto his body, making her utter a tiny noise of disappointment.

"Did you say something?" he asked, turning back to her.

"No," she said, shaking her head. *I did not ask you to turn around so I could get a good look at your naked chest. Purely for scientific reasons.* "Yes," she added. She would never get the chance to converse alone with a gentleman after today, not until she was older than Methuselah's mother. She might as well take advantage of it.

"You've asked me what I'm intending to do—"

"Which you haven't answered," he interjected.

"And I know there is some story to why you took Richard's commission in the first place.

You're far too talented to spend your time painting often-drunk viscountesses," she continued, as though he hadn't spoken.

"I'm an artist," he said, spreading his arms out.

"That doesn't explain it," she said, determined. "I've seen critical reviews of your work. You're one of the ones to watch, according to all the noted authorities."

"Noted authorities' praise doesn't put bread on the table," he pointed out. But there was something about his expression that told her there was, indeed, more to his story. She kept her gaze pointedly directed at him.

After a few long moments, he sighed. An exasperated sigh, the kind she often heard from Richard. "You're very stubborn, aren't you?"

She offered him a proud smile. "I am, yes."

He gave her a rueful glance, then sat down on the edge of the bed, turning his head to regard her. "I received a letter. It turns out there is a child who needs my help."

"Yours?"

He looked shocked. "No, of course not. I would never do to another what was done to me. Not that I know the circumstances of my birth. Just that I am, as your brother said, a bastard."

"Whose child is it, then?" she asked.

"My mother's."

"I'm sorry, what?"

"My adoptive mother. Apparently she had a child, and left the child with her sister. The sister has died, and the child is left alone in the world."

"Oh my goodness!" she exclaimed. "No wonder you were willing to paint Regina, and more than happy to take my money. Where is the child now?"

"Waiting for me to send word on *how to proceed*." He spoke the final words in a disdainful way, as though aware of how dehumanizing it was to wish to proceed with a human being. Dispatching them if they were inconvenient, or ignoring them if they were a bother.

Rather like the aristocracy usually did with their children, though her parents had not done that. Nor was Richard doing that, though Regina's behavior could be erratic. As evidenced by her screeching when Simeon turned her down, or whatever he'd done to make her upset.

That meant, too, that it was important for him to stay scandal-free, not only for his own sake, but for the sake of the child he would be taking care of.

She hoped Richard had been able to squelch the gossip, or Simeon and his new charge would suffer.

"Speaking of proceeding," he said, unaware of her dire thoughts, "I'll ask Smith to get the carriage ready. It shouldn't be more than another day of travel, and then we'll have arrived." He sounded eager to get back, and she couldn't blame him— he'd lost his commission, he was putting his reputation in serious danger by traveling with her, and he was desperate enough for money that he'd agreed to take her in the first place.

And then there was the decision of what to do with the unexpected child.

"Do you need any money?" she asked abruptly. "I could give you half of what I've promised, if you need it."

He gave her a puzzled look, then shook his head. "No, we have an agreement. You can pay me when we reach London." His mouth curled into a half smile. "Business partners, remember?"

He was altogether too honorable. Perhaps overcompensating for his low birth? But she knew she was fortunate to be traveling with him. And they had agreed that this was strictly a business arrangement, despite the whole "hand on belly" situation she'd woken up to.

It was unfortunate he wasn't one of the twenty-seven or thirty-two people who'd proposed. Not that she *wanted* to be married to anyone at all, but at least he was interesting. An artist, likely the handsomest man she would ever meet, and someone with a conscience. That was a rarity worth calculating when she had the time.

But right now, she did not.

After he left, she scrambled out of bed and got dressed, doing up as many buttons as she could reach and fixing her sleep-disheveled hair.

She looked a fright, but that didn't matter. All that mattered was the opportunity to prove she didn't need to be married to have value in the world.

It was not the first time she'd realized just how valueless someone in her position was. But it was the first time she was going to do something about it. Something beyond saying "no" when a gentleman proposed.

Fifteen minutes later, he was back, holding two mugs, steam rising up from them. "I brought tea. I thought we could both use a cup." He handed her one of the mugs, taking a sip from his. "Smith is getting the carriage prepared. He's already had his breakfast. Would you like to eat here, or get on our way and stop in a few hours?"

She drank from her mug, the warm liquid sliding down her throat. "I think we should get going, don't you?"

He nodded, as though he'd expected that answer. "Yes, we can make a lot of time today. Be in London by the afternoon, if we're lucky."

Which meant last night was the only night she'd ever share a bed with anyone, if her life turned out as she was hoping.

Waking up with his hand on her. Her one experience with that kind of tender touch, even though it was likely an unconscious gesture.

She already ached for the loss of the kind of life she had never had. What would it be like to wake up every morning with another person? A person who cherished you? Who cared for you?

She might never know. Because she knew herself, knew that she was far too odd, too intelligent, too *different* to be appealing. At least to anyone she might find intriguing herself; so many of the people, in general, she met were simply not that interesting to her, mostly because they weren't curious.

It didn't matter as much if they weren't as intelligent as she—she'd long ago accepted that very few people were. It mattered if they were *curi-*

ous, if they wanted to know things for the love of knowing things, of wanting to discover new information, have new adventures, even if they were just adventures of the mind.

"Are you done with that?" He held his hand out for her now empty mug. She hadn't realized she'd drunk all the tea.

"Yes, thank you. I'll—I'll be ready in a few minutes. I just need—" And she gestured to her back, then turned around so he could do up her buttons.

"Of course."

She held herself stiffly as his fingers worked swiftly and efficiently. Otherwise she might just be tempted to melt into him, to lean against that strong chest and tilt her head back on his shoulder. Not that her head could actually reach his shoulder; he was far too tall for that. But this was her imagination working, and her imagination liked to think her head could reach, if she tried.

"All done." He patted her back, and she spun around again, facing him.

THEY WERE ON their way within another fifteen minutes, both settled into their seats as the carriage set off at a brisk pace. Simeon had insisted on paying the fees at the inn, even though she'd made faces at him while he'd been handling it.

"I could have paid, you know," she pointed out after a few minutes.

"Yes, but what husband would allow his wife to pay for everything?" Simeon shot back.

She snorted. "The kind that wants to be my

husband." She turned her head away from him to stare out the window.

"I'm certain that is not the only reason any man wants to be your husband," Simeon began. Somehow, this intelligent, vibrant woman had gotten the idea that she was only valuable for her fortune.

She snapped her head back to regard him, one skeptical eyebrow raised. "I am equally certain that is the only reason. My fortune is stupendous, Mr. Jones, and my suitors have made sure to mention how I need their assistance to manage it all."

"They should have complimented your—"

"They've done that also," she interrupted, speaking in a dismissive voice. "Talking about how many children I appear to be able to bear. As though I was only meant for breeding."

"I was going to say," he replied, his voice choking with laughter, "they should have complimented your brain. That would be the way to your heart, wouldn't it?"

She stared at him, her brown eyes wide, her mouth parted as though she was going to say something, but couldn't.

"It's a remarkable brain," he continued, pleased he had surprised her. "I've never met anyone else who has it. My friend Fenton is close, but even he isn't as quick and sharp as you are. I am glad you are not going to waste it in marriage." He paused. "That you'll be doing something else instead."

Her expression froze.

"That is," he said, now feeling a bit befuddled, due to her reaction, "I assume you are going to

London to use that remarkable brain in some way. Isn't that true?"

She gave a slow nod.

"And I would say it has something to do with mathematics—also true?"

Another nod.

"We always knew Fenton would do something extraordinary," he said, feeling as though he was coaxing a bird out of its nest. "He had the good fortune to be born a male"—at which she snorted—"but he is also illegitimate, like the rest of us. He was placed with a family who didn't always understand him—nobody can, truly—but who encouraged him. Like my own adoptive mother. She told me never to take my talent for granted, to place it above all other things in my life." He shrugged. "Which is why I have succeeded so well thus far."

It took a few moments, but at last she spoke. "I do want to do something with my remarkable brain, as you put it," she said slowly. "I don't want anyone, any lady, that is, to have to be as beholden to her family as I am to mine. I want to help them gain financial independence."

"Short of completely dismantling the current system, how do you propose to do that?" he asked mildly. But inside he was anything but mild; in her he sensed the same dedication to her vision, to her talents, that he had. That few people other than fellow artists felt. It was a rare feeling, to know that someone you were speaking with had the same dedication to their craft. That his craft was paints, and hers was numbers didn't matter. It felt the same.

"Most ladies have access to at least a little bit of money," she replied. "I cannot do much to help the most destitute, beyond donating what I can. But if there is some money, I can advise them how to make it grow. How to budget, how to accommodate life's vicissitudes. I think it is what I was put here for."

"Your vision is even grander than Fenton's," he said in an admiring tone.

"And you care for this Fenton?" The way she spoke, she made it sound as though it was the most important question in the world. As though it amazed her that a person would like someone with that kind of mind.

"I do," he said firmly. "Fenton cannot be depended on to wear a pair of matching hose, but he can be depended on when you truly need it."

"Like lending a carriage for a trip to the country?" Her words were accompanied by a charming grin. Not *that* charming, Simeon had to rush to assure himself. He could not complicate his already complicated life by fancying any kind of deeper relationship with her—this was a business arrangement, nothing more. Even if it was the most enjoyable business arrangement he'd ever had.

He knew he was fully capable of falling in love with her in as short a time as they were to be together. Once he'd fallen in love over the course of four hours and thirty-seven minutes, and it had taken him weeks to recover.

Nothing was permanent, of course; in that he was similar to his adoptive mother, who swapped gentlemen callers like she changed out shoes.

But the temporary nature of his entanglements didn't mean he didn't feel as deeply. If anything, the intensity was magnified because of its expected brevity. And she had something greater to do than to dally with him—no matter that the dallying would be most delightful for both of them.

"My friend Letty—Miss Rogers—is to me like your Fenton." He'd forgotten what they were speaking of for a moment, and frowned in confusion. "Though I think she would say I am the one more likely to wear mismatched hose." She stuck her feet out in front of her. "I do check every so often, just to be certain."

He glanced down at her shoes, impossibly fragile things meant only for a young lady who did nothing but step from her bedroom to the tearoom, and back again. Another reminder that she came from one world, and he was from another. This was just an interlude in passing, one that would fade from their memories as time went on.

"People don't like people who are different," she continued. Sounding both proud and sad. "I've never found it easy to be around others, even around members of my own family. I do find it easy to be around you. And not just because you're so easy on the eyes. If only I could marry someone like you," she said with a sigh.

And then she clapped her hand over her mouth, her eyes wide.

Chapter Six

It was remarkable how long one could go without speaking, if one really concentrated on it.

She'd made that ridiculous comment, and then she'd briefly debated flinging herself out of the carriage onto the road—a few scrapes and bruises were preferable to having to sit there with her ill-conceived words—but that wouldn't get her to London any faster. Or safer. It would seriously damage her ability to do both, in fact.

So instead she'd resolved to be quiet. If she was quiet she wouldn't be able to say anything, would she? That was the very definition of *quiet*.

Something she nearly opened her mouth to discuss when she realized what she was thinking and pressed her lips together so she wouldn't.

This was the first time she'd realized she'd said something awkward as she was saying something awkward; usually it took hours, days, or even *weeks* for her to figure out why someone was looking oddly at her.

Hence her general discomfort in Society.

He didn't start any conversation with her, leaving her to her own churning thoughts; though why would he, when they barely knew one another and yet she was blithely talking about being paired up for the rest of their lives?

No wonder he didn't offer any comment on anything.

Not for the first time, Myrtle wondered how regular people walked around without making complete asses of themselves.

Or, more accurately, how people walked around making regular asses of themselves. Not spectacular asses like she'd done.

And what was the distinction? If she was a regular person, a person who was intent on living a regular life, who wasn't confounded by Society's rules and wasn't fascinated by math and other bits of knowledge, would she have even thought of what she'd said, much less said it?

There was a reason she was currently haring off to London in search of something else to do but be regular, she knew.

She was desperate to ask him more about his life, the child, his art. But she also didn't want to say anything at all.

They were *business* associates, she reminded herself. She was paying him for a service, a service that would be complete once they arrived in London and she could start finding ways to assist other women like her.

In fact, the less they knew about one another the better. So she'd have to forget how easily he mingled with the guests at Richard and Regina's party, how she envied him his friendships with his fellow orphans, what his back looked like, and how he had listened to her as she talked about herself.

How she'd woken up with his hand on her belly.

And remind herself, instead, how terrible it would be if anyone knew about what had happened over the past twenty-seven—or was it thirty-two—hours. Her lips curled into a small, secret smile at her own joke.

She woke up abruptly sometime later, the carriage's sudden stop forcing her to immediately know where she was, who she was with, and what she was doing.

"Are we here?" she asked in a sleep-fuzzed voice.

"It depends on what you mean by 'here,'" he replied. "We're in London. But I wasn't certain where you wished to go. Please tell me you have a place to stay."

Myrtle straightened, blinking herself more awake. "It does feel like we're the only two people in the world right now, doesn't it? As though this," she said, waving her hand in a gesture encompassing their general area, "is the only thing that exists." She processed his last words. "Of course I have a place to stay," she said firmly. If also falsely; she would head to the Allen town house, but she'd have to find other lodgings before the family arrived. She couldn't have them interfere, not when she'd gotten herself here.

"Thank goodness," he said, relieved. "And if I may point out, if we were the only two people in the world we wouldn't have Smith, who is driving the carriage in our mysterious world."

She rolled her eyes. "Fine. Be literal about it, if you must. I *meant* that in this carriage, during this time, we haven't been Mr. Jones and Miss Allen, we're Simeon and Myrtle, possibly married, probably not married, and traveling together with our own separate plans and goals."

It made perfect sense to her.

"I suppose that is true," he said, still sounding confused. Making him just like every other person she knew. Except for Letty and Lilah; her former governess would just ignore Myrtle's flights of fancy, and her niece would figure out how whatever Myrtle had said could directly apply to her, usually missing the initial point.

Like most girls her age, Myrtle thought. Though she didn't think she had been like that—at eighteen, Myrtle had made her debut, as Lilah was about to, but hers had been disastrous because she'd been obsessed with solving Polignac's conjecture, which stated there were infinitely many cases of two consecutive prime numbers with difference n.

Getting anyone she conversed with at the time to understand what prime numbers were, let alone what n represented, was impossible.

Needless to say, she had spent many an evening standing next to the wall wondering when she could go home. Wondering if there was a way for her to be like everyone else, until she realized she didn't *want* to be like anybody else. She just wanted to be like her.

"Miss Allen?" he said, reminding her that this was the end of this particular adventure. She was back to being Miss Allen, and she should call him Mr. Jones. "What direction can I give Smith?"

Even though she felt the tug of wanting to stay inside their own world. To talk about everything and nothing, perhaps have him laugh along with her—not at her, as happened far more frequently than she wished. But with her, as though they both understood the joke and found enjoyment in it.

"Ten Mayfair Square," she replied.

He nodded, then gave the direction to Smith, who started the carriage up again.

And the next part of her adventure was about to begin.

"I DO APPRECIATE you taking me, you know. And I'll need your address," she said after a moment.

"Pardon?"

"Your address. So I can send you the money I owe."

"Ah, of course." Simeon patted his pockets, but found nothing. "I can write it when we stop, I know I have paper with my art materials."

"Are you relieved you don't have to paint Regina, after all?" she asked.

She certainly did say whatever came into her mind; Simeon envied that. So much of his brain was occupied with what was the right thing to say at what time. He hadn't been aware of how much energy he spent making certain he was fitting in, saying the polite phrases, ensuring his welcome would continue. Because it would only take a moment, a lapse, and he could be blackballed by the only people who could support his art, who would make it possible for him to continue painting.

If he didn't have that, what would he have?

Nothing.

His art was everything, and he could not jeopardize it.

"Regina?" she prompted, making him realize he hadn't responded.

Why not just say what he thought, for once?

"I don't like doing portraits," he admitted. "It is necessary, at least until I am able to make a living only selling the paintings I actually want to do. Too often the sitter fidgets, or wants to talk, or has a different idea of what the finished portrait will look like. I prefer to implement my own vision."

"So you are forced to compromise because you need to survive?" she asked.

He nodded, then said in a cheeky tone, "You are quite clever, something that is rare to find in very attractive people." He used her words from a few days ago.

Her eyes widened in surprise, and her mouth fell open. "You don't—"

"I do. Of course I do." He gestured toward her. "I told you, if I could paint you, I would paint you as Artemisia. She fought alongside Xerxes," he explained, noting her confused expression.

"I would love that," she said dreamily.

"To be painted?" he replied.

"No, of course not," she said, sounding dismissive. "To fight alongside someone when both of you truly believe in the cause. That would be glorious."

"I presume you are going to engage in some sort of fight?" She was Artemisia. "That is, not alongside anyone else. Just yourself." Which made it all the more admirable—he knew it was hard to be on one's own trying to do what you thought was right.

She looked thoughtful. "I suppose you could say that. The fight isn't for a grand cause or anything. I just don't want to be forced into a life I don't want."

"I would say that is the grandest cause of all," Simeon retorted, thinking of his mother's constant reminders. "If you have a goal, a purpose, and someone wants to make it impossible for you to achieve it? That is well worth fighting for."

He glanced out the window again, noting the size of the houses had increased. "We must be getting close to your home." He felt an odd pang in his chest at saying goodbye.

"Do you think—" she began, then shook her head. "No, never mind."

He opened his mouth to ask what was on her mind when she began speaking again.

"Do you think you could kiss me?"

SIMEON WAS SELDOM, if ever, at a loss for words.

"I mean," she said, speaking so fast he could

barely keep up, "that since you do think I'm attractive, and I am unlikely to have the chance to kiss anyone nearly as handsome as you, I would like to seize the opportunity. I think it's important to be able to pivot, don't you?"

He still couldn't speak.

"Though if you don't wish to—"

"I do."

Well. It seemed as though he could say something, when it was important enough.

"Oh good. As I was saying, I want to kiss someone—anyone—because it seems like a thing people do, and I might not get the chance again. So," she said, tilting her head to regard him, "do you think we could?"

The carriage slowed, then stopped. Her expression fell.

"Oh. We are here already." She waved her hand in the air. "So never mind, it isn't—"

He took her by the arms and drew her close, placing his lips firmly on hers.

She froze for a moment, and he nearly drew back in apology, but then she let out a tiny sigh, grasping his shoulders and shifting herself into a more comfortable position.

Her mouth was soft, and warm, and for a moment Simeon just let himself stay there, feeling the tickle of her breath on his skin, relaxing as her fingers found purchase on his body.

And then she parted her lips slightly, and he licked them gently, his mouth curling up at her startled reaction. She didn't pull away, however;

instead, she made a happy little noise in her throat, widening her lips a bit more.

He slid his tongue inside, tasting the sweetness of her mouth, her soft warmth sliding through his veins like honey. If asked, he might not recall his own name, or where he was, or any of the enormous problems he faced. Right now, it was enough to be here, with her, giving her the best first kiss of her life.

Even if she hadn't explicitly said that was the case, he would have known this was the first. But it was because she was too direct, too honest, too intelligent, not to clarify precisely what she meant when she said anything.

Which meant he should stop thinking, for once. Just accept that if Miss Myrtle Allen said she wanted a kiss, then she actually wanted a kiss. She wouldn't hide behind what she thought she should be saying, or wanting. She just *did*.

Now her tongue was meeting his, both of them exploring as they kissed, Simeon feeling that delicious anticipation at the beginning of a relationship. Not that this was going to be one of his usual relationships; for one thing, she was about to leave this carriage, and it was unlikely he would see her again. But it felt the same, only perhaps more so because he knew when it was going to end. In a few moments.

But for now, all he could do was relish the sensations: her tongue in his mouth, her fingers clutching his shoulders, her soft, warm breaths sliding across his skin.

And then they heard the door of the coach opening, and they sprang apart, her holding her hand up to her mouth, her expression one of surprise. A good surprise, if Simeon had done his job well.

"We're here," Smith said, glancing between them. A tiny smile tugging at his mouth, as though he guessed what had been happening.

"Yes, of course. Mr. Jones, thank you for escorting me."

Her cheeks were flame red, and her eyes were nearly starry, they shone so brightly.

A good surprise for certain, then.

Chapter Seven

"Myrtle."

Myrtle froze at the doorway, her heart racing, and not in a good way. She clutched the piece of paper Simeon had given her, the one with his address, and her fist clenched around it in unconscious tension.

Richard stood in the foyer, his arms crossed over his chest, his expression furious.

How had he gotten here ahead of her? She shouldn't have taken time for that kiss. Perhaps she might've beaten him here.

On the other hand, then she wouldn't have been kissed at all. So never mind.

"Hello," she said cautiously, lowering her valise to the floor.

"Hello. That is all you have to say to me."

Not just furious. *Livid.*

"It is customary when seeing someone for the first time in a bit to welcome them," she replied. She was accustomed to dealing with Angry Richard, and had met Furious Richard on occasion, but had never seen Livid Richard.

Today was a day of firsts, then. First time being voluntarily silent, first kiss, and first Livid Richard.

She liked the middle one—a lot—but she had to say she wished she hadn't had the first or the last.

"The library," he said. "Now."

He spun on his heel and marched down the hall, her scurrying after. No matter what he said, he could not deter her from her plan.

She just had to weather his ire and stand firm.

"Shut the door," he said, when they were both inside.

She did, then leaned back against it, taking comfort somehow in the solidity of the wood. Bracing herself for what he might say.

"You left in the middle of the night with that man," he began. "Alone, with no chap—"

"I know all of this already," she interrupted. "Just skip ahead to the part where you tell me precisely how you feel, because I don't know any of that."

His eyes widened, and she wondered for a moment if they were going to pop out of his face. An impossibility, science-wise, but perhaps his anger would triumph over science.

"I am furious with you," he said, enunciating each word separately, as though tossing stones into a lake. "You ran off in the middle of the night with someone you didn't know."

She opened her mouth, but he held his hand up. "Let me finish. Someone you didn't know, an unmarried man with a . . . a reputation," he said, his cheeks burning red, "to hie off to London because you don't want what every other young lady in your situation does."

I'm not every other young lady, Myrtle thought.

And then he surprised her by adding, "But I need your help."

She blinked. "My help?"

He tilted his head to stare up at the ceiling, and she could see his throat move as he swallowed. "Yes."

Well, this was getting interesting. Not at all what she'd expected when she'd followed him down the hall.

"How can I help?" she said, advancing toward him. She took a seat on the sofa, stretching her legs out in front of her. "Come sit," she said, patting the seat.

Richard didn't move for a moment, but then he exhaled, loudly, and came to sit beside her, leaning his forearms on his thighs. "I need your help with Lilah's debut."

"My help?" She couldn't keep the surprise from her voice; Richard and Regina had made it abundantly clear that she was to stay away from anything pertaining to Lilah's debut because she was likely to do or say something that would reflect badly on her niece.

Myrtle couldn't help but agree, though of course that pained her.

"Regina broke her leg the morning after—the morning after the incident," Richard said, through tight lips. "She is in extreme discomfort, and is immobile for some time until she heals."

"Oh no, that is terrible! I am so sorry for her," she said. She didn't particularly like her sister-in-law, but she didn't want her to be hurting. Except for what she'd done to Mr. Jones. Though if she hadn't done that, Myrtle wouldn't have been here. Would not have been kissed.

So never mind, again.

She processed all that, and then her insides began to churn, and she felt her face tighten into a pained expression. "You're not going to ask—"

"You've got to guide Lilah through her come-out," Richard said. He was going to ask. Or rather demand. "You know how important this is to her, and naturally she doesn't want to wait until next year. She told me to ask you especially. For her."

"Oh no." Myrtle couldn't help her exclamation, though it wasn't answering the question. Not that Richard had phrased it as a question, had he? *You've got to guide Lilah through her come-out.* Definitely not a question. There was no possibility of denial.

"Believe me, I share your opinion," Richard said. "But there is no one else. If there was someone else, literally anybody else, I would not be telling you all this."

She wished the insult didn't sting as much as it did, though once again, she couldn't deny the veracity of Richard's words. She was a Societal disaster, and not particularly caring about that didn't make it any less true.

"The ball will be here in three weeks' time," Richard continued. "Lilah's wardrobe was already ordered, thank goodness, and she and I will return just before the ball." He gave her an assessing look. "You've got a little less than three weeks to get suitable clothing and prepare. You do know that this is what Lilah has been waiting her whole life for. You cannot allow for any kind of failure."

"This is me we're speaking of," Myrtle replied. "I know who I am, and what I am capable of."

"For once," Richard interrupted, sounding aggrieved, "just try to be normal. It's for Lilah. You can do it for Lilah, can't you?"

Myrtle felt a swell of emotion in her chest. When she spoke, her voice trembled. "I can. I will."

Richard put his hand on hers and squeezed it. "I know you can. I know you left for your own reasons, and we can talk about that later. I do want your happiness, you know that."

Myrtle nodded. "I do." There was a difference between loving someone and understanding them; she and Richard loved one another, but they definitely did not understand one another.

Both reasons were why she'd agreed to help and why she'd left in the first place.

And, just like that, her plans were pivoting again. Thank goodness she was so adept at change. She'd need to prepare for this new challenge better than she'd ever prepared before.

Her niece's happiness was at stake, and that was far more important than anything else.

Which meant she was going to need some help.

"I will do this," she repeated, "but I have a few stipulations regarding my assistance."

Richard gave her a wary look, one that was completely appropriate for what she was about to say.

But that didn't matter. Richard needed her. And she needed to make her own future—which meant she needed *him*. It was the perfect solution, one that made her giddy with excitement.

"Let's ring for tea, shall we?" Myrtle said, picking up the bell.

"Better make it something stronger," her brother replied, giving her a suspicious look.

RICHARD WAS NOT as elated as she was at the solution to the problem.

"I have hushed it up as best I can," he continued, taking a large sip of wine, "but it is bound to get out that Mr. Jones is the one who is rumored to have made advances toward my wife." His face was red, and his expression set, as though quite aware of how things were versus how they were gossiped about.

"And that is why he is the ideal person to help," Myrtle said easily, taking a sip from her teacup. Even though she was far from certain Richard would see it her way. But he didn't have a choice. Just as she didn't have a choice—she needed to help Lilah, but this was the only way it would work. "If people have heard the gossip, and see that both you and your sister are spending time with the gentleman in question, they will be less likely to think the worst of him. It is an excellent strategy," she said, with a note of complacency in her voice.

"If you do say so yourself," Richard replied dryly. Another swallow of wine, and then he pointed an accusing finger at her. Which would be effective if she wasn't so certain she was right. "As long as you understand that you will get none of your money if you end up marrying someone of whom I do not approve."

"You have been very clear about that," Myrtle said, selecting a biscuit and bringing it over to her plate. "And I have no plans to marry Mr. Jones." She lifted her gaze to her brother. "Or anyone. That is what we just agreed to, is it not?"

She'd laid out her stipulations one by one as though she was explaining a particularly difficult equation: one successful debut would equal a husbandless future but would require Mr. Jones's assistance.

He exhaled. "I remember. I don't know why I promised it—"

"Probably because I wouldn't help you otherwise, and it isn't as though you can make me marry someone I don't wish to." Even though he could, if he were cruel enough.

But she knew Richard wasn't cruel, just perplexed by his sister and what she wanted. The issue was that at some point his perplexity and frustration might lead him to make cruel decisions—but if she could help him marry Lilah off, and then prove she was adept on her own, he wouldn't be forced into that. He could continue to think he was doing the best for his family, and in Myrtle's case, if all went well, that would be true.

She'd have to calculate the odds for success another time.

"And," she continued, thinking it through, "if people see me with Mr. Jones as frequently as I presume we will be seen, they will think he is courting me, even though he is not."

"This is helpful how?" Richard said, taking another large sip. At this rate, he and Regina would drink the Leybourne wine cellar dry.

"Because then I will not have to spend time telling idiotic gentlemen I have no interest in them. I can focus all my efforts on Lilah." And on starting her own venture.

His eyebrows rose in surprise. "That *is* actually helpful."

"Don't be so startled," Myrtle said, stung. "I can be helpful."

"Yes, if I want my ledgers balanced or for you to talk about some arcane piece of mathematics so I can get to sleep more easily," he replied, sounding aggrieved. As though it was a burden to have such an intelligent sister.

"Balanced ledgers are necessary," she said tartly.

He inclined his head. "Agreed, but I pay someone to do that. It is not seemly for my sist—"

"We've been over this," she interrupted. "The point is we have a Season to get through, a Lilah to marry off, and you to allow me to do those things without too much of your interference."

She leaned closer, as though speaking in confidence. "Which means you do not have to participate much yourself. That is what you truly want, isn't it?"

He kept his gaze on her for a moment, and then he nodded as he exhaled. She could see the relief in his expression, even if he didn't admit it. "Yes. I just want Lilah to be happy, and I don't want to have to watch over her every moment."

"That is my job," Myrtle replied.

"Indeed. And you had best do it well, or we will have to find you a husband."

An implicit threat made explicit.

"My work is cut out for me, then," she replied brightly, willing herself to sound confident, even though she wasn't. But with his help—well, the odds would greatly increase, so perhaps confidence would be warranted.

She took a bite of flaky biscuit so she would stop talking, concerned she might inadvertently tell Richard something that would make him renege on this bargain.

Something like describing how wonderful kissing was, or how she had never known a gentleman's back, for goodness' sake, could be so appealing.

Thankfully the biscuit was delicious.

Chapter Eight

Simeon started at hearing the knock on the door. He'd come home and set up his easel immediately, sketching out his idea for the painting he'd spoken of to her. If he could pull it off, it might be the painting to take him into the next level of artists—people who could command enormous sums for their work, whose exhibitions would be spoken about by everybody who was anybody.

It was the kiss that had done it, that had sent the images of the painting shooting through his mind, though he hadn't realized it at the time. He hadn't realized much of anything at the time, in fact—just the softness of her lips, and the warmth of her body, and how engaged she was in all of it. So curious, so refreshing, so joyful.

It felt different from other experiences he'd had. But that was always true—each of his romantic encounters were different from one another, and he didn't want to diminish any of them in favor of this one.

Though this one felt oddly different, and not in the same way they usually did.

He shook his head in annoyance at himself, making as little sense as Fenton often did without the genius underpinning it.

Instead of thinking about it, then, he lost himself in his work—sketching the outlines of her face, hinting at her fierce expression. Her brows, which could knit together in concern only to rise up in humor mere seconds later. Her hands, gesticulating to an unseen army to fight for her. Which they would do, gladly.

And then he heard the knocking again, only louder and more insistent.

"Coming," he shouted, before going down the stairs to fling open the door, hoping that it would only be a brief interruption, since it felt as though he was on to something with his initial sketches.

"Miss Allen!" he said, jerking his head back as he saw who stood on the street. His muse. "You didn't need to come yourself with the money, you could have sent—"

"It's not that, Mr. Jones," she replied, then brushed past him without waiting to be invited up, immediately beginning the climb up the stairs. Just as she'd done when she'd barged into his room only the day before.

Where did she want him to take her now? Timbuktu? The South Pole? The moon?

He stared after her, then shut the door and began the ascent.

"Please do come in," he said dryly when they were in his rooms.

The main room was his studio, and held only his art supplies and a small sofa that he often used for modeling sessions.

"Things have changed," she announced, her tone making it sound very dramatic, and he kept his gaze on her face, waiting for her to continue.

"Well?" he prompted, when she remained silent.

And then her expression faltered, and he saw a hint of vulnerability in her eyes—not something he'd seen yet from her. Things must truly have changed for her to exhibit even a tiny bit of trepidation.

"I need your help." She sounded . . . almost lost.

"You don't need another ride somewhere, do you?" he said, injecting a lightness into his voice. Wanting to put her at ease. "Because I've already returned the carriage."

Her mouth curled into a slight smile as she shook her head. "No, nothing like that. That would be simple."

"Would you like to sit?" he said, gesturing toward the sofa.

"Yes, please," she replied. "This is your studio?" She settled herself and glanced around the room, clear interest evident in her expression.

"And where I live, yes."

"Oh, of course," she said. She leaned forward to glance down the hallway. "Your bedroom and kitchen are there?"

Simeon went to sit beside her, crossing his legs and stretching his arm over the back of the sofa.

"I don't think you came here to discuss the layout of my rooms," he said.

Her cheeks turned pink, and he smothered a chuckle.

"No, I did not." She lifted her chin and met his gaze. "Richard is here, and things have changed."

"Yes, you've mentioned that," Simeon replied. "Can you explain?"

"I need your help because my niece is coming out this Season, and my sister-in-law can't chaperone, and I have to do it, except I am a disaster." Only she spoke so quickly it sounded like, *Ineed yourhelpbecausemynieceiscomingoutthisSeasonand mysister-in-lawcan'tchaperoneandIhavetodoitexceptI amadisaster.*

"I'm sorry, but—what?" He held his hands out, palms up, in question. "Are you asking me to chaperone your niece? Because I am guessing that is the last thing your brother would want, given our recent interaction." He frowned. "As well as being entirely inappropriate."

"No, not that," she said, impatient. "Do keep u—never mind," she said hastily. "I want your help in navigating Society to make certain I don't do anything that will ruin Lilah's debut. This is so important to her, and therefore important to me, and I just know I will say something that people will talk about and suddenly Lilah will be twenty-four years old with no marital prospects."

"Like you, you mean?" he said in a mild tone of voice. "From what I can see, you are quite happy."

"But Lilah is not like me," she shot back. "She is

a normal girl who dreams of marriage and children and security."

"And you don't." It was not a question; he already knew she did not, and he found that remarkable. Intriguing.

And definitely not normal. He liked not normal. A lot.

But that wasn't the main point of what was happening.

"You want me to help you navigate Society? There is nobody else you could ask?"

She gave him a scornful look. "If there had been anybody else to ask do you suppose I would be here? You are literally my only friend in London, and Lilah makes her debut in a few weeks."

"What about your brother?" He spoke in a dry tone of voice. "I imagine he would not be pleased to see me, especially if he's seeing me with you and your niece."

She snorted. "What about him? He's asked for my help, and I'm giving it to him. I told him he was going to have to make certain Regina's behavior didn't affect you adversely, and there is an easy way to do that. Appearing with our family will make it clear that nothing untoward occurred, and that you have our support." Her face shifted into a sour expression. "He'll just be thrilled I might not mortify him and our entire family. Not that I care about that, mind you." She frowned. "Though that is not true. I do care just because it would reflect poorly on Lilah." She flapped her hand in dismissal. "I was going to prove to Richard that I could survive perfectly well on my own without a husband, and my accomplishing this will make it clear." Her face brightened. "When I get Lilah married off, or at least have her experience a successful Season, he'll see I am quite capable of not being married. He's promised he would adjust his plans. Pivot even, perhaps."

"What with never doing it and all," he remarked.

She glared at him. "This is not the time for humor."

He shrugged. "I think this is the best time for humor, in fact. If we can't enjoy ourselves while in the worst situation of our lives, then when can we?"

"That makes no sense at all, and you know it," she pointed out.

He gave her a knowing look. "Correct, but at least the sentiment for enjoyment is out there. I see no reason to suffer unduly." *Ever*, in fact, which guided his way of life—undue suffering was to be avoided, unless it was in the service of his art, in which case he would suffer everything.

But the opportunity she was presenting was too enticing to resist. The chance to not only rescue his reputation, but enhance it? Simply by guiding Miss Allen—Myrtle of the kissable lips—through a Season?

How hard could it be?

But then a thought occurred to him, and he had to ask. Even though it might mean he didn't get to take advantage of the enticing opportunity.

"What about your plan? I thought you wanted to set up some sort of Myrtle Money service."

"Myrtle Money," she replied. "I like that. Alliteration and all." Her expression sobered. "I'm just going to have to table those plans for a bit. Hopefully there won't be too many ladies who are facing financial ruin because of the gentlemen in their lives." She sounded mournful.

"Why not do both?" he asked, feeling the spark of inspiration hit him. "With my help, you can meet everyone you need to—you did say you don't have much of an acquaintance in London?" *You are literally my only friend in London.*

She snorted. "That is understating it." She gave him a speculative look. "But why would you do this in addition to that? You told me yourself you put your art and your talent ahead of everything else. Why take on more duties?"

Because I want to spend time with you. Because I want to see your pretty smile when I've helped you achieve your goals. Because I want to watch your remarkable brain working, something I seem to find as alluring as seeing another woman undress.

Though seeing her undress while using her remarkable brain might just break him. In a very good way, but he'd still be broken.

"Because I also want you to pose for me," he said. "We can do the whole debutante thing, and the Myrtle Money thing as well; we will find enough time for everything," he said, without explaining the details. "People are very skilled at frittering their time away. I do not."

She kept her gaze on him for a moment, as though wanting to question him more, but eventually she shrugged. "If I can repay you as easily as posing for you, then I will accept your help grate-fully. Thank you." And then she added, after an-other moment, "Friend."

SIMEON WOKE TO the sound of banging on his door.

"Jones!" a voice yelled. Sounding angry.

Simeon rolled onto his side, then pulled himself out of bed, not hurrying. Whoever was out there was irate enough to wait a few minutes while Simeon made himself presentable.

"Jones! I know you're in there!"

"Yes, because it's six o'clock in the morning," Simeon murmured. He located his trousers, then donned his shirt and grabbed the jacket he'd worn yesterday. He didn't bother putting his boots on, just tucked his toes into his slippers—the one concession to urgency he would make for his unexpected visitor.

The banging continued as he went downstairs. "Jones!" the voice called again.

The viscount. Of course it was him.

"Hold on, I'm coming," Simeon said, already annoyed.

"Open up!"

He undid the lock, then opened the door, hold-ing it wide.

The viscount stood on his step, looking as though he'd been up all evening—his clothes were rumpled, his face was unshaven, and his eyes were wild.

To be honest, Simeon had often looked like that, but always for far more pleasurable reasons than worrying about a relative.

"Come in, then," he said in a mild tone, turning to ascend the stairs.

The viscount followed behind him, clearly nonplussed at Simeon's reaction.

"Do you want some tea?" Simeon asked as they entered the main room. The canvas with his initial sketches of Myrtle was on his easel, but he doubted the viscount would realize who Simeon was painting—his early pencil work was mostly to get the emotion of the subject, not to draw any particulars. Unless he saw the brows—those belonged entirely to Myrtle, and could be mistaken for no one else.

So if he did see, and registered who the painting was of, he would most definitely be even more irked with Simeon.

Oh well. At least this was *interesting*. He'd rather be interested than comfortable. Though he did wish the viscount had waited for a few hours so Simeon could get some more sleep—he'd been so eager to start on his painting he'd stayed up later than usual.

"I don't want tea!" the viscount said. "I want you to explain yourself!"

Simeon arched a brow, aware that would likely annoy the man even more. "Explain myself from what age? You'll have to be more specific. If you're speaking of where I came from, that I don't know. All I know is that I turned up at the School for Scoundrels—the Devenaugh Home, that is—when I was about six months old."

"I don't mean that kind of explanation!"

Simeon regarded the viscount, then decided it was probably best not to continue to irk him. Myrtle was depending on her brother, after all, to accommodate what she wanted in order to successfully launch his daughter into Society.

Not for the first time, Simeon was grateful he hadn't been born into that world. Yes, having one's birth constantly brought up as a denigrating factor was unpleasant, but at least he didn't have to fuss about any of this kind of thing.

Until now, that was. Because he'd promised Myrtle. Because he was her only friend in London, and she was clearly terrified of encountering Society on her own.

Which really meant he needed to placate her brother—since she was a friend, he needed to be as staunchly loyal as he was to anyone he put in the friend category.

And even though the man seemed angry, there was something underneath that Simeon recognized—worry. Concern, perhaps? Maybe even love?

But from what he knew, Myrtle's brother would prefer to try to keep his sister in her prescribed box than let her express herself. Perhaps that, too, came from love. Not understanding someone didn't mean you couldn't love them—look at him, after all. He didn't always understand his starchy friend Bram, or his morally upright friend Benedict, but he loved them. And that wasn't even taking Fenton into account, whom no one understood. Not even Fenton himself.

So he'd try to be patient, and not irritate the man.

"As far as I understand it," Simeon said, donning a conciliatory tone, "your sister feels uncomfortable in her world. *Your* world. And since you have tasked her with launching your daughter into Society because the viscountess"—and then he paused, noting the viscount's change of expression—"is unwell, Miss Allen was hoping I could assist her. Smooth the way, so to speak."

The viscount appeared to be experiencing a range of emotions, from embarrassment, to irritation, to frustration.

"I would do it myself, you see," he began, "but I don't know the first thing about any of it. My wife was too—well, you know," he said, his face turning red. "So if you can help Myrtle, I suppose I will be grateful. It is most important to all of us that Lilah has a good Season."

"And that is why you have arrived here so early? To make certain I can succeed in what I have promised your sister?" And hadn't Myrtle said that her brother had already agreed? There had to be more to this visit than just Richard rattling his aristocratic saber.

Simeon's questions were a graceful way to extricate the viscount from his discomfort, and thankfully the man took it.

"Yes. Of course, yes. That is why I am here." He cleared his throat. "I also wanted to say, however, that my sister, despite her intelligence, is naïve."

Simeon stilled, wondering where the viscount would take the conversation. This felt like the crux of it, and he braced himself for whatever the viscount had to say.

"Her fortune remains under my control, and I will not hand it over to just anyone. I will not agree to her marrying anyone of whom I do not absolutely approve. That would include you, Mr. Jones, as well as any other money-hungry suitors."

The viscount's face grew hard, as though he was anticipating an argument.

Simeon would not accommodate him.

This was why he was here. To warn Simeon away from Myrtle, even though Simeon knew full well she had no intention of marrying anyone. Not even someone she'd enjoyed kissing.

"I have no intention of marrying your sister." The other man's expression eased. "She has made her feelings absolutely clear to me, and I believe she has made them clear to you as well." Simeon set his jaw. "Does this mean that if Miss Allen succeeds this Season with your daughter that you will accommodate her wishes for her future?"

To remain unmarried, to focus instead on her remarkable brain. To live life as she wished, to ensure that she was living up to her full potential.

As Simeon's mother always insisted he do. They were two talented peas in a pod.

"I have promised I will hear her out. Though that is not your business," the viscount replied in a completely condescending tone of voice. "What is your business is to make certain she does not enter into a disadvantageous match. With you, or with anyone—" He paused, and Simeon spoke.

"Or anyone like me. I understand your point entirely, my lord," he said.

Viscount Leybourne gave a firm nod, then held his hand out to Simeon. "Good day, sir," he said. "I trust you will keep this conversation confidential."

Simeon raised a brow. "You mean you don't wish me to tell your sister how you came to my house at dawn and insisted I adhere to certain stipulations when I am only endeavoring to help her?" he said dryly. He glanced down at the other man's hand, but did not clasp it. "I will not speak of this to her at all, no."

The viscount flushed, and snatched his hand back. He turned and walked quickly to the stairs without another word.

Leaving Simeon angry and anticipatory all at the same time.

"I CANNOT TELL you how excited I am!" Lilah exclaimed.

"Actually, I think you can," Myrtle replied, "since you've said the same thing at least a few dozen times."

It was only a slight exaggeration.

Thankfully, Myrtle had had a few weeks to prepare.

Lilah had only arrived the previous day, and had quickly set about responding yes to every single invitation she'd received, even though some of them were occurring simultaneously, making for an impossible situation until and unless someone invented cloning or time travel.

Richard had found himself suddenly immersed in work, a claim Myrtle found highly suspicious, but since he'd already tasked her with the job of launching Lilah, it didn't much matter.

Perhaps her brother was as averse to Society as she was?

She hadn't contemplated that. She'd been so busy feeling awkward and uncomfortable herself she hadn't wondered if anybody else did.

She and Lilah were in the breakfast room, a few footmen standing at attention behind them. Cook had made far more food than two ladies could possibly consume, and Myrtle was especially delighted about the scones and clotted cream.

Things were always better with clotted cream.

"What are we doing today?" Lilah asked. It was a rhetorical question, since she was in charge of their schedule. "First there is the luncheon at Lady Leigh's, she apparently knew my mother from her come-out? She said it would be an intimate gathering, no more than twenty guests."

Myrtle's stomach sank. Twenty guests were eighteen more than she wished to tolerate, since two of them would be Lilah and Myrtle herself. But it was essential to extricating herself from the life that otherwise would be intended for her. Richard had promised. And she would have Mr. Jones's assistance, though she didn't think he was one of the guests at the Leigh luncheon, unfortunately.

She just had to look at it as a mathematics problem. She would invest a certain amount of hours doing things she would prefer not to, and she would be rewarded with her own future.

It was a simple equation, though it seemed daunting looking at it now.

"And then we are to go riding in the park. Father has said he will join us there, since we are likely to run into some of his acquaintances."

At least she would get to be out in the open air—Myrtle did appreciate staying inside so she could work, but she found she got restless if she stayed inside for too long. It got difficult to sleep, she'd end up doing problems in her head instead of trying to rest.

"We're to have dinner at home, just us, since Father will be dining at his club."

"Well," Myrtle said, already tired from Lilah's recitation, "that all sounds wonderful."

Her niece gave her a narrow look. "You are lying, Aunt. You are terrible at lying. I know you are not looking forward to any of this." She reached over and wrapped her arms around Myrtle. "But I do appreciate it so much. Mother could not come, and Father is far too busy to help." She leaned back to look into Myrtle's eyes. "Besides, it would have been odd to have him be my chaperone. People would have talked about why Mother was not here. It's far more reasonable to have someone like you accompany me than a gentleman."

"Of course." Myrtle thought for a moment how to ask a discreet question, then realized she'd never been discreet in her life. "So what will you say if anyone asks why Regina isn't here?"

Lilah's expression tightened. "I'll mention her leg. I hate that she is not here, but I know why. And we all know that any kind of scandal might adversely affect my own opportunities. I heard about what happened with Mr. Jones. I overheard a row between Mother and Father."

"Ah, I see." And she did see; it was terrible for both Richard and Regina to be, she presumed, unhappy with one another when there was no possibility of getting out of it.

They were one of the primary reasons Myrtle didn't want to be forced into that situation. Not that she would take to Madeira-ing, as Regina did, or trying to control everyone else's behavior, as Richard did, but she did not want to be miserable for years on end.

It seemed like a slow death sentence, one that would stifle her until she died.

"Well," Myrtle said, patting Lilah's arm, "let's go prepare ourselves for the day."

"AND YOU, MISS ALLEN," said one of the many ladies gathering in the room prior to going into luncheon, "do you have plans this Season?" Her sly expression left no doubt about what she was referring to.

Myrtle's returning smile was tight. "My plans are to guide my dear niece through her debut."

She had found that it was best to answer difficult questions simply and firmly, so that hopefully the questioner would take the hint and drop the subject.

"But every young lady, surely, has aspirations for a home? A family?"

This particular questioner seemed to be particularly dimwitted.

"I have a home and I have a family," Myrtle replied, nodding toward Lilah. "I am too busy to consider anything else."

"Ah," the woman said, her expression growing sharper, "I do believe, however, you have met my brother? The Honorable Lawrence Pensworth?"

"I must have, since you say so," Myrtle said. Being honest, as she always was, though the answer seemed to upset the questioner even more.

"Since I say so? I suppose my brother is not memorable enough." The lady glanced around at the other guests as though seeking confirmation that Myrtle was being impossibly rude.

Perhaps she was, but she was also being truthful.

"I believe what Miss Allen meant to say," a voice said from the corner of the room, "is that she wishes to devote every speck of her attention to guiding her niece through the Season, and then she will allocate as many resources to herself after she is persuaded her niece is properly settled."

Myrtle exhaled in relief as Mr. Jones walked toward her. She hadn't noticed him there previously, but then again, she had been focused on navigating the event without mishap. Something that required her full concentration.

He nodded to her, then addressed the brother-supporting lady. "If you like, my lady, I could introduce your brother to several young ladies of my acquaintance. I have had the good fortune of getting to know them through various events like these, and I imagine many of them will find your brother quite . . . memorable," he said, darting a quick, mischievous glance toward Myrtle.

The woman gave one last glower toward Myrtle, then offered a warm smile to Mr. Jones. "That sounds lovely. I do expect you will be at all the usual parties?"

He bowed, an elegant gesture that made every other bow Myrtle had ever seen seem like those gentlemen were just adjusting a bad back or perhaps looking down at something on the ground.

Not that she was a bow connoisseur, but his movements were remarkable. So graceful it was a pleasure to watch.

For the first time, she actually wanted to have a dance with someone. Namely him. Because she imagined his dancing would be as supremely lovely as his bow.

He was replying to the lady, and Myrtle missed most of it, but she gathered the answer was satisfactory, because the lady gave one final nod, then drifted away.

"Thank you," she murmured, as he moved closer to her elbow.

"I didn't think the task would start so soon," he said, but he didn't seem put out by it.

"I find all of these things—"

"Dull," he finished for her.

"Indeed."

"Yes, your disdain is apparent on your face. You're

going to have to do something about that, nobody wants to think they're boring their listener."

She wrinkled her nose. "But how do I do that? I've never lied before." She considered that, then spoke again. "No, that isn't quite correct. I have lied, I'm just spectacularly bad at it."

He shrugged. "It is a skill like any other you've undoubtedly mastered."

She tilted her head. "Do you really think so? Comparable to when I learned sums, or was able to translate text from the original Greek?"

"Not quite the same, but nearly as useful." She couldn't tell if he was being sarcastic. That was the problem with complete honesty, if she was being . . . completely honest. It was difficult to discern if someone else was prevaricating when one was so firmly committed to the truth.

"I suppose I can try. I can practice." A thought struck her, and she continued. "It won't be like the Pinocchio tale, will it?" She touched the end of her nose. "Because I would not want to have this grow."

"I imagine if noses truly grew then every single person in here—excepting you, of course"—accompanied by another magnificent bow—"would not be able to enter because their noses would be so large."

She laughed at the image, and then noticed several of the other guests looking their way.

"I suppose I have to work on suppressing my honest reactions," she said. "I think I laughed too much."

He followed her glance, then took her arm and looped it through his. "I don't want you to suppress anything, Miss Allen. We'll just need to improve your acting skills."

Myrtle brightened. "That sounds less like lying, and more like something I would want to do."

He made a diffident gesture. "It's all in how you phrase it, after all."

"Like a game," she said, feeling more comfortable. "I like games and puzzles and such. I suppose this will be fine, after all."

"If we can all make our way to the table," their hostess said. "I have put the two of you together, Miss Allen and Mr. Jones, since you are obviously such good friends."

Unfortunately, their hostess was also the avid questioner and brother-haver.

Myrtle felt her light mood dissipate as they walked to the lunch table.

This was going to be more difficult than any mathematics problem she'd ever encountered.

Chapter Nine

"In here, please," Richard said, as Myrtle, Lilah, and Simeon returned to Richard's town house.

The luncheon had ended without any further mishap, thanks to Simeon. And then they had all gone riding, with Richard joining them and introducing them to various businessmen he knew, none of whom would be suitable as a husband for Lilah.

But Myrtle got to be in the fresh air, and she was wearing a fetching riding habit in a dark, mossy green that reminded her of ancient forests and dark pools of water, places entirely removed from Society ballrooms.

Simeon had insisted on accompanying them to the rest of the events scheduled for that day, since he'd said Myrtle was in need of a friend. Richard had scowled, but hadn't said anything.

What Myrtle knew Simeon meant by needing a friend was that she needed someone to smooth Societal waters for her, since she was floundering. Lilah hadn't noticed, but Lilah had all the usual self-absorption of a debutante, and likely wouldn't notice until it was too late.

Though she did like the idea of him being her friend.

"You'd better come, too," Richard added in a grudging tone, addressing Simeon. "Not you," he said to Lilah, who was starting to walk to his study.

She opened her mouth to object, but then saw his expression, and likely realized that whatever her father was going to say was going to be unpleasant.

Richard glowered at Simeon, but sat down at his desk with a reluctant expression, folding his arms over his chest. He gestured for the two of them to sit in the chairs on the other side.

"You are supposed to be keeping yourself respectable," he began.

"I am!" Myrtle shot back. "Just now I took Lilah to a luncheon, and we are going to—to do something," she said, entirely forgetting. Just that she knew she wouldn't enjoy it. "And we are meeting all sorts of people, many of whom are coming to Lilah's party." She donned a bright smile, trying to remember what Mr. Jones had said about lying—that was, playing a game. This game would be to convince her brother she was doing a good job of chaperoning Lilah, because if he didn't believe it, he would try to force his vision of her future onto her.

"I've already heard about your behavior," Richard said. "You have met a lot of people already, some of whom are talking about how scandalous you are." He spoke in a bluster, not nearly at livid levels, but close enough. "Just now, a few acquaintances reported—purely because they thought I should know, you understand, though of course that means everyone will know—that you've been seen going to Mr. Jones's house alone, without even a maid. To his house!" he added, unnecessarily, stabbing an accusing finger toward Simeon.

"Yes, of course I go to his house. I am a chaperone, Richard. I am not an eligible miss any longer." If she said it enough, perhaps it would be true. "I am posing for Mr. Jones. I am Arte—" And she gave Simeon a questioning look.

"Artemisia," Simeon supplied.

"I don't care who you are!" Richard said, aggrieved. "It's not appropriate for you to be alone with him, no matter who you think you are."

"I think I am your ancient sister tasked with launching my niece's come-out," Myrtle replied acerbically. "If I am wrong, please do let me know."

"You are not ancient," Simeon retorted.

She glared at him. "And you are not being helpful. Please remind my brother that I am not a marriageable lady, that he has promised—if I am successful in Lilah's debut—that I will be allowed to lead my own life."

"Leading your own life, as you've done so far, is not what one would expect from someone in your position." He sounded as stuffy as he'd ever sounded, and she wondered just who he had spoken to while they were in the park to get him so fussed up.

Not that it mattered; the fact was, he was near lividity, and she needed to understand why.

Myrtle waved a hand. "What are you saying? Just tell me directly, I cannot comprehend you when you make vague announcements."

"I am saying," Richard replied through gritted teeth, "that you are now an official scandal."

Myrtle brightened. "Oh," she said, clapping her hands together, "that is excellent news!"

Richard rolled his eyes up to the ceiling in exasperation. "How is that possibly good news?"

"Because," Simeon answered, surprising her with his quickness, "if your sister is too scandalous, nobody will want to marry her, so she will not be beleaguered with proposals. Twentysomething of them so far, am I correct?" he asked, glancing toward Myrtle.

"Thirty-two if one is being absolutely precise," she said.

"Which you always are," Simeon shot back, his amusement evident in his tone.

"But yes, you are correct about the scandalous part. Very clever of you."

"See, I can keep up," he replied with a grin.

"Stop flir—Wait a minute," Richard said. "I see a solution."

"I don't even see a problem," Myrtle murmured, but her brother was not listening to her.

Richard jabbed an accusatory finger toward

Simeon. "You will have to pretend to be engaged to her. To solve this."

"What?" Myrtle and Simeon said in unison.

Richard was already explaining. "If you are engaged, you will avoid the scandal. And then you can break it off when Lilah is taken care of. Myrtle will withdraw to the country to avoid gossip, and I will allow her access to her funds."

"Yes, you will *allow* me to have my own money," Myrtle said dryly. But she felt unsettled by Richard's suggestion—it wasn't fair to drag Simeon even further into this, no matter that they were friends. There was a limit to friendship, after all.

"Why would I do that?" Simeon asked, sounding wary.

Of course. He had as little desire to be wed as she did, and it would cause some discussion of his antecedents—even more discussion, that was—if it was known he was engaged to someone of her rank.

"Why would you indeed?" Richard said, looking smug.

Myrtle disliked that expression. It only boded ill.

"Because if you agree, I will pay you your lost commission."

Simeon snorted. "Your sister already paid me for its loss. Plus more on top of that."

Richard's eyes widened. "She did not. With what money?" he said, directing an accusing glance toward Myrtle.

"I have money of my own," Myrtle said. Wishing she didn't sound so defensive. "It's just not very much. Not enough to live on for the rest of my life, to be certain, but enough to give Mr. Jones money he did not deserve to lose."

Richard's face flushed, likely a reminder of his wife's poor behavior.

"Fine," he said. "I'll give you—I'll give you twice the original commission if you do this."

"Not enough," Myrtle said, determined to ensure Simeon got offered what he was due. After all, if he agreed—and she didn't see why he wouldn't, as long as she did—he should get as much money as possible.

"Tell me how much, Myrtle, since you seem to know what Mr. Jones wants." Richard's lips tightened into a thin line.

"Five times the commission."

"Five—impossible. The most I can offer is four. That is my final offer. Is it a deal?"

Simeon looked confused, and Myrtle resisted the urge to give him a comforting pat. "Just say yes, Mr. Jones. You will get a lot of money for pretending to be engaged to me, and then we can break it off and Richard will keep his promise." She turned to stare at her brother. "Because if he doesn't, I will tell everyone of this arrangement."

Richard flung his hands up in surrender. "Why would I not keep my promise? It is my suggestion, after all." He turned to look at Simeon. "And no offense, Mr. Jones, but it is not as though I want my sister to marry a—a—"

"A bastard?" Simeon supplied. He spoke through clenched teeth.

"Precisely," Richard said, sounding relieved. He'd apparently missed how angry Simeon was.

But Myrtle hadn't. She hated how his truth must make him feel, when people insisted on tossing it in his face so much. She wished she could speak to him about it, but that would be broaching a subject that was likely too personal, even though they'd kissed and shared a bed.

Not in that order.

"A bargain, then," Myrtle said instead.

IT TOOK ALL of Simeon's will not to punch Myrtle's brother in the mouth.

Even though the viscount had only spoken the truth—Myrtle was scandalous, people were talking, and Simeon was a bastard.

But he didn't have to like the truth. Not when it was spoken like that.

Instead of punching anyone, he'd stalked home, then headed to the only club that would admit him—the Peckham, also dubbed the Orphans' Club, because it allowed gentlemen with suspect parentage in, as long as they were good people with something to offer.

"Whisky," he said to the servant standing at the door of the common area.

Usually he and his fellow orphans—the Bastard Five—took themselves to a private room, where they discussed books and their own lives. But Simeon wasn't certain if the book club was happening this month—Theo's wife had just recently given birth, Bram and his wife were expecting, and Fenton was still off in Europe doing . . . something.

"Here you are, sir," the servant said, returning faster than Simeon would have expected.

The room was fitted with comfortable chairs, a few crackling fireplaces, and plenty of places for quiet discussions. It was here that political deals were made, business ventures were proposed, and most crucially for Simeon, art was commissioned.

The members mostly left one another alone, but occasionally someone would recall that Simeon was a celebrated artist, and ask him to advise on a purchase, or try to hire him for a portrait. He declined often, but sometimes his finances would require his assent, or the person would offer enough money—as Myrtle's brother had—to make it worth his while.

He took a sip of the drink, relishing how it burned down his throat. He wasn't one for excessive drinking, but he did appreciate a fine whisky.

"What has got you here today?" a voice asked.

Simeon twisted in his chair to see Benedict Quintrell, the unspoken leader of the Bastard Five. Benedict worked for the government in some mysterious fashion, which meant he could both keep a secret and be maddeningly oblique in his answers.

"I can't be at my club?" Simeon said, gesturing to the chair opposite.

Benedict sat, looking around for the servant, who bustled forward. "Same as what he's got," he said, before leaning forward to look at Simeon. "Something's not right. If Theo was here, he would say it's a woman. Is that correct?"

Simeon made a grumbling noise deep in his throat, then nodded. "Of a sort." He might as well tell Benedict everything. It wasn't as though he had any secrets from his friends. Except for the whole "poor as a church mouse" thing that he kept to himself. "There's a person who's asked me to pretend to be her betrothed, just for the Season."

Benedict's eyebrows shot up. "You? Whyever would anyone want—"

"A bastard for a husband?" Simeon completed, still angry about the viscount's disdain. "That should tell you how dire the situation is, to be honest."

"Who is it? Anybody I know?"

Simeon shook his head. "I don't think so—it's Miss Myrtle Allen, the sister of the viscount—"

"The Viscount Leybourne!" Benedict exclaimed. "I've heard of her. She is a remarkable mathematician."

"You know Myrtle?" Simeon blurted, astonished.

"Myrtle, is it?" Benedict said, now waggling his eyebrows. "No wonder you are being asked to be her betrothed, if you refer to her that way." He leaned against the seat back. "I've heard of her, though we have not met. Some have said it is a shame she is a woman, since her particular skills could be so useful in cryptography and such." Benedict shook his head in mild frustration. "I'm not sure where I've heard of her, just that she has immense talent. It would be a shame if she married for real."

Benedict's words made something tighten in Simeon's gut. Not because he wanted to marry her—no, not that—but because he knew how Myrtle would react if she heard Benedict's words. Words that implied that a married woman would no longer be useful for her skills because she now had a husband. Benedict didn't intend that specifically, of course; it was just Society that dictated that a wife's sole duty be to her husband.

No wonder Myrtle was so set against marriage. He hadn't truly understood before, but now he felt it. The inequity of the system, a system that declared that someone with Myrtle's intelligence was less helpful than the biggest male dotard because Myrtle was born a woman.

He'd been determined to do everything he could to let her have the future she wanted— one unencumbered by husband or family—and Benedict's words were a reminder that that determination was even more crucial.

"But why you?" Benedict said. "I knew Miss Allen was in town, but I assumed it was her usual round of maths and museums. This is unexpected." Benedict's knowledge of Society was unparalleled, mostly because most of the aristocratic gentlemen also dabbled in government, which was Benedict's expertise. "And for her to agree to be engaged to you—whether it is a pretense or not—is most definitely odd."

Simeon bristled. He wasn't certain why, just that he was sorely tempted to punch his friend.

In the mouth, as he'd wanted to do to the viscount just hours earlier.

Perhaps he was developing a pugnacious streak? Or, more likely, the time he'd spent with Myrtle had made him want to protect her, to shield her from people who would make insensitive comments like Benedict and her brother had.

"You should take a sip of that," Benedict added, a smile playing about his mouth. "You look as though you want to—well, I'm just glad we're in public."

Simeon glared, but did as Benedict suggested, taking another swallow that burned down his throat. Not as much as those words had, and much more pleasant, but similar, nonetheless.

"So what is the purpose of the subterfuge?"

Simeon gave his friend a level look. "She has asked me to assist with her niece's debut. Her mother, the viscountess, is otherwise indisposed."

Benedict's expression was knowing. "Ah, I've heard about the viscountess." He jabbed a finger toward Simeon. "Didn't you go to paint her portrait or something?"

"Humph."

"I see. And now you are tasked with pretending to be her betrothed?"

"Shh, keep your voice down. It won't be pretense if everyone knows," Simeon said in a harsh whisper.

"Good point," Benedict replied in an equally low tone. "But I cannot think of anyone better to guide someone through Society."

The rare compliment eased some of Simeon's discomfort with the whole situation.

"Just as long as you don't go falling in love with her," Benedict added.

Simeon's lips curled in distaste. "She's making her debut, she is far too youn—"

"You know I do not mean Miss Allen's niece. I mean Miss Allen."

"Right," Simeon said, wishing Benedict wasn't quite so observant.

"Do I have your promise?" Benedict pressed.

Simeon finished his drink, then turned and met Benedict's gaze. "I promise." Not because of Benedict. Not even because of himself.

But because of her. She needed to have the freedom to make her own future, not be bogged down with love, or confessions of love.

Which meant now he was embroiled even deeper into this ridiculous scheme, all because he had given her a carriage ride to London. And not even in his own carriage.

But the alternative—any of the alternatives—weren't possible, not if he was to consider himself a good human being. Could he have let her head to London on her own? Yes. Would he have let her? No.

Could he have let her manage her lively niece's debut on her own? Yes. Would he have let her? No.

Today, when he'd seen her expression as Lady Leigh had questioned her, he hadn't even paused. He'd just leapt in to defend her from people who were more accustomed to lying than she was.

She was ridiculously intelligent, yes, but she was also incredibly naïve. Because she was so honest she thought everyone else was, when that simply wasn't the case.

He had to protect her.

He had to pretend to be engaged to her. Not just for the money—though that helped, of course—but because otherwise she would inevitably be pilloried, and that would adversely affect her niece and Myrtle's own future.

She'd have to accept one of the twenty-seven— or thirty-two—proposals she'd received.

Simeon would not allow that.

"I would like to meet her," Benedict was saying. Making Simeon fiercely protective all over again, even though it was Benedict, for goodness' sake.

"Humph," was all he said as he finished his drink.

FOR ALMOST THE first time, Myrtle wished she had someone to confide in —someone besides *him*, of course.

Because it was him that was causing the ruckus in the first place. And Richard, too, though Richard would be the last person she would want to speak to about it all.

Mostly because it was his idiotic suggestion.

Why did she need taking care of anyway? Why did she need a pretend betrothed?

Because you are likely to tell the truth, and your expressions give you away even if you try to lie. Because people here like nothing more than a little scandal—or a lot of scandal—and your conduct can be seen as scandalous.

Because it is easier to be alone with him if people think you're engaged to him.

It was the last one that finally persuaded her— well, that and the fact that Lilah's future might be in jeopardy if she didn't agree.

She wasn't even thinking about her own future.

"It won't be that difficult," she said aloud, talking to no one. She had returned to her room, not wanting to spend any more time with Richard than was necessary. Lilah was still out with her friends, so she had a moment to herself.

Normally, this would mean she would plunge into some mathematics problems, perhaps open one of her books and read, but her mind was going too fast to do either of those things.

"And then when I break it off—because I will break it off," she reasoned, "I'll be seen as a terrible person who is flighty and possibly a bit loose."

That sounded fun, to be honest. To be seen as a person with scandal attached to her name rather than oddity. To be seen as someone who might dally with a gentleman and then decide the gentleman wasn't for her, after all.

"Perhaps," she mused, "I should try to be more outrageous." Then she frowned. "Though that might adversely affect Lilah, so never mind." She brightened. "But at least it means that Richard cannot say anything about my spending time with Simeon, since he is the one who concocted the whole scheme."

A scheme that would fall apart as soon as Lilah's Season was done—Myrtle fully expected her niece to be engaged at the end of the Season, but even if she wasn't, Regina would be recovered enough to chaperone next Season. And besides, by then Myrtle would be . . . where? Living with Letty, her governess, out in the country somewhere? Occasionally corresponding with her government contacts when they had a particularly difficult problem?

A few weeks ago, that was all she had wanted—well, that and her fortune. She was clear-eyed enough to know that she needed some sort of financial cushion, even if her various interests—helping ladies with their money, double-entry bookkeeping, and the like— did well enough. There was never enough, not when it was a single lady who had no intention of marrying.

Now, however, she wondered. "Not about anything in particular," she reminded herself sharply, "but just in general."

What would it be like, for example, to take up residence in London? Have the freedom to move about the city and live her life as she wished? Doing things married ladies were usually only permitted to?

She couldn't allow herself to envision that—not when there was so much to do now.

Still. If she *did* envision it, she might see herself living as Simeon's mother must have—doing what she wanted when she wanted. With whomever she wanted.

But would it change her future? As Simeon's mother had warned?

That was something to consider. She'd never wondered about what the sexual component might mean to someone's creativity.

"Perhaps I should," she said, smiling to herself. "Perhaps I should ask him his opinion."

Oh, this fake engagement situation was going to be so much fun.

"No," SIMEON SAID, for what felt like the sixty-fourth time, "it is not like that."

Myrtle glared at him. She was dressed in what seemed like a bedsheet, but what Simeon had assured her was a chiton, the type of thing Artemisia might have worn.

Myrtle thought Artemisia's taste was quite plain.

Simeon had surprised her when he'd asked her to pose for him. When she thought he didn't like doing portraits.

But this was different, he'd explained. It was a *painting*. Myrtle didn't see the distinction, but then again, he didn't understand why she found double-entry bookkeeping so fascinating.

Which was why, a few days later, Myrtle was wearing a bedsheet in Simeon's studio.

It was a very good thing they were pretending to be engaged, because even Myrtle knew this was shocking behavior.

"You need to hold your head up more," Simeon continued. "Instead of as though you're looking for the nearest exit."

"But I am," Myrtle pointed out, jerking her chin

toward the door. "My coachman should be coming soon. I am supposed to consult with Richard and Lilah on my wardrobe"—at which she frowned—"and I have to sit there while the two of them fuss over what color the flowers should be, or if they should serve biscuits and sandwiches in the refreshment room or just biscuits and tea cakes." Her frown deepened. "And that is not even taking into account having to appear at the ball at all."

"But that is why you've enlisted my help, isn't it?" Simeon said, walking toward her to tilt her chin up. She couldn't resist a shiver as his fingers touched her skin. "To navigate all of that?"

She peered down her nose at him. "You have an opinion on the color of flowers or what food best goes with biscuits?"

He gave her an amused look. "Of course I have an opinion." He made it sound as though only fools would not. "But why not make a game of it? A mathematical game?"

"How do you mean?" she asked, intrigued. Feeling less foolish already, thanks to him.

"I mean," he said, adjusting the bedsheet around her, "you could always choose the final of the options. Or add up the letters in each and divide them by the amount of items. Something like that. Something to make your brain sparkle."

She laughed at his words. "My brain does not sparkle," she said.

"Oh, but I assure you it does," he said, giving her a knowing look.

She was opening her mouth to ask what he meant when there was a knock on the door.

Drat, the coachman had arrived only when things got interesting.

She wrestled the bedsheet off herself and smoothed her gown as he made his way downstairs.

She heard the door open, then a yelp of surprise, followed by a woman's voice.

Oh dear. Should she not be here? The thought of him entertaining another woman—of another woman feeling free enough to just pop by—made her feel odd things, things she usually only felt after having eaten a suspect piece of cheese.

Hmm. Was it possible she was jealous?

She was pretend engaged to him, after all. Perhaps she should be actually jealous, if she was to play her part correctly.

She was practicing her outraged expression as she heard the footsteps coming up the stairs.

A young lady, a very young lady, appeared in the doorway, and Myrtle felt her mouth drop open. He was far more of a reprobate than she thought if he was gallivanting with someone who looked to be about Lilah's age.

"Miss Allen," he said, looking bemused, "may I present my ward, Miss Phoebe Jones."

Myrtle's eyes widened, and then she rushed forward, taking the girl's hand in hers, wishing she didn't feel quite so relieved there was no gallivanting, only custody. Her fake betrothal could remain a simple reality.

Not that she knew what that meant, just that she wouldn't have to trot out her outraged expression.

"It is a pleasure to meet you, Miss Jones," she said, meeting the girl's gaze. "I am"—and she paused, glancing back at Simeon for a moment—"Mr. Jones's fiancée."

Miss Jones smiled in return. "My goodness," she said, her smile widening. "I didn't realize. That is wonderful news."

"Yes, well, it is rather sudden." It was the first time Myrtle had ever heard him not be smoothly charming—he seemed entirely rattled. Was it the fake engagement or his ward's sudden arrival?

It was a good thing Myrtle herself was so good at pivoting, or she would be equally unsettled.

"I am looking forward to getting to know you," Miss Jones continued.

Myrtle felt a pang of envy for how lovely the girl was—blond hair, blue eyes, and a delicate, lissome figure. Her clothing was simple, but clearly high quality, and she looked just like every other young Society lady Myrtle had ever seen.

Except herself, of course. Which was why she was not eager to reenter Society in the first place.

Even though that was exactly what she was about to do.

Chapter Ten

Simeon felt as though he'd been hit on the head with a rock. A blonde, elegant rock.

This was far more stunning of a plot twist than the wrinkle the viscount had presented—pretending to be engaged to someone he already liked and wanted to kiss seemed like a natural extension.

Even if it was entirely made up.

But this. She was a grown human, his adoptive sister.

"Would you like to sit down?" Simeon said, gesturing to the chaise. He couldn't think about some of the activities that had occurred there, not with his new charge directly in front of him.

"This is the person you spoke of?" Myrtle asked. Her eyes twinkled, though he failed to find any amusement in the situation. "From what you said, I assumed the child was, well, a *child*."

"I turned seventeen years old two months ago," Miss Jones said. Her voice was high and precise, indicating she'd been taught elocution. How had he gone this long without knowing anything about her? "I've just arrived in town, and I am staying with relatives of my mother." Her face softened when she spoke. "I mean the woman who raised me. My actual mother's sister." She furrowed her brow. "I did not intend to come without accompaniment, but the girl who's been assigned to be my maid took ill, and I just couldn't wait to meet you. And you, too," she added, turning to Myrtle.

"Seventeen!" Myrtle exclaimed. "Then you and my niece Lilah are of an age. She has just arrived in town also. I can introduce you to her. She is making her debut in a few days," she added, a wrinkle of her nose indicating how little she was looking forward to that.

"That sounds delightful," Miss Jones replied. She made her way delicately to the chaise, sitting down with as much aplomb as any well-born young lady.

Things were not as he'd anticipated.

"Can I—would you like some tea?" Simeon asked. He gestured toward his kitchen area. "It wouldn't take a moment."

"Yes, please." She inclined her head just so.

"Allow me to assist, Mr. Jones," Myrtle said.

The two of them walked down the hall, his mind racing with what he'd expected compared with the reality.

He picked up the kettle and filled it, then lit the gas. Staring at the flames as they licked up around the bottom of the kettle.

"From what you said," Myrtle whispered, "I thought she was much younger."

"So did I," he shot back. "I had no idea she would be a fully formed human."

"Though," Myrtle replied, her brow wrinkling in thought, "it might have been expected. How long has your mother been gone?"

"Eight years."

"And Miss Jones was born at some point before your mother adopted you?"

"I gather so, yes. I mean, I know it wasn't after I'd arrived. I was twelve years old when she took me in. I would have noticed if my mother was with child. But I—from what the letter said—I thought—" he said, faltering.

"Do the math!" she exclaimed. "If your mother had Miss Jones before she found you, then she would have to be at least sixteen years old." She flung her hand back out toward the main room. "And she says she just turned seventeen, so that makes sense." She folded her arms over her chest. "What are you going to do now?"

Simeon could only stare at her. He hadn't anticipated this. Any of this.

Her expression eased at seeing his, and she reached a hand to touch his arm. "I will help. I can see you are a bit lost now. I am very good at adjusting to things, so you need not worry at all." Her voice made it sound as though she was talking to someone much stupider than she.

Then again, he'd assumed a person born to his late mother was a baby, so perhaps she wasn't wrong.

The kettle whistled, and Simeon was grateful

to be able to busy himself with making tea—
something he knew how to do, unlike dealing
with a grown person who somehow needed his
protection—and gathered the tea things as Myrtle watched with an interested expression.

"Here we are," he said, placing the tea things
on one of the low tables he used as props for his
paintings. "Tea."

He felt and sounded like an idiot. An idiot who
hadn't been able to, as she said, *do the math*. Of
course Decision Child wasn't a child; he'd just assumed, since he was assigned the responsibility.
He hadn't known the child's gender, even. But
here she was, a young, genteel lady—albeit illegitimate, like him—who required guidance and
care. And money to do all those things with.

"Mr. Jones and I have been talking," Myrtle began. He jerked his head to look at her. What in
God's name was she going to . . . ?

"And I think it would be marvelous for you to
make your debut alongside my niece," she said.

Miss Jones's eyes widened. "Make my debut?
But—" And then she glanced anxiously over at
Simeon, who felt an immediate wave of warmth
and sympathy. Was this how parents felt? And
why was he feeling this not more than ten minutes after meeting her?

"But nobody knows my family," she finished,
color staining her cheeks.

"No, nobody does." Myrtle directed her sharp
gaze toward Miss Jones. "You can be whomever
you wish to be," she said in a firm tone. "If anyone

asks—and people will ask, of course, it is in their nature to be rude—we will just say that you are Lilah's friend."

"But they haven't met yet," Simeon couldn't help but point out. "What if they don't become friends?"

Myrtle gave him that *do keep up* look, then returned her attention to Miss Jones. "Do you like parties?"

Miss Jones nodded, though she looked confused.

"What do you think about meeting pleasant people? Or meeting handsome gentlemen? Are you for or against it?"

"For, I suppose," Miss Jones replied.

"And sweets. Cake, pie, tarts, biscuits. Do you enjoy them?"

"Yes."

Myrtle turned to Simeon, a triumphant expression on her face. "There. You see? They have plenty in common, and they should get along delightfully."

"I don't think—" he began.

"No, you don't," she interrupted. "Just let me take care of it. Lilah will be so pleased to have a companion through her Season. Otherwise she just has me, and while of course I am wonderful, I am not who you want beside you at a party." That wrinkled nose again. "I tend to go on and on about pi."

"Pie?" Simeon said, confused. "But you just said—"

"*Pi*, not pie," she clarified, though that wasn't any kind of clarification at all. "The math kind of pi. That is, I like both, though I seldom discuss the baked good. Both are circular, however, and I suppose there could be an infinite amount of ingredients— but I digress," she said, looking almost abashed.

It was adorable.

And then Simeon froze. Adorable. He'd never thought anyone was adorable, nor been charmed by someone conflating desserts with math concepts.

But here he was. It was refreshing to meet someone with a far more chaotic mind than his. Someone who wasn't afraid to think, or say, whatever came to mind.

Even though that might be troublesome.

But it was an interesting kind of trouble, the kind that made his skin feel prickly, and made him feel keenly alive.

The kind he recognized, and absolutely should not acknowledge nor allow in, since it would complicate already very complicated things.

"What will your brother say?"

Miss Jones had taken her tea and was walking around the studio, examining the various paintings on display, so she was out of earshot.

She waved her hand in dismissal. "What can he say? He's the one who insisted we pretend to— you know," she said, waving her hands in the air. "And we should keep up the pretense in front of Miss Jones and Lilah, by the way," she continued, not stopping speaking, even for a moment.

"Young women love nothing so much as sharing salacious gossip, and then it would cause an even worse scandal than what Richard hopes to prevent." She shrugged. "This way, there is even more support for our subterfuge."

"You are so certain this is how it will all go."

"Of course I am certain. And wouldn't I be? What is the point of not being certain when there is an outcome you desire?"

Desire.

He shouldn't immediately think of things when she said the word, and yet he was Simeon, after all. Frequent lover of many, in touch with his sybaritic side, finding an odd camaraderie with this woman whom he'd met only a few weeks ago. Whom he'd kissed just once, but wanted to again. Especially when she was so unusual. So attractive in so many ways.

"What is it?" she asked. "Do you have a fever?"

He snorted. "No, not that. I just—"

"You know, it would go much better for you if you just say it," she said, giving him a pointed stare.

How did one just *say* things? He'd never just said things; his brain filtered what he could or could not say, and he'd navigated his life as though he were walking on a tightrope. That was how he could advise her so skillfully on how to lie.

"Simeon."

He took a deep breath. "I want to kiss you again," he said at last.

Her eyes widened. "Oh!" He saw her swallow,

and then saw when she regained her composure. "Is that all? Surely we can arrange that. We will be spending time together, after all. As long as we don't make it a habit."

"We won't," he said confidently. "That is—like you, I have no wish to bog myself down in any kind of entanglement that might impede my work. We can agree to indulge ourselves with no strings attached."

"That would suit me as well," she said, her eyes sparkling. "You are remarkably handsome, as you know, and it would be a delight to explore more." She paused. "Kissing-wise, that is."

Dear God. Did she know what she was getting into? Did he know what he was getting into?

No. No, he did not, but he was getting in, none-theless.

"I LOVE THAT color on you!"

Myrtle winced at Lilah's near shriek, even if it was about evening gowns. She enjoyed a good evening gown herself, but she didn't enjoy the volume with which Lilah was enthusing about them.

The four of them—Lilah, Miss Jones, Simeon, and Myrtle—were in Madame Lucille's Fine Fashion, a place recommended to them by one of Simeon's friends.

Madame Lucille herself looked to be only a few years older than Myrtle, and took the girls in hand right away, leaving Myrtle and Simeon to watch. And to hear.

"I didn't know they could scream that loudly," Simeon murmured.

The two of them were seated in Madame Lucille's front room as the dressmaker bustled about finding bolts of fabric to drape on one or both of the two girls.

As Myrtle had calculated, Lilah and Miss Jones had become immediate friends—Lilah was already an open, gregarious young lady, but she'd always regretted not having more friends her age. She'd made do with Myrtle, but her aunt was—on her own admission—too eccentric and often too peculiar to converse about the usual things. It was more often than not that Myrtle would get distracted by the *probability* of a new gentleman being actually handsome than by the discussion of the new gentleman himself.

Miss Jones was more reserved, but it seemed as though she was enjoying herself.

Neither of the young ladies questioned the engagement at all. Myrtle had been concerned Lilah would interrogate her extensively once the news had come out, but instead Lilah had talked about how many gentlemen had asked her to dance.

Myrtle had never been more grateful for a young lady's self-absorption. She knew it would be difficult to lie, especially if it was Lilah and her way of working at a problem.

Something she and Lilah had in common, she realized. Thank goodness it hadn't surfaced yet about this topic.

"Just wait until they get a few glasses of punch

in them," Myrtle confided. "Though I imagine your ward won't be quite as exuberant as my niece." As she spoke, Lilah appeared to be imitating the Queen, tilting her nose in the air and walking in tiny, mincing steps. Miss Jones's expression made it look as though she wanted to laugh, but wasn't going to let herself.

"Thank you for this," Simeon said. He nodded toward the feminine rumpus. "I honestly had no—I mean, you know that. Do the math, indeed," he said, chuckling. And then he sobered. "But she is not at all what I'd expected. I would never have thought of giving her a Season, what with her—"

"Being illegitimate?" Myrtle supplied. She shrugged. "Your Miss Jones is beautiful and clearly refined. Richard has agreed to include her in all of Lilah's events, and with his backing, she will be accepted. Perhaps reluctantly at times, but accepted."

Like her, she thought ruefully. When she'd made her debut, she'd been terrified; terrified she would not be popular, and just as terrified she would be.

Neither had turned out to be the case. Half of the unmarried gentlemen had been intrigued by her massive fortune, while the other half had not. Of the first half, about thirty-seven percent of them had wandered off when they'd actually spoken to her, and the remainder had persevered, with five actually offering proposals.

Myrtle would have done the math on her results if she'd felt there was a point to them.

"What are you thinking about?" he asked. "You're not regretting all this, are you?" He waved a hand toward where Lilah had swept Miss Jones into a chaotic waltz, while Madame Lucille laughed on the sidelines.

"Of course not," she replied quickly. "I get to have some beautiful gowns and eat delicious cake. Nothing to regret." She'd placed an order with Madame Lucille earlier, and she was very much looking forward to wearing her new clothes. "No, I was thinking about my debut. I expect it will be quite different from theirs."

"Because they both hope to be married at the end of it?" he queried.

She turned to regard him. "Has your Miss Jones said that? I know it is expected, but you wouldn't want to push her into anything she doesn't want."

"She said, and I quote, 'I want marriage, and a family, and a comfortable home. And if I don't have to read another Bible verse aloud to various livestock, I'll be happy.'"

Myrtle gasped in surprise, then smothered a giggle. "She read aloud to livestock?"

Simeon nodded, looking solemn. "Apparently my aunt wasn't that fervently religious, but she did think animals should be educated." How he said that with a straight face Myrtle had no idea.

She leaned back to regard him. "Your family is quite unusual, isn't it?"

His expression froze, but then she saw him release his breath. "You don't mean that pejoratively."

It wasn't a question.

"Of course not," she said, answering anyway. "I think it's wonderful." She glanced away, looking at nothing but her own thoughts. "I wish I had family like that. Or even friends. I've got Letty, Miss Rogers, my former governess, but she and I are as alike as cake and sardines."

"I'm your friend," he said. Making her chest tighten. "That's why we are together right now—because you knew you could come to me for help, even though we've only known one another for a short time." He leaned closer still. "And because we're friends, we can trust one another."

She felt tears gather, and tried to calm herself. It would not do to burst into grateful crying at a dress shop.

Not that there was an appropriate venue for grateful crying, but this place seemed particularly inappropriate.

"Thank you," she said in a quiet voice. "I am pleased to be your friend."

Chapter Eleven

*T*here wasn't nearly enough kissing, as it happened. Simeon tried not to think about it too much, but that just meant he thought about it all the time. Because he was trying so hard not to think about it. He'd never felt this kind of fascination before—she was so chaotically delightful, and he liked watching her brain career from one topic to the next, all the while running mathematical formulas in her head.

Like tonight, for example.

They were at her niece's and Miss Jones's—he found it hard to call her "Phoebe," even though she was now under his care, God save her—first official party. Their actual come-out ball, held at the Allen town house, would be in a few days; this was just a dress rehearsal, so to speak, for the social events to come.

Both girls looked lovely, clad in their debutante white, with matching expressions of overwhelmed glee.

Meanwhile, Myrtle was hiding in the corner,

wearing a glorious gown of pink silk that made her look like the most delicious confection.

Simeon dearly wished to taste her.

"You have to come out from there," he said, nodding to her. She had tucked herself behind a large pillar, and was peering out at the crowd. Her expression was one of intense interest, and he wished he had his paints with him so he could capture it.

Also he'd like her to look at him like that.

"At the very least," he continued, "you should stop hiding and come out so everyone can see your gown. Lucy worked hard on it."

"I am not hiding," she retorted. "I had every intention of going out there and saying hello to all those people, but then I started thinking about how many ingredients it takes to make a dish."

He had no idea what she was saying, which must've shown on his face.

"I mean, cheese is cheese, is it not?"

He nodded, still befuddled.

"And cheese is delicious, but it is not a dish. But if you combine cheese with macaroni and butter and some other things, you have a dish." Her expression turned thoughtful. "But what is the minimum amount of ingredients needed to prepare a dish?"

And then her expression shifted, and she smiled as she looked down at herself. "This gown is beautiful, however."

Her smile was that of a woman who knew she looked good. Or at least that she was wearing beautiful clothing; she seemed not to pay attention to her appearance, beyond blithely informing him all of her suitors focused on her dowry, not her looks.

Another thing he'd like to do: demonstrate to her just how attractive she was.

Tonight, for example, her eyes sparkled, her clear and obvious intelligence shining from them. Lucy had cut the gown so as to show her geometrical curves, her breasts, creamy mounds that caught his attention. Her gown had whorls of embroidery on it, black thread on the pink.

"It's the Fibonacci sequence," she said in a proud tone of voice, noticing his focus.

"Pardon, what is what?" he said.

"The Fibonacci sequence," she repeated, gesturing to the embroidery. "Madame Lucille thought it would be fun to add an element that was meaningful to me on the gown." She shrugged. "I suggested the Fibonacci sequence."

Had he compared her to Fenton? She was miles ahead of Fenton in her brilliance, so much so that he was nearly daunted.

And he wasn't daunted by anything. At least not since his mother had told him that not only was he the best artist she'd ever seen, he was also the handsomest person she'd ever seen, and he should take advantage of the latter to raise up the former.

"What is that?" he asked.

A brief frown crossed her features, and he wondered if he had disappointed her by not knowing.

"It's a series of numbers in which each number is the sum of the two preceding numbers," she explained, even though he did not understand.

"Those are numbers?" he said, nodding to the embroidery.

"It's a visualization of them, yes," she said, as though that made it clearer.

It was not clearer.

But he was fascinated.

"Oh look, Lilah and Miss Jones are coming this way," she said, extricating herself from her barricade.

"I see," Simeon said in a low tone. "You won't come out if I ask, but dangle a couple of excitable debutantes and you pop up like a jack-in-the-box."

She gave him a sour look. "It is my responsibility to watch out for these two," she said, her tone deliberately haughty. "I would be failing in my duties, and would therefore be failing my brother, who entrusted Lilah's care to me. And failing you, who has entrusted Miss Jones's care to me."

"Don't forget, you're supposed to be meeting people yourself," he reminded her.

Another sour look. "I know. I just— it's all so"— and then she looked vulnerable, and he wanted to protect her at all costs, even though that was obviously the last thing she wanted—"so awkward. That is, I am so awkward." She paused as she considered her words. "I mean, I gather I am awkward, though I often don't realize it until much later. And the thought always occurs at the most inconvenient time, like when I am in the bath or on the verge of falling asleep."

"We can practice, if you like," he suggested.

A narrow look. "Practice? How can we practice not being awkward? Is it like practicing lying?" She frowned. "It sounds as though there is far too much practice and not enough doing." Of course she'd just want to launch into things without thought. She'd call it a *pivot*, while he would call it *reckless*.

"Well," he replied, deliberately using a patronizing tone that was bound to irk her, "if you practice doing something you are not good at, the idea is that the practice will make you better at it. You didn't spring forth as a baby knowing how to do sums, did you?"

She wrinkled her nose. "No, of course not. But there is a difference between behavior and mental processes. One is much easier than the other."

"So you'd like to just . . . give up on the former?" he said, a tone of challenge in his voice.

She bristled. "Of course not."

"And we can practice other things," he suggested, more for his benefit than hers. Because he dearly wanted to kiss her, and he wanted her to kiss him back.

She blinked in surprise. "Oh, I thought—that is, I didn't think—"

"That I wanted you?" He wanted her so much he ached with it. But he wouldn't tell her that; it would either intimidate her or deter her, and he didn't want either of those possibilities.

He wanted her to leap into his arms with as much enthusiasm and alacrity as she'd leapt into the carriage a few weeks ago, relying on a stranger she'd just met to take her to London.

And then they could practice all the rest.

SIMEON WAS UNEXPECTED, even though he was not unexpected in an unpleasant way; rather, he was similar to the cake she'd eaten on the floor of Richard's ballroom, back when she'd decided she'd rather leave than succumb to anyone else's expectations for her future. Like the bursts of candied orange studding the top of an already delicious cake.

And, she had to admit, he was more delicious than any cake she'd encountered yet.

She'd never been challenged as much by anyone in her life as she was by him—challenged to come out from behind the pillar, challenged to meet people and present herself as someone to trust with financial concerns. Even though she hadn't done a lot of that in actuality.

Challenged to explore the side of her she'd only ever thought about when she was by herself, late at night, in the dark.

Though she had been the one to ask for the kiss in the first place. So perhaps she already had the ability to do things that were not as comfortable for her as mathematics or pretty gowns or cake.

She definitely had the desire.

He stood beside her, speaking with Lilah and Miss Allen. He wore evening clothes that looked just a bit more dashing than what every other gentleman was wearing—due partially to his handsome appearance, but also due to the trousers being cut just a little bit snugger, the jacket more expertly fitted. His waistcoat was made of a vivid material most gentlemen would eschew; it was a bright blue, with sparkly buttons studding the front.

If she hadn't seen his bare back, she would say he likely looked as good as he ever had in his life, but the memory of all that skin covering bone and muscle kept drifting into her mind.

"Are you all right?" Lilah asked suddenly. "Because you just gasped, as though you were holding your breath or something."

"Or something," Myrtle said, feeling her cheeks heat. "I'm just pondering the axis of the room multiplied by the number of people in attendance." It made no sense, none at all, but it was clear Lilah didn't understand most of what Myrtle said, which she was counting on.

"Ah, of course," Lilah replied vaguely. "Oh, Phoebe, look! They just brought out more of those tiny sandwiches!"

The girls made some sort of girl-like shrieking sound, then scurried toward the refreshment table.

"I feel suddenly very old," he said. "I don't know that I've ever been that exuberant about sandwiches in my life."

"You just haven't had the right kind. And I shouldn't talk, what with my fascination with cake," Myrtle replied, turning to look in his eyes.

What she saw there made her want to gasp all over again. And forget entirely about sandwiches, and even forget about cake.

She saw the desire, the heat, even though she had very little concept of what happened after the kissing—just that he certainly did, and it must've been quite pleasurable, given his expression.

"I haven't, have I?" he said, and she knew he wasn't speaking about sandwiches at all.

"You're very—that is, I—"

He raised one eyebrow. "Have I managed to make you speechless? That is a rare thing indeed. You have something to say at any time."

His tone made it clear he was complimenting her—not what she was used to hearing when others had said the same. Usually they accompanied their words with an aggrieved tone, as though she should be quiet just because, when it was obvious she always had an opinion, and likely a more informed one, too.

But he—he wanted to hear what she said. And also wanted her not to speak.

This was so very unusual she wanted to dismantle it all on the spot and analyze each element, figure out what made it so different.

But since they were in the middle of a ball, for goodness' sake, she couldn't do anything of the sort.

"Would you like to dance, Myrtle?" he asked, still using that low, silky tone that made her insides tremble. "Because I very much want to touch you, and the only acceptable way now is for us to dance." Oh, she wanted to dance. She'd wanted to dance with him since she saw how incredibly graceful he was.

"But won't Lilah and—" she began, only for him to take her in his arms. She went willingly, she wasn't an idiot.

"Lilah and my ward are busy devouring sandwiches," he said, nodding toward where the girls stood. "They will be fine in the time we dance together. You can continue being the diligent chaperone after."

She uttered a rueful snort as the music began. "I don't know that I'm very good at being a chaperone at all," she admitted. "I keep getting distracted by things in my head. I just want to be certain Lilah doesn't make a mistake. Nor your Miss Jones either," she added.

He shook his head as he began to guide her through the steps of the dance. "You won't let her. When it's important, when someone's life is on the line, you will take heed and assess the situation. Won't you?"

It wasn't truly a question; she knew he knew the answer, and was just bolstering her confidence. She appreciated that.

"I will," she said. "I suppose I did that with myself, didn't I?"

"You did," he replied.

They were silent then while they navigated the steps—Myrtle was out of practice dancing, but he more than made up for her, gliding them elegantly around the floor. She caught a few people staring at them, and she wanted to rush up and agree: *He is splendid, isn't he? And he is surprisingly intelligent. A very good artist as well.*

"—types of ladies you wish to meet?" she heard him say.

"Pardon?"

He gave her a sly smile. "Do keep up. I was asking what types of ladies you believe would be the best recipients of your skills. I can make introductions this evening, if you want." He gazed around the room for a moment, still not losing his place in the dance. Remarkable. "I know most of the people here."

She considered his question. "I suppose it is ladies who are under someone else's control," she said slowly.

"In other words, all of them," he replied.

"Unfortunately, yes. But the ones that might need the most help are ladies whose husbands are not as responsible as they should be. At least financially."

"Again, unfortunately, most of them," he said with a grimace.

"I need to approach them with care," she continued. "I don't want to insist they do what I say, or I will be just as bad as their spouses. I want them to trust in me, and that trust will expand to include themselves. At least I hope so."

"I believe you can do it," he said, and she heard the sincerity in his words.

"Thank you, friend." She offered him a warm smile, and he returned it. Making her feel, at least for a few moments, as though they were again the only two people in the world, even though there was a ballroom full of people.

Chapter Twelve

"Aunt Turtle!"

Lilah's voice came from down the hall, startling Myrtle from her work. She'd been collecting the names of the gentlewomen Simeon had introduced her to over the past week leading up to Lilah's ball, writing down her impressions and how she thought she might be able to help them.

Lilah had discovered her uncle Joseph's nickname for Myrtle and had been using it to excess. It surprised Myrtle that she found it endearing, rather than annoying, like when Joseph did it.

It made her feel part of the family, she supposed, where she'd always felt as though she was some sort of alien mathematics creature come to reside amongst the normal people.

"What is it?" Myrtle said, putting aside her notebook. It was morning, and she hadn't gotten dressed yet. She was sharing Lilah's lady's maid while in town, and Lilah's care naturally came first.

Lilah burst in, her face alight with excitement. "You have to come see for yourself."

What could it possibly be? Myrtle wondered. Something that would both excite Lilah and be pertinent to Myrtle's interests. The intersection between the two generally came down to gowns, sweets, and backgammon, oddly.

She didn't think any of that was what was making Lilah so excited. For one thing, they'd just had a delivery from Madame Lucille, so it couldn't be more gowns. It was too early in the morning for sweets, and there was no time for backgammon, Lilah had informed Myrtle loftily not two days ago.

"Come down right away!" Lilah said again, beckoning Myrtle. Myrtle threw on her wrapper, then bustled downstairs, flinging her hair onto her back.

Simeon stood in the foyer, an expression she couldn't read on his face. He held something in a bundle in front of him, a bundle that wriggled.

Her steps slowed, and she felt her eyes widen as she walked toward him. It wasn't appropriate at all for her to appear in front of him in her night rail and wrapper, but they were both a little too far for that to be a concern.

Not that anybody else knew that. Nobody knew, for example, that she had traveled alone in a carriage with him, shared a bed, and seen his beautiful naked back.

Though all of those things were impossible for her to forget.

So she tucked her wrapper more firmly around herself and tried to assemble the few scraps of propriety she could find.

"Good morning, Mr. Jones," she said in a deliberately formal voice. "I have to say, I am—"

"Show her, Simeon!" Lilah interrupted.

He lowered the bundle to the floor and opened it, releasing a small dog that immediately bounded over to Myrtle to sniff at her skirts.

"I thought—I thought you could use another friend," he said in a low tone, while Lilah was calling to the pup. "And this poor fellow was in need. I spotted him yesterday as I was returning from the art shop. He doesn't appear to have an owner, and I thought the two of you could be of use to one another."

Of use to one another. What a gentle way to indicate he knew both of them were likely lonely. Hadn't she just been wishing she had a friend to talk to?

This pup would do quite well.

Her chest tightened, and she felt her throat close as well, and knew she was perilously close to tears.

"What will you name him, Aunt Turtle?" Lilah said, having succeeded in luring the dog to her side.

He was scruffy-looking, with a medium-brown coat, a hook-shaped tail, and bright brown eyes. His paws were white and brown, while his belly was all white.

"I don't know," Myrtle said, bending down to pet him. She glanced up at Simeon, who now looked relieved. Because she liked the gift? Because it meant she had someone else to talk to?

Because now she wouldn't be completely friendless when they broke their engagement?

"What do you suggest?"

He shrugged. "Is there some sort of mathematical function that might work? Fibo-something or whatever?"

"Fibonacci," she corrected. She looked back at the dog. "I don't think that would suit him. I'd like something less complicated. He is a dog, after all —"

"That he is," he said with a smile.

"And dogs like to nap and run and eat and be petted. They don't want to spend their time thinking about numbers."

"I suppose not," he replied, looking at the anonymous dog.

"That dog we met before"—she said, then realized that Lilah and her inopportune curiosity were in the room—"I mean the dog we met near Madame Lucille's. That dog was named Bow Wow, and I like that type of name."

"Bark?" he suggested, his eyes crinkling in the corners as he smiled.

"Yap?" Lilah added.

"Woof," Myrtle said in a decided tone. "He will always live up to his name, and he need not be concerned about anything but his doggie needs."

"Woof," Simeon repeated, his mouth curling up into a warm smile.

He'd given her a dog. A *friend*. When he'd

known, by her own admission, that he was her only friend within a few hundred miles' radius or so.

And to be honest, Letty was her only other friend, and who knew if they would have become friends if Letty hadn't been her governess.

Not for the first time, Myrtle recognized how hard it could be to have a brain like hers. It kept her isolated from others, always made her wonder if there was actually something wrong with her. If she just tried to fit in better with others, could she? Did she want that?

And then there was him. He'd never tried to make her feel odd; in fact, he'd seemed to revel in her differences, and found a commonality with his own artistic genius.

They were both isolated in their own ways, she realized. He had started out at a deficit because of his birth, and then had grown in his distinction because of his talent.

She had begun well enough, she supposed, but then her oddities had become gradually revealed until she felt exceptionally different—and not always in a good way—from the rest of her family.

"Would you like to take Woof out for a walk?" he asked. He nodded toward her attire, which she'd entirely forgotten about. "After you change, of course."

She startled, then glanced down and chuckled, meeting his gaze after a moment. "I would very much like to take Woof for a walk," she replied. "Give me ten minutes?"

He nodded, then lowered to pet Woof. "We'll just be here," he said.

She ran upstairs, glad to have a friend who understood her, one who brought her more friends without judging.

And then felt suddenly sad at the thought that after the Season was all over, after Lilah was properly settled and Myrtle had begun her business, that she would have no cause to see him again. She would have Woof, and she would have her own future, but he wouldn't be a part of it.

She shouldn't be nearly as sad as she seemed to be—she had met him only recently, after all.

But she had to put all that emotion aside. There were things to do now. First and foremost, she had to get dressed, then she had to make certain Lilah was on her way to a settled future, and finally she would have to persuade enough ladies that she had the skills to assist them with their finances.

All before the Season ended and Richard changed his mind about her future.

But first to put some clothes on and take Woof for a walk. With her handsome friend who was not only handsome, but intelligent, charming, and dangerously kind.

Simeon was still smiling as Myrtle went back upstairs to change. Woof poked his nose into Simeon's hand, demanding pets, and Simeon obliged, glad to be able to accommodate the humble request.

His admittedly soft heart couldn't resist rescuing the little dog when he'd spotted him. It was only later that he realized he could do something for both the dog and for Myrtle; each needed a friend, and each would be suited for the other.

He'd been worried at first that she would reject the mutt, but he shouldn't have been concerned; her eyes had widened, and then she'd looked at him as though he'd turned on the sun for her when he had only given her an animal.

And not even a very prepossessing one; Woof was clearly of mixed heritage, likely a bastard, like Simeon. His fur was brown and white, and one ear was raised up, as though he was asking a question.

Perhaps as simple as *when can I eat?* or *will you play with me?* But also perhaps as heartfelt as *is this my new home?*

He wrapped his hands around the dog and brought him up to his chest, murmuring nonsense. For every time he looked ahead to an uncertain future, for every time he made do with twice-used tea leaves, he was able to help somebody. In this case, his money wasn't required—a rare occurrence—but usually, he had to accompany his beneficence with funds.

She returned within a few minutes, certainly even fewer than she'd said, and soon they were outside on the pavement, Woof looking up expectantly at them.

"Where should we go?" he said, sweeping his hand out to indicate the entirety of London.

He was grateful that they didn't require a chaperone—there was another advantage to the whole pretend betrothal thing.

She considered it. The expected *wherever you want to* reply was not for her; no, she wouldn't rely on anyone else to decide what she was to do. That was clear.

And unusual. He admired it.

"Hyde Park, I think," she said, her mouth twisted into an adorable pout. "I imagine there might be some prospective clients there, wouldn't you say?"

"Good thinking," he said, holding his arm out for her.

She took it, and he tugged her close to his side, liking how well she fit, even though she was over six inches shorter than he.

"By the way," she began as they started to walk, Woof trotting alongside, "do you know how it is that Miss Jones came to live with your mother's sister rather than your mother? Surely, if she took you in, she had the resources to provide for a child."

Simeon took a deep breath. "I was wondering that myself, and I didn't want to ask Miss Jones—Phoebe—directly. I didn't know, I *don't* know, what she was told about our mother." Even saying *our mother* felt odd. Of course the whole situation was odd. "I was concerned, if I asked her, that she might resent me for having what she did not, or make some assumptions about our mother's behavior."

"And those assumptions would be?" she asked.

He exhaled. "My mother was . . . complicated," he said at last. They had stopped without conscious thought, and stood together, the occasional passerby walking past. They were about a quarter mile from the park still.

"She was completely focused on her art, and later, on mine. In looking at when Phoebe was born, it would have been just around the time she was beginning to reach another level of notice. She probably assessed what she was capable of doing, and decided she would rather give up the baby to her sister than compromise her art."

Myrtle was silent.

When he heard what he'd said, he knew it had to be true. His mother spoke often about what she'd given up to devote to her talent, and while she hadn't ever mentioned Phoebe—he wished she had, he'd have persuaded her to bring her back—he knew how she thought. She was ruthless in support of her talent. She wouldn't have let a small thing like a child interfere with her ambition.

"I wish I could say I understood that," Myrtle said. Her voice shook a little. "But I cannot." She turned to look at him, and he could see the tears gathering in her eyes. "To put your own satisfaction ahead of someone else's existence." She made a helpless gesture. "I can see if it was something like having a child stay at school for a holiday if there was something critical happening at the same time. But to irrevocably alter someone's life because it wasn't convenient?" She swallowed, and he could see how emotional she was. "It's not right."

It's not right.

The words hung in the air around them, shimmered as though they were palpable.

Simeon felt his own throat tighten and close, anger roiling up in him. What he was angry about, he wasn't sure; a combination of anger at his mother for choosing to be so selfish, for encouraging him to be so selfish, at her for making him believe that his art was more important than another person's life.

A bit at Myrtle for making the truth apparent, though that wasn't fair. But he still had to acknowledge, at least to himself, that that emotion was there.

"I've upset you," she said, putting her hand on his sleeve. She glanced around as though to see if anyone was about, then raised her gloved hand to slide it along his jaw. Grimacing in exasperation, she yanked her glove off and repeated the action. The smooth warmth of her hand was a comforting caress.

He didn't think about his reaction, he just turned his head and placed his mouth on her palm. Kissing it softly.

She inhaled, and he jerked away, worried he'd upset her in return.

But that wasn't upset he saw on her face.

Her eyes gleamed the way they had in the carriage when she'd asked him for a kiss. Her lips were slightly parted, and he could see her chest rise and fall with a rapider-than-usual breath.

"Oh," she said, her tone both sensual and curious. Like her.

And then Woof barked, breaking the moment, and the two of them stared down at the dog in surprise.

"We should get him to the park," she said, her voice shaky.

"Yes," Simeon replied. Trying not to resent the poor innocent canine for having ruined the moment. "Yes, we should."

Chapter Thirteen

*M*yrtle felt as though she was on fire from the inside out. Burning not only with how the feel of Simeon's lips on her skin had affected her, but also with a frustrated anger at his late mother, at the selfishness of artists in general, and wanting to get on with—with everything.

They walked quicker now, Woof slightly ahead of them, sniffing everything he could find.

"Where did you rescue him?" she asked, as much to keep her mind from racing as to find out the answer to the question.

"Near my rooms," he replied. "I was returning from purchasing new paints"—*for his art*, she thought to herself, art that he was as committed to as she was to her plans—"and he was in one of the alleys I cut through when I am in a rush. He was standing near some trash, and he looked rather lost—at least, as lost as a dog can look. I waited with him for ten minutes or so, but nobody came to find him. He was dirtier than now, I got him food and a bath before I brought him to you."

Her heart warmed again at his thoughtfulness. At finding her a friend, since he knew he was her only friend in London. Lilah didn't count, what with being a relative and someone who rarely ever actually listened to Myrtle when she spoke.

Plus, with any luck and their combined efforts, Lilah would be getting engaged soon enough, so she would then be part of her new husband's family, not beholden to Myrtle and her wishes.

As it should be. That was what Lilah wanted, and that meant Myrtle wanted it, too.

And now Myrtle had Woof. He would be her friend when Lilah was gone and Simeon was no longer part of her life.

But first she had a debutante to launch, a business to start, and a handsome gentleman to kiss.

Not in that order.

A part of her was still in shock that he'd been so firm that he desired her—her, Miss Myrtle Allen. Not because she didn't believe herself to be relatively comely or anything; she knew her face was pleasing, and her figure was alluring in its curves.

But she'd seen the beauties most handsome men tended to gravitate toward, and those ladies were not encumbered by oversized brains that constantly wanted to analyze and process. Not that those ladies were stupid (though some of them were); it was that their focus had always, rightly, been on their beauty, so they hadn't developed their brains as Myrtle had.

"What are you thinking about?" he asked.

You. Me. Passion.

"Nothing, really."

He snorted. "I don't believe that for a minute. Perhaps something I wouldn't be able to understand?" He had a joking tone, but she heard a note of uncertainty.

"You would be able to understand all sorts of things, if someone were to explain it to you," she said.

He turned to look at her. "Are you saying I— never mind, what are you saying? I know you don't mean to imply I am not intelligent." That uncertain tone again, and she wanted to take her words back right away.

At some point in her life—perhaps on her deathbed—she would remember to think before she spoke.

But that thought wasn't helpful now.

"I did not mean to imply anything of the sort," she replied firmly. "I meant that if you are not taught certain things that it is improbable that you would understand the concepts. I imagine you were not taught any sort of complicated mathematics?"

He shook his head. "No. The most complicated thing I learned was how to charm a merchant into accepting fifteen shillings when we owed a pound."

"And I am confident you were well able to do that," she replied, feeling on firmer ground now.

A reluctant smile curled his mouth. "Yes. Often."

"Just as I would not be expected to be able to

paint well if you handed me a brush and a palette." She shrugged. "It is all a matter of practice."

"Isn't that what I said to you about mingling in Society?" He gave her a cheeky grin as he spoke. "And lying?" he added.

"You are keeping up," she shot back.

"I always will, Myrtle. I always will."

It was both a threat and a promise.

SIMEON KNEW WHAT pleasurable things felt like—melting butter on a perfectly toasted piece of bread, the feel of silk against his skin, stepping back from the canvas just when he'd added the perfect detail to his painting—but he hadn't known that flirting with Myrtle would rank up alongside those things.

And there was more depth to it than merely toast or luxurious fabric; it felt similar to when he was working on what he knew would be a good piece, something worth the time and effort he expended on it.

She was worth it.

He was already anticipating what it would feel like, the natural continuation of their relationship. How she'd have to let her remarkable brain stop thinking, just for a moment, under the onslaught of his caresses. When he made her stop thinking and just feel.

"Now *you* have an odd look on your face," she observed. "What are you thinking about?"

You. Me. Desire.

"Noth—" he began, when he heard someone call his name.

"Mr. Jones! Over here, Mr. Jones!"

He turned to see Lady Flora—Aunt Flora, now, to him and his fellow orphans, the Bastard Five—waving enthusiastically.

"Ah, I see a friend of mine," he said, unnecessarily. "Would you care to be introduced to her?" he asked. It was purely a polite question, he didn't expect her to consider it. He expected her to agree immediately, as would be the norm of most polite people.

But she was constantly a surprise, wasn't she? She took a moment, squinting as she peered at Aunt Flora. "Yes, I would," she said at last.

He released the breath he hadn't realized he'd been holding, then walked her over to where Aunt Flora sat on a bench with a few other ladies.

All of them looked up eagerly as they approached, and Simeon braced himself for what might emerge from Myrtle's mouth. Though that wasn't fair. She wasn't cruel or mean; she was just . . . *honest.*

"Good afternoon, Lady Flora," Simeon said, taking the hand Aunt Flora extended. He bent over it and brushed his lips across it, then glanced up at Aunt Flora with one of his best rakish smiles.

He knew it was one of his best because he'd practiced a few times when he'd been stuck on a painting—it seemed to help spur some sort of creativity, mostly because he felt like an utter ass doing it, and he would rather do anything than continue to feel like such an idiot.

"Good afternoon, Simeon," she said with a bright smile.

He'd met Aunt Flora when his fellow orphan Bram had been introduced to the lady who was now his wife, Aunt Flora's niece. Aunt Flora had adopted them all as her nephews, and Fenton had actually invited her to live with him—she was there now, even though he was away.

"May I present Miss Allen?" he said, indicating Myrtle. "She is Viscount Leybourne's sister, in town to present her niece." He cleared his throat. "And we are, uh, engaged."

Aunt Flora leapt up immediately to embrace Simeon, him meeting Myrtle's amused look over the older woman's shoulder.

"Engaged!" she exclaimed. "Does Bram know? Theo probably doesn't, he and the duchess are still mooning over their new baby." It might have sounded as though she was being dismissive of such doting, but in reality she was the most softhearted of all of them, and worried constantly about little Theodora, who'd been born only a few months earlier.

"We're not making a fuss over it, though," Simeon continued, as he extricated himself from Aunt Flora's embrace. He nodded toward Myrtle. "Miss—that is, my Myrtle is acting as chaperone for her niece, who is making her come-out. We will be figuring out our details after we get Lilah settled."

"Oh, excellent," Flora said, smiling at Myrtle. "Though you look far too young to be a chaperone," she added. "Though not too young to get married," she added with a wink.

"I'm twenty-four, my lady," Myrtle replied. "I don't know if there is an age restriction on chaperones— it seems to be that as long as the chaperone is slightly more responsible than the chaperoned that it doesn't matter." She tilted her head in thought. "And that is true in this case. I am slightly more responsible than my niece." Her expression shifted, and then she added, "I think there should be an age restriction on brides, actually. Who is to know at age seventeen or eighteen who one wants to be with for the rest of one's life? I feel fortunate that I didn't seem to take when I debuted, or I might currently be miserable, instead of out here in the park with you and Mr. Jo—that is, with my fiancé."

Aunt Flora gaped, and then her smile widened, which didn't seem possible. She looked over at Simeon. "I like her." She nodded to the lady sitting beside her. "Scooch over, there's a dear, and let Miss Allen sit for a moment so we can get to know one another better."

The friend scooched, as asked, and Myrtle settled herself, her expression placid, as though this was entirely expected.

Woof went and snuffled around the ladies' skirts as Aunt Flora regarded Myrtle.

Aunt Flora met Myrtle's gaze. "I wish you had been around when I was young—I might not have made the mistakes I made, simply because I didn't realize there were other ways to approach the problem."

"There is always time, as long as one breathes, my lady," Myrtle replied simply. "In fact, I hope to put my skills to use for breathing ladies, to guide them with their finances. I find it intolerable that we are not in charge of our own monies."

Aunt Flora stiffened, and Simeon recalled that her own late husband had been irresponsible with her money. Perhaps it was a fortuitous thing that he and Myrtle had run into Aunt Flora.

"I absolutely agree with you, young lady," Aunt Flora said, and the other ladies around them all nodded vigorously. "Are you accepting clients? Because I would like to have you take a look at my finances and advise me." The other ladies all chimed in with their requests, and Simeon saw how pleased Myrtle was, and that made him want to puff out his chest in pride.

Not just because she would then look at him, and his chest, but also somewhat because she would then look at him, and his chest.

But also because he was delivering on what he'd promised: introductions to ladies who could use her services. And he hadn't even planned on that, which made it all the better.

"I would very much like to, my ladies," Myrtle replied, glancing at each of the ladies in turn. "Perhaps we could arrange a meeting?" She looked at Simeon. "Would you be able to host such an event? I don't think Richard would appreciate it."

"Of course he can," Aunt Flora answered. "I would host it myself, but it is rather awkward, since it is not my house." She tittered. "I am living in Fenton's home at the moment, and he is away, so I cannot ask him. It'll have to be at Simeon's. Simeon is nothing if not accommodating." Her mouth curled into a knowing smile. "And it is entirely respectable, since you are betrothed." She beamed at Simeon. "So smart of you to have chosen a woman who can think for herself."

Not that he'd chosen her; her brother had made the bargain, and he'd realized it was the best path forward for both of them.

Left unspoken, of course, was that his marrying someone of Myrtle's social status was a coup for someone with his uncertain birthright. Aunt Flora was as egalitarian as the next somewhat ill-used older lady, which meant she wanted everyone she loved to have financial and emotional security. She was kind, but she was no fool. Nor was she a radical.

"I would be delighted to host," Simeon replied, though he had to figure out who he could borrow chairs from. And likely serve something besides his usual eggs and toast.

"Thank you," Myrtle said, meeting Simeon's gaze. Her eyes were warm with gratitude, and it didn't matter that he would have to scurry around town locating seating and biscuits and Myrtle's favorite cake; she wanted something, and he was going to give it to her.

"THAT WAS WONDERFUL!" Myrtle enthused as they left the park.

Lady Flora and her friends had settled on a date

for their meeting, and Myrtle practically buzzed with excitement. She'd had to push her own future plans to the back of her mind while she concentrated on Lilah, but it did seem—as Simeon had said—that she would be able to do it all.

She just had to partition her time. She was a mathematician; it should be simple enough. Time to attend to Lilah's debut, time to work on her own business, time to pose for Simeon.

All manageable.

"I should have thought of introducing you to Aunt Flora earlier," he said. "She is precisely the sort of person who would benefit from your help."

Myrtle hadn't dared to think, not really, that she would be able to succeed at what she wanted. A 37 1/2 percent chance of success was less than half.

But now, with her first actual meeting set up, and with Simeon's charm smoothing her path, she felt a spark of hope. Perhaps there would be happiness for her, after all, without following the traditional path most other young ladies did.

"She came along at precisely the right time," Myrtle assured him. "I am feeling as though Lilah's and Miss Jones's debut will go relatively well, and we've got most of the major things sorted. If I had met Lady Flora earlier, I might not have been able to pay so much attention."

He gave her a warm smile. "Thank you for saying so. I know it can be difficult when you want to do something that's a little bit different from everyone else."

She took his arm and leaned against it. Woof

sat at their feet as she spoke. "Tell me about your choice. How did you come to know you could be a successful artist?"

He gave a rueful chuckle. "I'm not successful yet. I still think about money, and sometimes I have to forego certain items in order to pay for my art materials."

"What kinds of items? I could help—"

"No," he replied, cutting her off. "You paid me to escort you to London, and you paid three times what I was to originally get from your brother." He snorted. "And then you bargained with your brother on my behalf. All of that money will go a long way, since I have so few expenses."

"But you will let—" she began.

"Yes. Though isn't the whole point of you setting up your business because you don't have enough money yourself?"

She wrinkled her nose. "Yes, but I have more money, I believe, than you do. It is all a matter of perspective, isn't it?" She exhaled in frustration. "I know I am more fortunate than most people. I *know* that. But that doesn't mean I have to be satisfied with my good fortune. I want to improve upon it, or more accurately, I want to make my good fortune suit me." She shrugged. "Which means no marriage, no encumbrances, and a way to help others like me."

She felt him nod in understanding beside her. And she knew he understood—he'd made his way in the world very similarly, though he'd started from a much worse place than she.

"Back to you," she continued. "What gave you the confidence to pursue your goals?"

It was a rephrasing of her question so he wouldn't cavil about the particulars. Rather like rearranging a mathematical formula, as Myrtle would say; the elements remained the same, but it allowed the solver to look at the problem in a new light.

"I didn't think I had any choice but to," he said. "I had one talent: my art. My mother saw that, and did her best to encourage it." He paused. "It's only now that I realize that encouragement enacted a terrible price."

"Miss Jones?" Myrtle said.

"Yes. My mother had made that decision before I came into her life, but I hate that I might've kept her from changing her mind and bringing Miss J—Phoebe back. It feels so unfair that I got to know and love my mother and Phoebe never did."

"But she had a stable upbringing?" Myrtle ventured. "Unlike you?"

He murmured agreement. "She has spoken only a little about it. I won't get the whole story until we know one another better, I don't think. It sounds as though her childhood was the precise opposite of mine—she was loved for who she was, not who she could be, she didn't have to wonder if she was going to be able to eat that day, and my mother's sister, who raised her, was calm and, it sounds, rather dull. Unlike her sister."

"You don't crave calm dullness, then?" she teased.

He shook his head. "I wouldn't know what to do with myself. I like my routine, but it's neither calm nor dull; I paint, I see my friends, I do . . . other things." Which immediately piqued her curiosity.

They were getting closer to his lodgings now, and she glanced around her with interest. His neighborhood was so different from Richard's town house; there were all sorts of people here, not just aristocracy and servants, and she liked getting glimpses of regular life. The kind of life she might be leading, if all went well.

"What kinds of other things?" she asked.

He turned his head slowly to look at her, and she felt a shiver run through her. "What kinds of other things do you think, Myrtle?"

"Oh," she sighed, and his gaze darkened.

"I've gone far too long without kissing you," he said, his voice low and sensual.

That shiver was now a flame, even though that didn't make sense at all. A shiver was a muscle movement, while a flame was born of fire. Certainly, both were nouns, but other than that they had nothing in common.

Still. Shiver to a flame.

"If you want that," he added. "Because it is important that you be able to choose for yourself."

"It is. And I do," she said.

They'd arrived at his door, and he quickly unlocked it, gesturing for her to ascend the staircase. He followed close behind, his presence activating all her senses.

Except for the taste one. That would come later.

Woof was there, too, but was more interested in sniffing everything.

She flung her reticule and bonnet on the settee, then reached for him, pulling his head to hers. He made a startled noise, but soon enough his arms were wrapped around her, a solid band, and their mouths met in a clashing, fiery kiss.

Chapter Fourteen

This kiss wasn't like the first one.

That had been tentative, exploratory, and deliciously frustrating.

This one was a battle, one where each wanted the other to succumb to the passion first. Simeon knew he had far more experience than Myrtle, but by God, she must have been thinking about their first time a lot, since she dove in with all the confidence and artistry of someone who had kissed more than once before.

She fitted herself against him, anchoring her hands behind his head as she rose up on her tip toes. Her body was unreservedly pressed against his, and he was distracted by her soft warmth, by the way her full breasts pressed against his chest.

Her hands were sliding along his shoulders, squeezing as her tongue darted in and out of his mouth, teasing and tasting in equal parts.

He growled, and pulled her even closer, which he hadn't imagined was possible. He slid his hands down her back to her bottom, where he grabbed a handful of delicious flesh, grasping it hard. She made a little squeal of pleasure, and drew back for a moment. Her eyes, when they met his, were even starrier than the first time they'd done this, only now her lips were curved into a smile of satisfaction. Like a cat who'd managed to wheedle an extra bite of chicken from an indulgent owner.

"What?" he said, jerking his chin toward her. *Why are you so smug?* he wanted to ask, but one word was all that came out of him.

"This is so much fun," she said simply. "And I can tell you like it, too." Her gaze dropped to his mouth, and she licked her lips as she looked, and he wanted to reach down and yank up her skirts, taking her to the nearest wall and fucking her senseless.

But even though she kissed with the skill of a much more practiced woman, she was still an innocent, so he wouldn't do that.

Not exactly.

It wasn't a question of if they'd fuck, it was *when*. And he'd make certain her first—and second and third—time was enjoyable. He wanted to see that blissful look of pleasure on her face after he'd made her come. He wanted to taste her everywhere, especially *there*. He wanted to take his time, which was impossible to do when standing. One required an ample bed and plenty of stamina.

He had both, but now wasn't the time.

"Now it's my turn," she said, her gaze sliding up to meet his. "What?"

His mouth was dry. He'd never gotten so heated up so quickly before—usually he was most definitely in charge, and he led the action. Here, with her, he was unsure just who was leading.

And, surprisingly, he liked it that way. He liked not knowing how this would go today—whether there would be more kissing, or perhaps some touching, maybe a bit of fondling.

He definitely wanted to fondle, but he would let her lead. For now.

"What?" she repeated, tugging his hair for emphasis.

He shook his head to clear it. Though he couldn't clear it, not with her body pressed against his, not with her interest and passion so clear, as if she'd just said it aloud: *I want you. I want this.*

And she had actually said it earlier.

She nudged him, a reminder he still hadn't answered.

"It's—I'm just not accustomed to all this."

Her expression was one of disbelief.

"Let me explain," he said, hoisting her up into his arms and walking them over to the settee. He sat, settling her across his lap. She wrapped her arms around his neck, then looked up at him, her face alight with anticipation. Of all sorts of things, he imagined.

MYRTLE LIKED HOW all of this felt—to be kissed with what she presumed was savage abandon, and to reciprocate with the same savagery. To be picked up with confidence, and then flung across his lap, his arms draped possessively around her body.

Interesting. She'd never thought she'd like the feeling of being subdued, but it turned out she did.

"You were going to explain?" she said, wriggling her bottom against him. He uttered a strangled groan, at which point she realized not only did she like being subdued, but she also liked feeling powerful.

She was a woman of nuance, she already knew that. But it was always enjoyable to discover new facets to one's personality.

"Keep still," he growled, and she immediately stopped moving.

"Explain?" she said. Not moving.

He tightened his hold on her, then looked off into the corner of the room. Woof had discovered some sort of treat, but she didn't think he was looking at the dog—his gaze was unfocused, as though in thought.

"I have . . . quite a history," he began. "Experience, I mean."

"I know that. Everyone knows that," she replied, emphasizing her words by tugging on his hair. "You're a rake of the first order. So much so that news of you reached Richard's country house, where I could hear about it."

He seemed nonplussed by her casual acceptance. "But what I mean is, I haven't ever felt as though there were new things to learn."

"You think *I* am going to teach you new things?"

Now she couldn't keep the incredulity from her voice.

"Not about that, no, but in how it all feels when it happens." He shook his head in frustration. "I'm not explaining myself well—"

"Even though you said you'd explain," she said dryly, and he pinched her. Not so much that it hurt, just as a bit of a warning that she should not continue her impertinence.

Which of course meant she was absolutely going to continue it.

"As I was saying," he said in a stern tone that made her all fluttery inside, "this is different."

"Because I don't know what I am doing?" she asked.

He snorted, then followed that with a caress of her bare neck, making her shiver. "I think you know exactly what you are doing."

She wanted to preen, but preening meant wiggling, and she didn't want him to stop holding her. She wouldn't mind if he scolded her again, to be honest, but she wasn't sure what the line would be between his rebuke and just tossing her off his lap.

She wanted to stay here, thank you very much.

"And what am I doing?" she said, surprised to hear herself sounding almost arch. Had she ever sounded arch in her life?

Likely not.

He didn't reply, just uttered one of those growls again, his fingers digging into her skin.

Now she did shift, turning so she could face him, putting one knee down on either side of his legs. Placing her hands on his shoulders for balance.

She felt both powerful and vulnerable this way; powerful because she was literally atop him, but vulnerable because that part of her, the part that was making itself known below, was open, spread out over his lap. Which, she knew, contained a part of him that might be interested in the proceedings as well.

It was all rather like a puzzle, as she thought about it: pieces fitting into one another, clicking into place like when one solved a math problem.

She was about to share her insight when he yanked her close, putting his mouth on hers. He was very much in control even though she was straddling him.

His hands moved to her waist, and his fingers—his long, artistic fingers—slid up so they were achingly close to her breasts. She moved closer, and his fingers were there, on top of her tender flesh, even though the fabric of her gown separated them.

But that was a minor impediment, so she brought her hand to her bodice and dragged the fabric down, exposing herself to his touch.

"Please," she said, breaking the kiss to beg him, "please touch me."

That growl again, and then he bent his mouth to her skin, brushing his mouth across the tops of her breasts as his hand caressed the soft fullness.

Myrtle knew she was larger than the average female, and she had always viewed that as a negative; gowns were harder to fit, people stared more, and she had to worry about excessive bouncing on the rare occasions she danced.

But now she wouldn't trade her breasts for anything, because his hands were telling her, by touch and feel, how much he liked them. He squeezed and palmed the willing flesh, his mouth moving lower and lower still until he sucked her nipple into his mouth and she gasped.

"You like that," he murmured, and it wasn't a question.

She nodded frantically, and he chuckled before resuming his exploration.

Myrtle didn't know how much time had passed, to be honest; just that there was plenty of kissing, touching, and making a variety of noises that indicated a lot without actually saying anything.

Until, finally, he pushed her away, panting. "We have to stop or—or we won't ever stop." His voice was ragged, frantic, and she felt a secret thrill that she was responsible.

"It's like mathematics," she responded, her mind feeling unmoored. Like how she usually felt, but more so—it was as if everything was heightened, as if every sensation was increased geometrically.

He gave a snort of disbelief, and she struggled off his lap, pulling up her untidy and disheveled clothing as she did so. "Mathematics," he muttered as he tucked his shirt in.

"Well, that was enjoyable," she said, relieved to hear her voice didn't betray just how delirious, confused, and strange she felt. Not all bad things, but the intensity of each feeling made her want to lie down.

Preferably with him.

"But we can't do that too often, or we will both forget our purposes," she continued, ignoring his narrowed gaze. How could he be troubled when all of that had just happened?

"Enjoyable?" he repeated, his tone sharp.

"Mmm-hmm," she confirmed. "So enjoyable that it would be easy to lose one's focus. Submerging into the pleasure instead of setting up one's business or pursuing one's talent." She tilted her head in thought. "Perhaps that is why you haven't achieved the level of success you know you are capable of—too distracted by all of this," she said, gesturing between the two of them.

"You think I have not succeeded in reaching the limits of my talent because I've been too occupied with sex?" he said, his expression one of disbelief.

She shrugged, unperturbed by his ire. "Perhaps."

OF ALL THE accusations thrown at him over the years he had never heard he was not focused enough on his work—too often the opposite had been said. And he'd been proud of that, since it meant he was living up to his promise, both artistic, and the one he'd made to his mother to make his art his first priority.

But now here Myrtle had the audacity to say his

sexual indulgence—the only indulgence he, well, indulged in, was possibly impeding his path.

"Why would you think that instead of another reason?" he asked, not bothering to keep the annoyance from his voice. He knew she could handle that—something he appreciated, in fact, even if he was currently annoyed.

She shrugged again. "Because you are so talented there has to be a reason that you are not as famous as you should be."

"Oh," he said, feeling chagrined. "Though it might be that I am not concentrating enough," he admitted. Though now that he'd kissed and touched her, and she had done the same to him, he didn't know if he could give it all up, even if it was in service of his art.

So maybe what she was saying was correct, after all.

"I propose we do an experiment," she continued. Her face was alight with excitement, and it wasn't only because of what they'd just done. "How about we spend one week doing all the things, and then another week where we do not?" Her tone made it sound as though she was conducting a lecture. "If we did it the other way around we wouldn't know what we were missing in the first place. Everything else would be the same—you would help me with Lilah's debut, I would pose for you—we just wouldn't do anything that second week. We could see if your work noticeably improved." Her expression was pleased. "We would have many controls, and only one variable."

"And you? Would you apply the same experiment to your work?" he said.

She wrinkled her brow. "I suppose. Though I cannot entirely concentrate on one or the other as it is—I have to help Lilah and I also have to start setting up my future business. I need to do both simultaneously. It's not the same thing."

"So perhaps—if we are to conduct an experiment—your test will be to see if you can continue on your current course and add all of this," he said, gesturing between them, "to see if your work improves, stays the same, or deteriorates."

"And you will see if your work improves, stays the same, or deteriorates."

"Excellent." He gave her a wolfish grin. "And we will have a good time while we are doing our experiment. Tell me this is the most fun you've ever had doing an experiment."

"We haven't even begun!" she exclaimed.

"But from what you know," he said, making his tone silky. Like a caress. "From what you have already experienced, surely you can make a reasonable guess."

It seemed as though she couldn't resist smiling. "I think I could, yes."

"And your answer?" he prodded.

She rolled her eyes. "Yes. Yes, I think this will be the most fun I've ever had doing an experiment."

HE KISSED HER again instead of speaking, and she lost herself in his mouth, the way he held her, how perfectly everything seemed to fit together.

She couldn't help but move closer, and he uttered a strangled groan deep in his throat, but only held her tighter, so she presumed the groan was one of pleasure.

But—just to be certain—she shifted a bit more, and he groaned again.

She liked conducting these types of experiments. She definitely liked how possessively he held her, as though she might pull away, and he wanted to claim her.

She wanted to be claimed.

And she also appreciated that he was holding her as though she was strong, not a delicate flower who needed soft, gentle caresses.

Her whole body ached to be touched, to be grasped, to feel vanquished by his strength.

While she resisted, because resisting felt far more fun than succumbing.

So she concentrated on kissing him with the same ferocity with which he was kissing her. Their whole experiment—admittedly an experiment she'd proposed—was about equality, of seeing if moments with or without all of this would have an impact. And if the experiment was to be valid, it needed to be balanced on either side, so each could find a reasonable answer to the problem.

Which was why she placed her fingers on the strong column of his neck, stroking the skin there. He only wore a cravat when he went out, so there was far more skin than she would encounter with any other gentleman.

If she did such things with other gentlemen. Which she wouldn't; that would be introducing a variable that would alter the experiment.

Plus there was the whole "I only want to do this with him right now" element.

Eventually—a few minutes, an hour, a month—she drew away, hearing their breaths in the nearly empty room, feeling the warmth between them.

"Day One of the Experiment," she said, sounding breathless.

His lips curled slowly, his gaze seeming as though it was devouring her. "Day One. What will happen on Day Two? I wonder."

Chapter Fifteen

Day Two was the day of Lilah's official come-out ball, the kickoff to her—and Phoebe's, now—actual Season.

Lilah had stormed into Myrtle's room early that morning, worried that there would not be enough for the guests to eat —without Regina in the house, the menus and such were handled by Cook and the housekeeper, together, and they did their best, but they didn't always get it right.

"And what if there aren't enough flowers?" Lilah continued, as Myrtle blearily watched her pace the room. Woof had spent the night sleeping with her, a warm bundle pressed up against her side, so she'd slept better than usual, and was having trouble concentrating.

Also, Lilah was fussed up about nothing at all, and Myrtle knew she could untangle everything when she was fully awake.

She reached for her dressing gown and put it on, shoving her feet into the slippers at the edge of her bed. "Just a moment, please," she said to

Lilah, putting her hand out in a conciliatory gesture.

"I don't have a moment!" Lilah shot back, irate. "The ball is in nine hours, and there is so much to do by then!"

Myrtle gathered Lilah in a hug, pulling her tight. "It will be fine, dearest," she said, stroking her niece's hair. "The most important thing, and the only thing you can control yourself, is that you look as beautiful and poised as possible, and I know you are going to do just that."

Lilah's breath shuddered against her, and she tightened her hold even more. Sometimes she forgot that Lilah was only eighteen years old, and this was likely her first time without her mother, who was, while admittedly erratic, also her mother, who cared for her. Lilah had never anticipated having this kind of debut—with just her father and her aunt.

It would require some pivoting, which Myrtle was expertly adept at doing.

She drew back and regarded Lilah, while still holding her arms. "Let us break down the problems. Things are always easier to parse when you look at the elements and not the thing's entirety."

Lilah nodded, her eyes moist with tears. "Uh—uh, yes," she said in a shaky voice.

"Your main concern is that your guests will not feel as though they're being properly cared for, is that correct?"

Lilah considered it for a moment, then nodded again.

"And the elements of a successful event are . . . ?" Myrtle lifted her eyebrows in question.

"Good music, good food, a comfortable space, and pleasant guests."

Myrtle beamed at her niece. "That is an excellent answer. All of that, yes. So let us clear the things that are not in our control—the space and the music—and I will ask about the food. Oh, and the flowers!" she added. "We can't guarantee the guests are pleasant, we have to just hope."

Lilah's face crumpled, and then she flung herself back into Myrtle's arms. "Thank you, Aunt Turtle. I didn't know if you could—well, thank you."

Myrtle knew what Lilah hadn't said—she didn't know if Myrtle could handle practical, logistical things; in point of fact, Myrtle didn't know if she could either. But this was something that her niece needed, and she was here precisely to assist her niece, so she would have to adjust her scope of what she thought she could or could not do, and go make inquiries of the kitchen and the household staff about food and flowers.

Simeon would know about both those things, she thought. He already had opinions on flowers, and any person with taste—both literal and figurative—had to have opinions on food.

"I will just get dressed and go sort everything out," she said, shooing Lilah back to her own room.

Simeon preferred not to think about how quickly he dropped what he'd been doing to assist Myrtle. He told himself it was because it affected Phoebe and Miss Lilah, but he knew that was only secondary.

"Thank goodness you're here," she said, greeting him as soon as the butler opened the door. Woof trotted along at her heels, and Simeon took a moment to appreciate how perfect the two looked together—Myrtle's hair was nearly as untidy as Woof's pelt, and they both had a frantic energy.

Simeon suspected that Woof's had more to do with wanting to find treats, but the result was similar.

"Thank you for coming," she said, helping him shrug off his coat. He gave it and his hat to the butler, who nodded before making a quick exit. Whether because it was that he was very good at his job or Myrtle had been making herself a nuisance while she waited, Simeon didn't know.

"Come through here. First we have to see to Cook."

"What is the problem?" he asked in a mild tone.

"Lilah is concerned we don't have enough food for tonight, and I've never hosted a large gathering like this one before—"

"And I have?" he interrupted.

"No, but you know things," she said, making a vague, helpless gesture.

"You know things, too, Myrtle."

She gave him a warm smile in return.

After navigating the circuitous route to the downstairs, they entered the kitchen, Woof still with them, and the kitchen staff all looked up at their arrival.

"Good morning, miss," the woman who was

obviously in charge said. "Is there something amiss?"

"Miss Allen knows you have it all in hand," Simeon said smoothly, giving Cook his low-to-medium-range smile, "but she wishes to know the details herself, so she can assure Miss Lilah, who is naturally a bit nervous this morning." He increased the intensity of his smile, which made Cook's eyes widen as she staggered back to lean on the main table in the middle of the kitchen.

"Of course," Cook said, sounding dazed. "There are two hundred guests expected, and we have three hundred mini-sandwiches, five hundred or so canapés, along with an assortment of cheeses. Enough for one hundred people."

"Can you do the ma—" Simeon began, but Myrtle spoke before he could finish.

"That means you have provided food for each person to have one and a half times what anyone would expect them to eat," she said in a decisive tone. "Excellent."

Simeon turned to regard her, impressed again with how quickly her brain worked.

"Yes, precisely, miss," Cook replied.

"And the beverages? Are those calculated the same?" Myrtle continued, sounding much more confident than she had when she'd met Simeon at the door.

"Yes, miss. The same. We also have ordered additional bottles of champagne and Madeira."

"Though Regina won't be in attendance," Myrtle murmured. In a louder voice, she said,

"Wonderful. And do you plan on serving any desserts?"

Cook's expression was shocked. "Of course, miss. I would not dream of not having desserts."

"Oh good. Cake?" Myrtle said in a hopeful tone.

Simeon smothered a grin at how enthusiastic she sounded.

"Three kinds."

"Well, that all seems fine. Thank you." Myrtle gave a grateful nod to the staff in general, then strode out of the kitchen, Simeon trotting along behind her similar to Woof.

Simeon waited until they were a safe enough distance away, then he reached for her arm. "Come here," he said, pushing her against the wall. He planted his hands above her head and lowered his mouth to hers.

For a moment she didn't respond. Then she wrapped her arms around him and gave herself to his kiss, returning his fierce passion in equal measure.

There was something intoxicatingly dangerous about kissing here, where someone might stumble upon them. The passageway was dimly lit, giving it another frisson of danger.

He pressed his body against her, his already stiff cock rubbing against her front, dying for release, but instead sweetly frustrated.

She had one hand on his arse and was squeezing, hard, while the other hand was in his hair, pulling him close to her. The sharp twinge of pain only heightened the sensation of being lost in her mouth, lost in this moment, just the two of them in this narrow, dark hallway. Just two people who were intensely attracted to one another and weren't shy about showing it.

He had never lost himself so much in another human while kissing them—he knew his own name, but just barely, and he couldn't recall why he wasn't supposed to be with her. Not when it seemed like the best idea he'd ever had.

Their tongues were tangling and stroking one another in an erotic mirroring of what his cock wanted to do to her pussy, and he ached, he ached, and all he wanted was for both of them to be satisfied.

His hand slipped between their bodies, and he expertly found her mound, then began to rub and palm it as she writhed against the wall.

She broke the kiss, flinging her head back, her eyes closed, her lip in her teeth as she gave soft moans that only heated his motions.

"You like this."

It wasn't a question.

"Mmm, yes, don't stop—don't—" And then she arched her back, thrusting herself more into his hand as he kept touching her.

He could tell she was close. Here, in the passageway between the kitchen and upstairs. He was going to make her climax, and he was going to see her face as she did, and he had never wanted anything more in his entire life.

"Ahh," she said at last, and he captured her moans with his mouth, pressing his whole self against her, his hand still there, but not moving.

"What was that for?" she said at last, after her rapid breathing had subsided.

"I like seeing you use your brains," he murmured. "There is something so magnetic when I watch you do sums faster than someone with an abacus."

She chuckled. "I fear I would be under constant attack, then, if we spent more time together, because that is what I do."

"I know," he said, pressing his lips to her ear. "And it is incredibly provocative. To me, at least."

"I am glad you think so," she said, her voice husky. "Because I very much enjoy what you do to me." Again, that blunt frankness he admired and envied. That she could just tell him how she felt made him marvel. What would it be like if he could tell her how he really felt?

Better yet, what would it be like if he really knew himself?

"Tomorrow is Day Three," Myrtle said in a sly tone. "I wonder how good it will be, given all of this."

"You'll just have to wait and see," Simeon said, his words a promise.

THE COME-OUT BALL was a complete and total success. Neither Lilah nor Phoebe lacked for dance partners, there was plenty of food and drink, and even Richard managed a smile once every hour or so.

The best part, of course, was getting to spend time with Simeon, who was not only coaching her how to lie, but also making it so much fun that she didn't notice it was work.

"Here comes Lady Sandington," he murmured. He'd arrived early, receiving a glower from Richard, but had ignored that to compliment Lilah and Phoebe. Both girls wore debutante white, but Lilah's dark hair was dressed in a cloud of curls, while Phoebe's blond hair was simply pulled back with a flower adorning her chignon.

"Lady Sandington," Myrtle repeated.

"Yes, and you're going to say you enjoy her singing."

"But I've never heard her sing," Myrtle replied. "How can I—Oh, right."

"Good. Here she is."

Myrtle stepped forward, reaching to take the other lady's hands in hers. "Lady Sandington, such a pleasure to see you again. I wanted to let you know"—and then she shot a nervous look back at Simeon, who gave her a reassuring nod—"that I greatly enjoyed your performance the other day."

Lady Sandington's face eased into a wide smile, making Myrtle feel as though this lying business actually did some good, if it made another person feel more confident. "Which of the songs was your favorite?"

A moment of panic, and then Simeon responded. "The question is, which one is your favorite to sing?" he asked smoothly, making Myrtle give him an admiring glance.

Not that she wouldn't otherwise; he looked exceptionally handsome, even for him. He wore elegantly stark evening wear, a black jacket paired with black trousers and a crisp white shirt. He'd slicked his hair back, better showing the handsome planes of his face, and he wore no ornamentation other than a diamond stick pin.

Other gentlemen looked unkempt and over-dressed next to him, even though they were tidy enough. It was just the beautiful severity of his appearance that made her catch her breath.

"I think my favorite is 'Juanita' by Caroline Norton," Lady Sandington said at last. "If you don't think that is too radical, that is."

"Not at all," Myrtle responded quickly, even though she had no idea about why the song was radical or who either Juanita or Caroline Norton was. Just that if a lady thought something was too radical, chances were very good Myrtle would be all for it. "That would be my choice as well," she said, earning a look of approval from Simeon.

Eventually, Lady Sandington drifted away, her cheeks still pink with pleasure for the compliments.

"You did very well," Simeon said. "The important thing about lying, in general, is to keep as close to the truth as possible."

"But I didn't know anything about that lady's singing," Myrtle objected.

"You don't know the specifics, but you know things in general—that people like to be told they have done well, and that getting them to talk about themselves makes them like you more."

"That is a very cynical way to look at it," Myrtle said.

"Not cynical—I like to talk about myself as well. Like how handsome I am, or how well I paint. Or kiss," he added, quietly, so only she could hear him.

"You are incorrigible," she said, but she couldn't keep the admiring tone from her voice.

"You wouldn't like me so much if I was corrigible," he shot back.

She had no choice but to laugh. And to agree—and when had she started liking him so much? At first she'd assumed he was a vain rake, like so many other handsome gentlemen who didn't have to do anything but smile and people did things for them. But he'd put his actual talent, not just his appearance, to good use, making a living and building a reputation for himself as an artist.

"But to get back to the lesson," he said, sounding more serious. "The secret to a good lie is to stick as close as you can to the truth, don't swallow or touch your skin, and make eye contact with the person you're lying to."

"What if you're lying to a crowd?" she asked.

"One step at a time," he said with a laugh. "You're not advanced enough for that yet."

"Did you see me, Aunt Turtle?"

Lilah popped up seemingly out of nowhere, her face alight with excitement.

Might as well practice now, Myrtle thought.

"I did! You were wonderful."

"I wasn't certain of all the steps, but Mr. Hopper said I learned very quickly."

"I didn't realize you didn't know all the steps,"

Myrtle said. Which was the truth, since she didn't even know what Lilah was talking about.

"I am having a wonderful time," Lilah continued. She reached forward to take Myrtle's hand, squeezing it in hers. "Thank you for this. Father wouldn't even notice me dancing, much less tell me I did well."

"It's a good thing I am here, then," Myrtle replied, feeling smugly satisfied.

"It is. Oh, there's Phoebe!"

And Lilah was off again, leaving Myrtle and Simeon alone.

"Goodness. I didn't realize it was this easy. I'm going to have to do it more often," she said.

Simeon's expression was thoughtful. "Please don't. You are so refreshingly open and honest, there aren't very many people like you. Actually, there is nobody like you," he said, sounding as though he was speaking the truth.

Even though Myrtle didn't know if he was or not, since he was so adept at diplomacy and she was skeptical of gentlemen's compliments in general, even if this one was not accompanied by a desire to take her fortune.

"Thank you," was all she said. It didn't matter if he spoke the truth or not, not in this instance; all that mattered was whether she would decide to believe him or not.

And now she would. After all, she wouldn't ever have the attention of such a handsome gentleman—of any gentleman, actually—in a few weeks, so she might as well enjoy it while it lasted.

Chapter Sixteen

Day number four was much less fun, Myrtle thought sourly.

It had begun well enough; she'd woken at a reasonable hour, early enough that she knew Lilah would still be asleep. She was able to work through some more pages in the Peacock, taking notes in the margins of the book. She liked algebra well enough, though geometry was her passion; something about all the angles and the relationship between them spoke to her. But algebra had its good parts as well—the equations usually balanced one another out, and she liked the stealthy use of letters mixed into the sequences.

But then Lilah had burst into her bedroom and announced that a "grand group" of people would be going to see Madame Olechka, the self-styled "Mesmerist of Mayfair," a woman who promised she would be able to hypnotize others into bizarre behavior.

Myrtle wanted to retort that she had been ac-

cused of behaving bizarrely her entire life, and
nobody wanted to come see *her*.

But she thought that might be beside the point.

And since Lilah required a chaperone, that
meant Myrtle had to attend as well.

Putting the Peacock reluctantly aside, she rose,
glancing over at Lilah, who was bouncing up and
down in her excitement. She couldn't help but
smile then; Lilah's enthusiasm was nearly con-
tagious, though Myrtle was already anticipating
some awkward moments.

On the other hand, those awkward moments
were not likely to be from her, so perhaps there
was an upside?

"What does one wear to visit a mesmerist?" she
said, making her way toward the wardrobe.

Madame Lucille had delivered an entire Season's
worth of clothing, especially suited for Myrtle's
coloring and shape. It was an honest pleasure to
get dressed every morning and night, since beautiful dresses were almost as much of a pleasure for
her as mathematics and cake.

Lilah shrugged, clearly not interested in offering any advice pertaining to her aunt's clothing.

"I'll take care of it," Myrtle said, tugging Lilah's
arm and guiding her toward the door. "Just go
and get yourself ready, and I will meet you downstairs in an hour."

"You look lovely," Lilah exclaimed as Myrtle
descended the stairs fifty-seven minutes later.

Myrtle had chosen another gown that evoked—

in her mind, at least—geometry. Its fabric was cream silk, with brown velvet ribbons stitched on at right angles to one another to create a maze across the gown.

It had enormous belled sleeves tied at the wrists with the same brown velvet ribbons, and the waist was emphasized with multiple layers of brown ribbon.

The gown enhanced her already enhanced curves, and for a moment she wondered if it was all too much—but then again, what was the point of having beautiful gowns styled for one's figure if one didn't wear them proudly?

Lilah was wearing a white day dress with lace trim, and carried a lemon-yellow shawl, while she wore a bonnet with yellow ribbons and paler yellow shoes. She looked every inch a beautiful debutante, and Myrtle's heart squeezed a little at seeing how joyous her niece seemed to be.

Traipsing out to see some charlatan demanding audience members quack like a duck or whatever would be worth it, if it made Lilah so happy.

"Phoebe sent a note to say she and Mr. Jones would meet us there," Lilah remarked, and Myrtle noted how her own breathing quickened, and she immediately felt more interested.

Hmm. There was obviously significant chemistry between them, chemistry that could affect her lungs and other parts. Her mouth, for example, suddenly felt tender, as though her lips were recalling how it felt when he kissed them.

And her breasts were—well, she shouldn't

think too hard on that, or she might spontaneously combust. Not that she believed it could happen, despite what Mr. Dickens might say, but it seemed more possible if she kept thinking on certain things.

So she had to wonder if she was thinking smarter and harder because of their mutual exploration, or was she befuddled by it and getting too distracted?

On the one hand, she was thinking about what made people respond and react to one another as a way to gauge human relations. On the other hand, she just couldn't stop thinking about kissing him.

So she'd have to continue the experiment to be absolutely certain.

"Aunt Turtle?"

Lilah's voice—sounding impatient, leading Myrtle to think she'd spoken a few times—cut through the miasma of her mind, and she straightened, wrapping her arms around herself in an attempt to silence her body's wishes.

"Yes, what?" she said.

Lilah gave her a narrow glance. "You are thinking of something."

"Always," Myrtle snapped back, though she felt a blush come to her cheeks. "I am always thinking of something. You'll have to be more specific."

"You're thinking of something now. Something that makes your face get hot." Lilah stepped close to peer into her aunt's face. "What is it, hmm?"

"You're not supposed to be observing anyone

but yourself, what with being an eighteen-year-old debutante. Every thought is supposed to be focused on you."

Lilah raised a brow. "I can do both at once. I am quite talented."

Myrtle couldn't help but laugh. She looped her arm through Lilah's, gesturing to the door. "Shall we go see what bizarre behavior we can get up to?"

"A usual Wednesday for you, then," Lilah observed, making Myrtle laugh even harder.

"PLEASE?"

Simeon often wished he wasn't so softhearted. But never more so than now, when Phoebe was standing in front of him with enormous, pleading eyes, her hands clasped in supplication.

She was a remarkably even-tempered girl, quiet and modest. He'd asked her how she was enjoying the Season thus far, and she hadn't replied with anything but mild pleasantries.

But this was something else.

"Madame Olechka is famous for her abilities. I've never seen anyone who is able to control someone else's actions"—*except well-born men in Society*, Simeon thought dryly—"and I'd like the chance to see for myself. And," she added, twisting her hands together more, "Mr. Hopper will be there. I met him the other night. Please?" she said, but she didn't need to. He was going to cave.

"Yes, I'll be happy to escort you." He was proud that his tone exhibited only enthusiasm, given what he was feeling inside. Perhaps if the whole artist thing didn't work out he could explore work as an actor.

"Miss Allen and Lilah will be there as well," Phoebe remarked.

Well. She could have led the conversation with that instead of trying to persuade him that some random charlatan was able to mesmerize people into feeling things they hadn't planned on.

But he didn't want to share that with her, since he didn't want to share that with anybody. Even himself.

Something he would force himself to examine later on.

MADAME OLECHKA'S PERFORMANCE was in a cavernous space that was spare on ornament, but made up for because of its immense size.

There were a lot of people already there by the time Simeon and Phoebe arrived, but it wasn't difficult to spot Myrtle and Miss Lilah. Myrtle was talking animatedly with another one of this Season's debutantes, while Lilah was gazing mistily up at a handsome gentleman whom Simeon immediately distrusted.

"Lilah, we're here!" Phoebe called, making her way toward them. Lilah's attention snapped away from the gentleman, making Simeon a little less anxious. Not that he was Lilah's chaperone, but he understood gentlemen better than any of the ladies, and he wanted to be certain that anyone Lilah became acquainted with beyond a dance was someone worth knowing.

"I'm so glad you came!" Lilah exclaimed, running up and grasping Phoebe's arms. "Aunt Turtle," she said, glancing behind to where Myrtle was walking toward them, "says she will keep an open mind, but it's clear what her actual opinion is."

Myrtle had joined them by now, and winced as she heard Lilah's words.

Simeon bit his lip to keep from laughing—Myrtle's face was entirely expressive, and the fact that she hadn't actually laid out all the reasons to mistrust the mesmerist had to mean she loved her niece very much.

"I just don't think that science works that way," she said in a meek tone.

Simeon jerked his chin toward her. "If I were to say I believed in this nonsense you would waste no time disabusing me. Why is it different for her?"

Myrtle glared at him, and he felt a rush of satisfaction. He didn't want her to bend, ever, even if it was for a good reason. He didn't know when it had become so important to him that she stick to her resolutions, her values, but it had. He needed her to speak her mind, to share her truths in a way very few people did.

"I already know how you feel," Lilah pointed out. "But we're here because it should be fun, no matter what we believe." She gave her aunt a narrow look. "You do believe in fun, don't you?"

Myrtle's lips drew into a wide smile, and the open, honest joy Simeon saw there shook him—

like a beautiful piece of art, or a particularly evocative bit of music.

She was art and music. Her frankness, her intelligence, her wit, and yes, her curves spoke to him in a way that made him wonder how he'd existed without her for so long.

Or how he would survive when they were no longer acquainted.

Because they'd promised one another that they would never put their gifts aside—his art, her brain—for anything less important. Not for love, not for security, not even for happiness.

Because to waste the talent they'd been given would be a tremendous loss of their potential.

And it was unfortunate he was having all of these thoughts now, when they were standing in a large building with a few hundred fellow humans waiting for a conjuring trick.

"Of course I believe in fun," she was saying, casting a quick, sidelong glance toward Simeon. "It is just that my idea of fun is not yours."

Lilah wrinkled her nose as Simeon tried not to laugh. "Because yours is mathematics and science and books," she said in a scornful tone.

Simeon held his hand up. "I might agree with the first part, but I absolutely will not tolerate demeaning books. Books open up a world for us that we normally cannot go—worlds with new ideas, fantastic characters, and unimaginable bravery."

"Mr. Jones is in a book club," Myrtle explained.

Simeon gave her a surprised look. "I hadn't realized you remembered that."

"I listen to you," she said simply.

It warmed him—he had to admit—that Myrtle, with her brain stuffed full of complicated ideas and theorems spent any time saving room for what he'd mentioned in passing. That she took note of it, and understood when he defended one of the few pleasures in his life. A pleasure that didn't relate to his art or to his body.

"What books do you read anyway?" Lilah asked, with a challenge in her voice.

Simeon shrugged. "Fiction, mostly. Bram's wife, Lady Wilhelmina, has been trying to get us to read a book about the stars, but thus far we've been able to put her off. I think this month we're reading some Spanish romance from a few centuries ago. In translation," he added, "since none of us reads Spanish."

"Margaret Tyler's *The Mirrour of Princely Deedes and Knighthood*?" Myrtle asked, as though the information was already at the forefront of her brain.

Simeon turned to look at her, stunned. "How did you know that? I thought all you knew was numbers and formulas."

She looked smug. "I like to relax by reading things that aren't numbers and formulas, you know."

"I didn't know," he said, unable to keep the admiration from his tone.

"Aunt Turtle should go to your next book club!" Lilah exclaimed, and Simeon froze.

Not that he wouldn't want her to go; it would be a pleasure for her to meet Benedict, for example, who always assumed he was the smartest person in the room. Or Fenton, who actually was the smartest person in the room, but whose brain worked nearly as oddly as Myrtle's did.

But the first and only time a person who wasn't an original member of the Bastard Five had attended their meeting—that person had ended up married to Bram. Simeon didn't want to tempt fate, nor himself, by bringing her to meet his closest friends. To exchange ideas with them, to watch them interact, and to know that they would all have opinions about her and be able to tell he had deeper feelings for her than he should.

He didn't think that would be a good idea.

Not for him because he shouldn't have allowed himself to even get into this kind of state about her, to be thinking about her when he wasn't with her. He'd never done that with any of his romantic partners in the past.

But also and especially for her. She'd been very clear about what she wanted, and what she did not want, and she did not want a permanent fixture in her life. She wanted to be free to work on her own thoughts, to devote herself to the work of her brain, not to anything as mundane as home and family.

Even though Simeon was beginning to wonder if those things were really as mundane as he'd always believed.

"That sounds delightful!" she was saying, and Simeon's chest tightened. It wasn't as though he could explain why he might not want her to come—she had already said he was her one friend in London, and if this was an opportunity to make more? He could not deny her.

But still.

"Of course," he forced himself to say. "We're not quite certain when the next meeting is, since Bram is away with his wife—they're expecting, you see—and Fenton is—" He made a vague gesture in the air, indicating he wasn't quite sure about Fenton.

"Well, you will tell me when it is scheduled for," Myrtle said brightly. "I did enjoy the Tyler, and it would be a pleasure to discuss it with people who read it as well. I've never found anyone in my actual life I could speak about things with. Mostly," she continued, her expression growing dimmer, "I read what others have said about a thing. But until you, Mr. Jones, I hadn't been able to discuss anything live, as it were." Her smile, when she turned to look at him, was radiant. And he felt like the worst kind of heel for wanting her to stay away so his heart wouldn't get too broken.

For one thing, that would be cruel; for the other thing, he suspected it would be too late.

He wasn't able to see the future, as Madame Olechka might claim she could, but he strongly suspected life would take a turn for the worse when they were in the second part of their sexual experiment, when they weren't able to touch one another.

And he likely already knew that he wouldn't mind, not as long as he was still able to speak with her. Falling in love with her brain—because he had to admit he was in love with her, he couldn't lie to himself anymore—was far more dangerous than just falling in love with their physical experimentations.

He was in so much trouble.

Chapter Seventeen

Myrtle's smile faltered when she saw Simeon's expression. It had felt so wonderful to be invited to be part of his book club, but it seemed as though there was something wrong; did he not truly want her there? Did he regret ever meeting her in the first place?

Myrtle knew well enough she was not suited to be friends with most people; they were put off by her intelligence, her blunt way of speaking, and she didn't much care for them either.

But Simeon felt different. At least, she *hoped* he felt different. That was to say, she liked how he felt—particularly physically—and she wanted to keep his friendship long after Lilah was married and this whole situation was over.

But what if he didn't feel the same?

That would not be under her control, she reminded herself. Too often she thought that if she could just use enough brainpower she could solve things.

"That is," she said, aware he hadn't replied to

her earlier comment, "I would like the opportunity, but I would not want to impose."

Lilah snorted. "How could it be an imposition when it is likely very hard to find enough people to want to talk about such dull subjects?" She poked Simeon in the arm. "You and your friends are likely not prepared for Aunt Turtle."

Myrtle wished, not for the first time, that her niece was a little less opinionated. Though there, at least, she did take after her aunt, so Myrtle should not be hypocritical about it.

"It will be an honor," Simeon said, but it didn't sound as firm as Myrtle would have liked. But perhaps, because she was so out of her element here, she was more self-conscious about not fitting in. About not being wanted.

She wanted herself. She liked herself, and her brain, and her appearance. But she was intelligent enough to know that not everyone did.

And sometimes, like in these kinds of situations, she felt more out of place than usual.

"We'll discuss that later," Myrtle said, adopting a bright tone she hoped would fool him.

His eyes narrowed. "Miss Allen, I think we should go fetch some refreshments." He turned to address the girls. "You won't get into any trouble if we just go over there, will you?" he said, jerking his chin toward a woman who stood behind a table filled with various beverages.

"No, of course not," Lilah and Miss Jones replied.

"Excellent," he said, holding his arm out for Myrtle.

She took it, wishing her pulse didn't flutter when he touched her, even at something as innocuous as looping her arm through his.

"Are you all right?" he asked, as soon as they were out of earshot.

"I was going to ask the same thing of you," she replied. "If you don't want me to go to—"

"It's not that," he interrupted. "It's—it's everything. The more I do with you, Myrtle, the more I want to do. And that is not good for either one of us."

"What do you mean?"

Now it felt as though her pulse was fluttering and her heart was beating more quickly. Apparently her bodily reactions were very in tune with what her brain wanted. Good to know, she noted. That fact would come in handy if she was faced with imminent danger, for example.

"I mean," he said, pulling her closer, "that I find I want to spend time with you. To speak with you, to learn how your brain works."

"Good luck with that," she muttered.

"And I know that neither of us wants any kind of further entanglement, I mean more than we are already entangled. Not to mention your brother—"

"What did Richard say? When did you speak to him?"

"He came to see me soon after you did. Very early in the morning, in fact. He made it very clear that if you do not marry anyone to his liking, he will not release your money." He shook his head. "He seems like a decent enough fellow, but he is like most of your class—very concerned with breeding, and correct behavior, and all that."

"He should learn by now that I will do what I want," Myrtle said, most of her earlier flutteriness gone because of her idiotic brother.

"I think he does know that," Simeon replied, laughter in his tone. "And this is his only way to circumvent that. But having spoken to you, having listened to you, I know you want to make your own life. So my inconvenient wishes to spend more time with you are just . . . inconvenient."

She turned to regard him. They had reached the beverage table by now, but neither one of them glanced at the drinks for sale. "I like how direct you are," she said. Her cheeks were flushed, and she knew it was because of him, because of his open admiration. The flutteriness was back in full force. "It is rare, if not nonexistent, to find someone who will just say what they are thinking."

"Except you. I think I learned it from you, to be honest," he replied. "I certainly have never been concerned about saying what is on my mind. In fact, I've actively avoided it until now." His gorgeous mouth was drawn into a warm smile, and she wished they were alone so she could lean forward and kiss it.

But that was a bit too far, even for her own usually impulsive self.

Instead, she had to settle for her words. "Along that topic, for us to keep a good control over our experiment, we will have to find some time today to—" And she made a vague hand gesture that she hoped he would understand.

His eyes gleamed. He didn't have to say anything to let her know he absolutely did understand, and what was more, was eagerly looking forward to it.

"We have to watch this Madame Olechka— what is taking her so long to appear anyway— and then get our respective charges safely back home. And then we can—"

"And then I can pose for you."

His eyes widened in surprise. "I hadn't thought we would do that first, but—"

She shook her head. "I might be too distracted to pose after. But before, with all of that lovely anticipation . . ." she said, ending her words with a long sigh.

"I do like how you think," he said, and now his tone was fully admiring. "I like it all the time, but I especially like it now."

She smiled up at him, feeling her heart catch at just how beautiful he was. And he was hers, at least for the next few weeks. At least hers to explore with; she would never lay claim to anybody else, not when she knew how precious and rare true freedom was. He had his purpose, his art, and she had hers—her brain.

She had to keep that in mind—regardless of anything else, even without Richard being a controlling arse, or what Society would have to say about an aristocratic lady's involvement with an illegitimate artist—they each had their chosen paths, and marriage was not an option. Not now, and most definitely not with one another. Perhaps in the future she would find a gentleman who was content to let his intelligent wife bustle here and there being intelligent, but there wasn't a possibility of two geniuses cohabitating. One would invariably have to let the other shine, and she knew that it was likely—the world being what it was—to be her.

She would not accept that. Not ever, not even if it meant waking up to his beautiful face every morning.

It was a hard reality, but it was something she knew in her bones.

And even if she didn't know it, he did—he had said as much. They were in agreement. Everything they were doing now was temporary.

It made her sad, even though the current situation was quite pleasant.

Thankfully, Madame Olechka made her appearance just as she was about to share her thoughts and feelings with him—he didn't need to bear the burden of her conflicted emotions.

"Welcome, everybody." Madame Olechka stood on the small stage at one end of the room, a tall, thin woman of middle age, wearing a gown bedecked with various gems, an enormous headdress atop her hair. The headdress, to Simeon's eyes, looked vaguely Eastern. Her entire look was very clearly and artfully constructed, a representation of what most British people would think a Russian mesmerist would look like.

"This evening, I propose to open a world the likes of which you have never seen," Madame Olechka continued. Her accent was heavy, but intelligible. The crowd surged forward, Miss Lilah and Phoebe stepping closer as well. He and Myrtle stood at the back, along with a few other clearly skeptical audience members.

"The mind is a wonderful thing." Madame Olechka directed hard stares toward each section of the audience. "Most of us do not know the extent of what is possible in humans' capability—"

"Speak for yourself," Myrtle muttered, and Simeon suppressed a laugh.

"But tonight you will see just what we are capable of." Madame Olechka walked to the edge of the stage. "Mesmerism is a powerful art, and it should not be used by amateurs." She glared at the back of the room where the obvious skeptics stood. "Mesmerism can cure diseases of the mind, and it can also summon behavior that a person would not normally do. For this demonstration, I will need a volunteer," she said, and many of the audience members flung their hands up in the air to indicate their willingness to participate. "But I want someone who does not already believe," she added, and several of the hands dropped. She raised her head and looked over the crowd. "You, my lady," she said, jerking her chin toward Myrtle. "I want you to join me on the stage."

"You don't want me," Myrtle replied, her voice firm.

Madame Olechka gave what Simeon could only describe as a menacing smile. "Oh, but I do. Come here, please."

"Do go on up, Aunt Turtle," Lilah urged. "It will be fun! Imagine if she makes you cluck like a chicken!"

As though that was something to be desired.

"You don't have to," Simeon said in a low voice, but Myrtle shrugged as she met his gaze.

"I might as well," she said. "It is not as though she can force me to do anything I do not wish, after all. We both know how powerful my mind is," she added, a note of humor in her tone.

"Indeed," Simeon said, and swept his hand out to indicate the path to the stage.

She strode forward, not a hint of hesitation in her walk. Once on the stage, she stared out with a proud demeanor, as though aware that she was not who the audience members would have wanted to see up there, but knowing she was fully capable of whatever task the mesmerist would give her.

Simeon was as proud of her as she was of herself. Myrtle never shirked from anything tossed her way—whether it was a Russian mesmerist, a gaggle of fortune-hunting suitors, or refusing a life that would not suit her, or not denying what she was truly destined to do. She was ready to accept any challenge.

What would it be like to be partnered with someone that confident, that intelligent, that determined?

He could not dangle that possibility in front of himself like that. He'd already reminded himself that she was not for him, and vice versa.

All he could do was admire her for now, and hope that they remained friends after everything was done.

"Please tell me your name," Madame Olechka was saying.

"Miss Myrtle Allen," Myrtle replied in a clear voice.

"Miss Myrtle, can I ask you to close your eyes?" Myrtle obliged.

"And if I may, I will put my hands on your shoulders?"

"Go ahead," Myrtle said.

Madame Olechka placed her hands on Myrtle's shoulders, shifting slightly to the side so the audience had a clear view of Myrtle's face.

"I want you to breathe deeply. In and out, like this," Madame Olechka said, inhaling audibly.

Myrtle complied.

"And now, I want you to think of the place you would most like to be."

Myrtle's expression grew wistful, and Simeon wondered where she was thinking of—back in the country, free of importunate suitors? In his studio?

Traveling to London in the carriage with him?

Though that was arrogant, to think that her ideal location was somehow related to him. Then again, he *was* arrogant, so he might as well think that.

"Are you picturing it?" the mesmerist asked.

"I am."

"And now, I want you to describe it."

Myrtle took a deep breath. When she spoke, it was in her normal tone of voice. Nothing to indicate she was yet affected by the mesmerist's actions.

"I am in a ballroom," she said, and Simeon's eyes widened. He hadn't thought that would be her ideal place. "And I am dancing with—with someone," she said, faltering. "He has me in his arms, and I am twirling and laughing and enjoying the music."

"Excellent," Madame Olechka said. "And now, can you demonstrate how you would dance?"

To Simeon's shock, Myrtle did just that—her eyes still closed, she turned in a circle, her movements rhythmic. Her arms were curled as though around an invisible partner and she was smiling.

The audience gasped, and Lilah turned to look at Simeon, her eyes alight with excitement. He couldn't keep his gaze off Myrtle for long, however, and he watched her, rapt, as she continued to spin.

"Thank you, Miss Myrtle," Madame Olechka said after a moment. "When I count to three, you can open your eyes again. One, two, three," and Myrtle's eyes snapped open, her expression placid.

The audience erupted into cheering, and Myrtle smiled, then bowed to the mesmerist before making her way back to where Simeon stood, still stunned.

"That was fun," she whispered. "I wanted to make certain the girls got what they wanted to see here."

"So you weren't—" he began.

"Of course not. But it suited everyone to think so, and I thought it would be harmless fun." She gave him a knowing look. "Besides, now you know what I truly want."

"That was a very roundabout way of telling me you'd like to dance with me again," he said with a laugh.

She beamed up at him. "I am nothing if not complicated, Mr. Jones," she replied.

That she was. As well as being the most remarkable person he'd ever met, and that included his friends.

So much trouble.

Chapter Eighteen

$\mathcal{M}$yrtle grinned as she ascended the stairs to Simeon's studio. Lilah and Miss Jones had clamored to join a large party that was going to the theater, and there were enough chaperones to make it acceptable. Then she'd stopped at home to gather Woof, who greeted her with sloppy kisses and lots of jumping about.

Now they were alone, with the anticipation of what was to come.

Simeon immediately went to work setting up his easel, positioning the canvas just so and frowning as he worked. She was free to look at him, since he was too engrossed to notice her regard.

As it should be, she reminded herself.

"Why did you go along with all of that?" he said suddenly, startling her. Apparently he was paying more attention than she'd thought.

"I wanted to do something for Lilah, something she could hold over my head," Myrtle replied. "She doesn't want to be me, not at all, but I can sense she is sometimes intimidated by who I am."

She offered him a diffident smile. "So if I could make it seem as though I was vulnerable it might make her feel more confident herself."

"She hasn't seemed to lack confidence," Simeon observed.

"No, not when it comes to her debut, or being sought after, or popular—that I know she knows. But I want her to feel confident in her own abilities. I can't force her to do mathematics, or be interested in any of the scientific puzzles that I am, but I can let her know that even very smart people can be influenced like I was just now."

"Even though you weren't."

She wrinkled her nose at him. "No, but she doesn't have to know that. I want every woman, not just Lilah, not just Miss Jones, to know that they are as valuable as anybody else. Even if they do not adhere to what Society expects."

"Like you," he said.

"Yes." His comment made her chest constrict. How often would she be reminding herself that she wasn't like most other people? That most other people found her odd?

But he didn't. Or at least he found her odd in an intriguing way.

"You can get dressed," he said. "I'm ready to begin."

"Oh!" she replied, heading to the storage chest where he kept the linens she draped around her in service of the painting. "I didn't realize."

"No, and that is why I told you," he said,

amusement lacing his tone. "You don't have to know everything, you know."

She paused in her movements. "It feels as though I do," she said honestly. "If I don't know everything, something might happen that would upend my life. Or someone else's life; I don't discriminate. What if I hadn't known my sister-in-law was prone to wandering the halls when she drank? And that therefore you would have to leave immediately? If I hadn't known that, I wouldn't have been able to take advantage of the opportunity to leave, and Richard might have coerced me into making a decision I didn't wish to."

"I doubt that." He met her gaze. "You are very determined, you know."

"I will take that as a compliment," she said as she finished the draping process.

"You should."

His words made her warm, and she wished the posing part of the afternoon was finished so they could get on to the other things—she hadn't kissed him since the day before, and she found she missed it.

She could not get accustomed to it, however. After less than a week, they would stop. And there was no guarantee they would start again, since it might turn out they were both more productive without it.

SIMEON FOUND IT nearly impossible to concentrate on the painting. He had been blocked before, before her, so he couldn't entirely blame it on her.

Though he strongly suspected that wondering how she'd react if he licked her nipple instead of focusing on his work might have been due to her.

"Keep working," she said, sounding as though she knew he was distracted.

He glanced up at her. "How did you . . . ?"

"Because you got that look on your face, the one I've only seen when . . ." she said, her words trailing off as her cheeks turned pink.

It was endearing. Not a word most people would use to describe her, but she had many facets. More than he'd imagined when he'd first met her, bursting into his room in the middle of the night to demand an escort to London. He'd thought of her as adorable before, in fact, something he knew would annoy her if she knew; she kept those parts, the tender, vulnerable parts of her, carefully hidden.

Visible only to someone who cared to look deeper.

"When . . . ?" he prompted, and her face flushed even more.

"You know," she said reprovingly.

"Of course I do," he said, a sly smile curling his lips, "I just want to hear you say it."

She raised her eyebrows. "Is that an appealing thing?" she asked.

He hadn't ever considered it in that way, but—"Yes. It is."

"Well, then. When you are kissing me to distraction and putting your hands everywhere, and I am doing the same to you." Her tone was a unique mix of provocative and demure, and he felt his pulse quicken.

"I need to finish this for the day," he said in a rough voice, slashing at the painting with quick, fervent strokes.

"Do you suppose the anticipation is helping or hindering?" she asked. "For scientific purposes, I mean."

"Helping." He spoke in a curt tone, too focused on painting the lines of her gown as it fell. Artemisia, as he'd pictured her, stood on the shore of a vast beach, her ships and crewmen surrounding her, looking to her for guidance. He couldn't necessarily describe in words how appropriately Myrtle suited as a model for the fierce warrior, but he could paint her. He hadn't gotten to her expression yet, but her confidence and leadership were imbued in every brushstroke of her gown and body. He knew, he just knew, he was creating something that would be superior to the rest of his body of work, which he already knew was impressive.

And it was all because of her—because he was inspired by who she was, and what she wanted.

"There, that's it," he said, stepping back from the work.

"Can I see?"

She didn't wait for his reply, but tossed the garment onto the settee and walked toward him, her eyes alight with excitement.

Instead of letting her look, however, he stepped in front of the easel, bending down to grab her knees, hoisting her over his back so her round arse was right in front of him.

"Simeon!" she yelped, slapping at him.

"Simeon what?" he replied in an innocent tone. "I thought we agreed—"

"I didn't agree to be hauled around like a sack of potatoes," she said, though she sounded pleased, not aggrieved. "You should put me down."

"Or I should do this," he retorted, putting his palm right on the soft roundness of her and grasping it hard. "You have the most squeezable arse, you know," he said in a conversational tone. "I'd like to bite it."

"Is that something people do?" she asked in an interested tone.

Instead of replying, he brought his mouth to her and bit—not hard, but just enough to make her squeal.

"I gather they do," she replied, and then she grabbed his arse, uttering a satisfied groan.

He walked to the settee and flung her onto it, then immediately clambered on top of her, effectively caging her with his body.

Her eyes sparkled, and her cheeks seemed as though they were glowing. As he watched, she dragged her teeth over her bottom lip and then licked it, making his cock react.

Everything she did seemed to enchant him— he'd had plenty of lovers before, and none of them had undone him as much as she. And they hadn't even fucked yet. Not that he knew if their bargain extended to that—he'd leave that up to her,

though he would take the responsibility of protection on himself if it came to that. It wouldn't
ever be right to bring an illegitimate child into the
world, as he well knew, and it also would not be
right to force her into marriage when that hadn't
been her intention.

"Are you going to sit there and think or are you
going to kiss me?" she demanded, and he grinned
before lowering his mouth to hers.

EACH SEXUAL ENCOUNTER made Myrtle worry that
she wouldn't be able to live without such things
in the future—and that was the better of the two
options.

The other option, that she wouldn't be able to
live without *him*, was something she didn't want
to contemplate. Though here she was, contemplating it.

His mouth was firm and persuasive, his lips
opening to allow his tongue entry into her mouth.

She let him in, but immediately twined her
tongue around his, unwilling—even now—to let
him completely guide the action. Even though
she was keenly aware he had far more experience
than she. But these things didn't seem to require
experience—they needed emotion and allowing
oneself to fall into the moment, both of which she
seemed very good at doing.

She slipped her arms around him, rubbing her
palms on his strong back, sliding them down to
his trim waist. One of his legs was on the settee
beside her, while the other was planted on the

ground, holding him upright. She put her hand on his thigh, feeling his muscles tighten, and was wondering if she should remove it when he put his hand over hers and pressed it down into his flesh.

"Touch me, Myrtle," he said, his voice ragged. He guided her hand so it was just there, there where she knew his sex organ was. She didn't know the more familiar terms for it—she knew there had to be some, given how important the appendage was to humanity and sexual relations and all of that. She'd have to ask.

At another time, of course.

Because right now her hand was on him, and he was showing her, with his own hand, how he wanted to be touched. He had resumed kissing her, more savagely, less adeptly, and she knew it was because he was even more lost in the moment.

She had done that to him. Myrtle the Awkward. Who wasn't awkward when it came to all of this, which pleased her immensely.

He wrapped her fingers around the length of him, even through the fabric of his trousers, and she tightened her grip as he gasped into her mouth.

And then he'd thrown her hand off, and was doing something down there, just for a moment, and then he'd clamped her hand back on him again, only this time there was no fabric in the way.

It was just his skin and hers. Her fingers on his

long, thick shaft. It was warm and throbbed against her, and she resumed the motion again, sliding her hand along his length with smooth, hard strokes.

His back arched, which pushed him more into her hand, and then he broke the kiss to fling his head back, his expression one of intense concentration as she kept up the movement.

"Like that?" she asked, her voice breathy. Parts of her were exquisitely tender as well, and she squirmed against him to find some relief.

He chuckled, then put his palm on where she ached the most.

"Don't stop," he commanded, and she kept up the rhythm, sliding her hand up and down him.

Meanwhile, his hand pressed against her, and she was grateful he had enough experience to know just what would feel the best. This was them with most of their clothing on, and she already felt as though she was rocketing to the stars; she could only imagine how it would feel if they had no fabric between them, if it was just skin and muscle and flesh.

And mouth and breasts and chest and other parts.

"Does that feel good?" he asked, his voice low and resonant.

"You know it does," she said.

"I do," he replied in a smug tone. "I just want to hear you say it."

"It feels so good, Simeon," she said. "I am grateful for your expertise."

He snorted in surprise, and she smiled up at

him, still moving her hand on his length, still keeping up her firm touch as his breathing got harsher and noisier in the quiet of the studio.

"You don't know what you're doing to me," he said in a rough voice.

"I have a fairly good idea," she replied, and he gave a strained laugh in response.

"Don't stop," he said again, and she watched his expression tighten even more, and his whole body seemed as though it tensed, and then he was shouting, and liquid was spurting out over her hand and she wasn't at all worried she was doing something wrong because he was clearly in the throes of passion. Of ecstasy, if she were to be specific.

Eventually, his breathing slowed, and he collapsed onto her chest, uttering a few soft groans.

"That was magnificent," he murmured, and she felt the swell of pride all over again. She had done that to him. She had followed his lead and taken things into her own hands—so to speak—and brought him to his peak.

She wished there was someone she could boast about this to, but of course she could not.

He withdrew a handkerchief from somewhere, and cleaned up the mess, his motions careful and meticulous. When he was finished, he pressed his mouth against her neck, his lips tickling her skin, and she couldn't help but utter her own moan, feeling the tremors rush through her as though his hands were everywhere.

And then he eased back to drop onto the floor,

at which she frowned. "What are you doing down—" she began, only to stop speaking as his hands slid up each leg.

"Wait and see," he said, his voice dangerously soft.

"Oh," she replied, focusing on his strong fingers as they glided up toward that inexorable spot. "Oh, Simeon, I cannot wait."

Chapter Nineteen

Simeon was a generous and accommodating lover. It was important to him that his partner be as satisfied as he when it came to bed sport. But he had never felt this urgency before—the need to make her climax, to watch her face as she came.

It was all because her delightfully curvy body was attached to her even more attractive brain.

A brain that he wanted to make quiet for a moment so she could just feel. He didn't know she craved that, but he had to think she might—the opportunity to just be, to let herself bask in sensuality rather than constantly thinking.

At least, he liked those moments, and he knew they were likely similar enough she should as well.

His fingers dug into her thighs, and he spread her legs wider, taking a moment to pull her skirts up so they bunched around her waist.

She was flagrantly, openly displayed for him— she wore drawers, but her pussy was bared, and he could see the glistening results of his touch from earlier.

"Mmm," he murmured, then bent his head to place his mouth on her upper thigh, right near the crease of her hip and leg. She trembled, and he glanced up at her, concern in his gaze. "Is this all right?"

Her lip was between her teeth again, and she gave a vigorous nod of her head. "I don't know what you are planning, to be honest," she said, "but I know I will like it."

"You will," he promised, before sliding the fingers of his right hand up her leg, petting the soft hair there before brushing her clitoris. She gasped, and he repeated the action, making her writhe on the settee.

Then he touched her more firmly, rubbing the button of her clit as his palm pressed in below.

"Oh, God, Simeon," she said, and he smiled up at her.

His cock was still recovering from her touch, and he was startled to feel it twitch in response, but he shouldn't have been surprised by how strong his reactions were to her.

There was something about her in particular that seemed to make his whole body vibrate. To make him want to do everything in his power to please her, to satisfy each and every one of her wishes.

That one of her wishes was that she be allowed to live on her own without any kind of entanglement was something he would most definitely not think about now.

He stroked her open, spreading the lips of her

pussy and putting his mouth there. Tasting her juices, the distinct, musky odor invading his nose. She yelped, jerking more upright, and he glanced up at her again, his eyebrows raised in question.

"Carry on," she said, her voice a breathy rasp. "As you were."

He chuckled against her skin, then began to lick her, sliding his tongue over her clit and through her soft folds. She had—unconsciously, no doubt—clamped her hands on either side of his head and was holding him in place. As though he would want to be anywhere else but here.

Her hold was strong, and almost painful, but he relished that—the sensation of the pain combined with the spent pleasure still coursing through his body, and the anticipation of her finding her release all combined to make for a euphoric experience that he'd never felt before.

She tensed, her legs narrowing, and he was enclosed within her body, her legs touching his shoulders and his arms, her hands in his hair, his mouth on her clit, licking and sucking with a fervent rhythm that he could feel reverberating through her body.

And then she tensed more still, and froze, and he felt the pulses of her climax as she shuddered, her breath catching as she gave a stifled moan.

He gave her one last, long lick, then drew back, still banded within her body, to look up at her.

What he saw there made his heart squeeze.

Her expression was astonished and joyful, as though she couldn't believe there could be something like she'd just experienced. He'd given her that—something she didn't already know about, something that wasn't part of her arsenal of information.

It was revelatory to see her face. To see the expression of wonder, of pure delight, and know that he'd done that to her. For her.

"Oh my," she said at last, her voice breathy, and not at all like the matter-of-fact tone he'd come to expect from her. "Oh my."

"You liked it?" he asked, unable to keep from sounding smug.

She gave him a narrow look. "As though you don't know."

"I want to hear you say it. Please?" he asked.

"I liked it." She inhaled. "I loved it. I never knew—" She shook her head, and it wasn't hard to read her emotions. As always, but especially now. "I never knew that kind of feeling was possible. I am supremely annoyed nobody ever told me."

That was the Myrtle he knew and lov—No. He couldn't admit that, not even to himself.

"I imagine that would be a difficult conversation to have," he said. He drew up his right arm and rested it on her thigh, leaning his cheek on her warm skin. The scent of her surrounded him, and he never wanted to leave where he was or what he was doing.

But of course he would have to. Eventually.

She snorted. "You are right. I can't even begin to think about how that would sound."

Suddenly, he wanted to hear her say it. To say all the salacious things he had done to her. To ask for more things to be done to her later on. Their week wasn't over, after all.

"How would you describe it?" he said, striving for a noncommittal tone.

She gave him a wry look, as though aware of what he actually wanted.

"You mean what would I say if someone were to want to know what just happened here?" She withdrew her fingers from his hair to make a vague gesture.

She looked so delicious, he wanted to eat her up.

"Mmm-hmm," he said, taking a moment to kiss the soft inner skin of her thigh.

"Well, I suppose I would first explain the various parts involved. So that the later action was entirely clear."

"And what parts are those?" he asked innocently. Unable to resist darting a quick glance there, at where she still glistened.

"Well," she began, her expression mischievous. "I suppose first I would speak about—what do you call that?" she said, pointing down toward his penis.

"You don't know?" he asked, surprised.

"Why would I know? It is not as though it is a mathematics problem."

"Oh, but it is," he replied in a silky tone, easing up to sit beside her on the settee. He drew her into his arms and leaned back, holding her against his chest.

Her skirts were still pulled up, and her legs were bared to his sight.

"One cock—my penis, in more scientific terms—plus your pussy, also called your vagina, equals one spectacular experience."

"Or one hand plus one cock," she said, and he tightened his hold on her. His cock was responding with alacrity to her words, to how warm and soft and lovely she felt in his arms.

He wanted to fuck her senseless. He wanted to fuck himself senseless.

He wanted—

Just then there was an aggressive knock on the door, and they both leapt up off the settee, her shaking down her skirts, him tucking his shirt in and buttoning up the placket of his trousers.

The intensity of the banging increased.

"Just a moment," Simeon called. He glanced at Myrtle, whose face was still flushed, her eyes sparkling. It was obvious what had been happening, but there was little he could do about that.

"I'll just go see who it is," he muttered.

He ran down the stairs, flinging the door open to reveal possibly the worst person to be standing on his doorstep at this particular time: Richard, Viscount Leybourne. Myrtle's brother.

"Good afternoon, my lord," he said, immediately donning his most charming persona.

The viscount was not charmed. "Where is she? Where is my sister?"

Simeon was opening his mouth to make some sort of excuse when Myrtle called down.

"I'm up here, you oaf. As you know, since you've been trying to knock the door down."

Simeon gave an exasperated sigh—why couldn't she have just stayed silent?—and indicated the viscount should go upstairs.

"I'll speak to you later," the viscount said, making it sound far more like a threat than a promise.

"Good afternoon, Richard," Myrtle said in a relatively calm tone.

Though she was anything but—the past hour or so had opened her eyes to all sorts of things. She had never known that such pleasure was possible, and she knew enough about human biology to know that they hadn't even done the act that most people were speaking of when they spoke knowingly and furtively amongst themselves.

It wasn't the same type of feeling she got after she'd solved a particularly thorny problem, but it ran along the same track of emotion—as though she'd conquered some previously insurmountable obstacle and was standing, triumphant, atop the answer.

"Good afternoon?" Richard replied, sounding incredulous. "Is that all you have to say?"

She frowned, puzzled. "Is it not a good afternoon?" *She'd* certainly had a good afternoon, but she didn't think Richard wanted to hear about that.

"You know what I mean!" he exploded.

"Honestly, I do not," she said.

"Please sit down," Simeon said, indicating the

settee. She glanced at him, eyes widened, and he blanched. "No, not there, let me get you a chair."

It would be even more awkward to have her brother sitting in the same spot she'd been in just moments before, with his head underneath her skirts. Or more accurately his head where her skirts had been. She wouldn't misrepresent what had happened. Facts were very important for a mathematician.

A few moments passed as Simeon found a seat for Richard, whose expression was livid-adjacent, but not quite fully livid.

"What is the matter?" Myrtle asked, when it seemed Richard had finally settled.

"What is not the matter!" he replied.

She rolled her eyes. "That is not an answer."

"My lord, if you could explain a bit more—" Simeon said, sounding conciliatory.

Richard huffed out a breath, but seemed to calm somewhat.

"Even though we have established the two of you are engaged, people are still talking about how much you are together."

"Given most of the marriages in your world, I'm not surprised," Simeon said, then looked startled. Likely at his giving a candid response. When normally he would impress diplomats with his suavity.

Myrtle giggled. "Isn't that what you wanted, though? To have everyone think we are besotted and in love?"

Which—which she might be, if she was being honest with herself.

Which she always was.

Damn.

"What is it?" Simeon said, his attention turning to her. She should have known he would notice her change of expression, and of course her expression would have changed—her face was like a piece of paper, all her emotions written across it like a confession.

I love you.

I have fallen in love with you.

Love.

Damn again. This wasn't part of the agreement, and she could not allow her feelings, her true feelings, to reveal themselves.

How ironic was it that she would be utilizing his tutelage in how to prevaricate to lie to him? To protect him from the truth of her heart?

Well. She was intelligent, she could definitely do this. Even though she had been fairly abysmal at it in the past.

"Myrtle?" Simeon's voice sounded concerned. Of course, she hadn't responded to his initial question. Instead she'd spent some time lecturing herself about her response to her own revelation.

No wonder he was concerned. So was she.

"I am fine. Richard, you're going to have to make your mind up," she said, turning her attention toward her brother. Not toward the gentleman she'd just discovered she was in love with, even though all she wanted to do was drink in his beauty until that was no longer allowed to her. "Either you want us to pretend to be engaged, or you want us to—to what? Pretend to hate one another?"

Richard's expression tightened. "Why does it have to be one or the other? Can't you just . . . ?" he said, waving his fingers in the air.

"Just—tolerate one another?" Myrtle said in an acerbic tone. "You know me, Richard, I am incapable of tepidity."

"That is true enough," Simeon chimed in, looking startled at himself again.

"Then you'll have to make some sort of public spectacle."

"That I can do," Myrtle said. "What kind of public spectacle do you want?"

Richard took a deep breath. "Well, it seems Lilah's come-out is going well, though she has shown no preference in suitors. But I am not concerned any longer that she will not take; she is firmly established, and if we return next Season, she will be fine. Regina will be able to accompany her, no doubt." And then he looked uncomfortable again, as though aware that that might not be true. But apparently he was willing to take that risk; Myrtle would have calculated the odds, if she'd had time.

"Meaning?" Myrtle prompted, irritated that he was taking so long to get to the point.

"Meaning he wants us to have a very public break." Simeon turned to regard Richard, and Myrtle felt the coldness in his stare, even though he wasn't looking at her. "You want us to ensure that everyone knows your sister is free. Isn't that right?"

"I won't," Myrtle said. "That would ruin Simeon's reputation—"

"If I had one to ruin," he interjected, and she waved him off, unable to keep speaking. Unable to keep from letting her emotions seep through the words, even though she'd just told herself not to. "I will not be responsible for that. Mr. Jones has helped us enormously, we both know I would have said something by now to put most people off of Lilah. Even though she would have had nothing to do with it." She frowned. "How is it that one innocent person can be tainted because of another's actions?"

"Oh, I don't know, how about you ask the bastard?" Simeon said dryly.

She laughed, while Richard looked shocked.

"Excellent point. But the fact remains," she said, speaking to her brother, "I will not be party to anything that will make Mr. Jones look bad."

"Then how about something that makes *you* look bad?" Simeon suggested.

"I love that idea!" Myrtle said, clapping her hands. Richard uttered some sort of snarl, but didn't speak otherwise. "I could jilt you in front of everyone, and—and I could have some sort of reason that would make you look wonderful and me look terrible." She frowned in concentration. "I'll need to think what it is, though," she said. "And we'd need to be certain it wouldn't affect Lilah next year."

"It won't," Richard vowed. "The scandal would have died down by then."

"So we've got time." Simeon glanced over at Richard. "Unless you have us on a schedule?"

Richard had the grace to look ashamed, then muttered an incomprehensible reply.

"But I don't want all this hanging over our heads," Myrtle said, even though a part of her wished to extend the pretend engagement for as long as possible—long enough, perhaps, to realize she'd been lying to herself when she said she loved him.

Even though she never lied.

Because she knew she loved him. She loved him, she would always love him, and she could never have him. Because that would be the death of all the things he wanted for himself, and she was cognizant enough to know that mere love would never replace those ambitions.

"Let's schedule this for ten days from now," she said casually, as though she wasn't condemning herself to future unhappiness. "That should give us enough time to think of a good way to end it all." In ten days, they'd have completed both halves of their experiment—sexual relations one week with none the following week—and thus would have accomplished something, at least.

And then she could close the door on this aspect of her life. She wasn't destined to pivot to love and marriage and family, she knew that now. Not when the person she wanted those things with didn't want any of them.

Fine. It would all be fine.

Chapter Twenty

Simeon felt as though someone had knocked him on the head with a shovel.

That, or the inebriated dictionary known as Myrtle, Miss Allen, had entered his life with aplomb.

She and her brother had left about an hour ago, and Simeon had spent the past fifty-seven minutes pottering around his rooms, with no discernible purpose in his random movements. He was angry at himself, furious with Myrtle's brother, and not sure how he felt about Myrtle herself.

That was. He knew what he felt for her, but he didn't know how she felt about *him*—even though she was usually so transparent. He knew she liked what they were doing together, sexually, but he didn't know what she felt about it, about him, beyond that.

And if she was so able to blithely agree to her brother's ridiculous stratagem then that gave him his answer.

He shouldn't be upset about it. They both

knew what they expected of one another coming into all of this: they would never put their talents second. They would forgo pleasures ordinary people indulged in because it wasn't good for their art. Or at least as important as their art—in his case, his painting, in her case, her mathematical mind.

"Simeon?"

Phoebe hesitated at the door, her expression concerned.

"Yes, of course. I'll make tea." It wasn't an answer to, well, anything, but he had been mortified to discover that having tea really did clear his mind. His and millions of his fellow citizens.

Phoebe followed him down the hall to the kitchen. "I wanted to speak to you about something, if it is convenient."

He stopped and turned to face her. All of his attention immediately focused on her—his own problems were meaningless, at least until he understood why his sister sounded so odd at the moment.

"Tea can wait," he said decidedly, taking her arm and leading her back to his studio room. It was late afternoon, and the sun coming in through the large windows was shadowed, making the room seem more elegant and mysterious somehow.

What would Myrtle look like here in the nighttime? Lying on the settee, her gorgeous curves on display as candlelight flickered on her skin?

But that was not keeping his attention focused on his sister.

"Come sit," he said, drawing two chairs up to the small side table he usually just used to place his teacup or spare paints. He didn't want to distract himself by sitting on the settee where they'd so recently done so many things.

And yet not enough.

"Tell me," he said. At least now he knew that if she needed funds he could provide them—Myrtle had paid him what she'd promised, and once the Season was over, her brother would also pay him. He wouldn't have to worry about money, no matter who asked, for some time yet.

"I want to say first that I am very grateful you have been so kind, taking me in so unexpectedly."

He nodded, then reached forward to take her hand. She offered him a warm smile.

"But I think it is time for me to go home," she said. She gave him a look as though she expected him to be angry.

"Are you not enjoying yourself?" he asked.

She shook her head. "It's not that. It's just that—I haven't told you everything. From before, I mean."

"Let me guess," he said, giving her hand a fond squeeze. "There is someone at home that you miss."

Her cheeks turned pink, and she gave the smallest of nods.

"We had hoped to be married, but then my mother died, and there was so much to take care of. He is the son of one of the farmers there. We've known each other since we were little. Wellsie—my mother, that is—left me her house and farm, and I want to go back and live there.

I like it here, don't mistake me, but that is where my home is. I was raised there. In everything but giving birth to me, Wellsie was my mother." Her expression grew concerned. "You are not offended, are you? You've been so kind, and it has been wonderful knowing I have a brother."

"Mrs. Wellsford left you enough?" Simeon said, prepared to empty his coffers for her, if she needed.

"She did," Phoebe confirmed. "I didn't know that the reverend assumed that I was bereft."

"You're very reft, it seems," Simeon quipped.

"Indeed." She laughed. "Wellsie was a very thrifty woman, and apparently your mother—our mother," she corrected, "sent money for my upbringing, but Wellsie held it in store for me rather than spend it."

"Well," Simeon said, surprised, "I didn't know our mother was so conscientious."

Phoebe leaned forward, giving him a searching look. "She sent letters, too. Not that Wellsie shared them with me. I was too young. But she kept them. I read them when I was going through Wellsie's things. She—your mother, that is—talked about how talented you were, and how much she regretted making the choice she did to send me away." Her voice softened. "But she also said she knew it was the best decision, since she could barely manage taking care of you."

"Why didn't you tell me any of this when you arrived?"

Phoebe took a moment before replying. "I didn't

know you," she said simply. "All I knew was that my mother—my birth mother, not Wellsie—had sent me away, but had kept you."

"That must have hurt," Simeon observed. "I wish she hadn't made the choices she did. I would have liked to watch you grow up—you are a strong young woman."

Phoebe's smile was wistful. "I would say I wished that as well, but then I would have missed out on having Wellsie as my mother. I loved her."

"And you don't need anything from me?" Simeon said, still prepared to give her money, if she needed.

She took a breath. "All I need—all I want—is your love and support. And for you to come to the wedding, if you are able."

"I would not miss it for the world," Simeon promised.

Finding another family member was remarkable for anybody. But finding another family member when you'd long ago felt as though you were the only one was extraordinary. He would not relinquish Phoebe as his sister, even though she was planning on returning home, far away from London.

"Thank you," Phoebe replied, rising from the chair. "I will just go pack my things. There is a coach leaving in a few hours."

"So soon?" Simeon said.

She nodded. "I would like to get home. I am needed there." And her face lit up, as though thinking about her intended, about the life they would have together.

Simeon envied that more than he could say. Even though he had his own purpose, one devoted to his art, he wished he could have both art and family. Even though he knew that to be impossible.

Unless the family was somehow different from what he imagined families to be.

Would that even be possible?

And why was he thinking about that?

He could answer the last question, at least. It was her. It was all her. Being with her for the rest of his life, watching her face light up when she was happy or express confused adorableness when she didn't understand something. That would be a life he would enjoy. Even if it meant he didn't achieve everything his art seemed to indicate.

Likely why his mother had warned him so strongly against falling in love, against putting anything or anyone ahead of his talent. Because it was alluring, to think of what could be.

But the truth of the matter was that Myrtle would never agree. She was too strong, too independent, and too determined to live life on her own terms to want to compromise an inch of what made her so thoroughly Myrtle.

"Goodbye, then."

Phoebe's soft voice cut through the clamor of despair his brain was circulating, and he turned to regard her, a deliberate smile on his face.

"Thank you. You'll write?"

She nodded. "I will. As soon as I get home. I will let you know when the wedding will be also." She put her palm to his cheek. "I hope you are able to find your home as well."

She withdrew her hand and was walking down the stairs before Simeon could even think of a response.

His home was here, wasn't it? Did she see something lacking?

But he knew the answer. He had a house, but not a home.

And he also knew that answer would not change.

"I'LL HAVE TO lie," Myrtle said.

Woof looked up at her, a questioning look on his face.

"Yes, I do see your point," she replied. "It is very difficult for me to lie. But this is a lie I need to sell convincingly. He cannot know I have feelings beyond what we've expressed. Nobody can. They all have to believe I am a heartless woman who has decided her sole pleasure is all she will accommodate."

The phrase would have been true before she arrived in London, if she had swapped *sole pleasure* for *intelligence*.

But now those words seemed lacking, somehow.

"I have something to announce," she began. She and Woof were in her bedroom, thankfully alone. Except for one another, that was. Lilah was off spending Richard's money, and Richard was off mismanaging it, too stubborn to accept his sister's financial assistance.

She spent a brief moment mourning the loss of double bookkeeping.

"Announce . . . where was I?" she said, looking at Woof intently. "Right. I have come to realize that I cannot marry Mr. Jones. Mr. Simeon Jones because—why can't I marry him anyway?" she mused, then froze when she realized what she'd said.

Why can't I marry him anyway?

"Never mind that," she added hastily. Woof did not seem to notice her momentary digression. "He is an honorable and upright gentleman, and my desire not to wed him has nothing to do with his character." She pondered that last bit. "Or perhaps it does," she continued, a burst of energy fueling her words. "He is faultless, while I—I am faultful. Full of faults? I am not sure. How would you phrase that?" she said, glancing again to Woof.

Woof responded by lying down and stretching his body across the carpet.

"You are no help," she said reprovingly. "But you are adorable, so I will forgive you." She began to pace, her thoughts coming nearly too quickly for her to vocalize them. "The point I need to make is that he is not at all to blame for the broken engagement. If anything, he is to be commended for—for something. I'll have to figure that out later," she said, dismissing the thorny question.

"I'll need to break the engagement well enough

that his reputation remains intact, and that mine is tarnished enough for fortune hunters to be leery of approaching me." She brightened. "It would help if Richard would look disapprovingly while all of this is happening. I am certain *that*, at least, is achievable."

If only she didn't have to go through all this rigamarole. If only she could just—be who she was, without having to prevaricate. Which meant lying.

She didn't want to lie.

So that meant having to face what she'd been avoiding thinking about. The fact that—the truth that—"I love him!" she yelped, startling Woof. He gave a short bark in response, then resumed his former posture.

"I love him," she said again, only quieter this time. "And I am not sure what to do with that information. I cannot pivot to not loving him—despite my ability to pivot, you understand," she said in an aside to Woof. "And I cannot pivot to expressing my feelings, since both of us have been very clear as to our priorities."

She frowned.

"This is the worst kind of mathematics problem to have—one staying at one, with no additional one making two." She flung her hands up in the air. "It doesn't even make sense. And yet here I am. What am I going to do?"

Woof had no answer.

"You are absolutely correct," she said. "I will

have to lie convincingly enough that nobody suspects I have done the worst thing possible for me and fallen in love with him."

She would have to utilize all the skills he'd taught her without his knowing she was doing so. The trickiest problem she'd ever had to solve yet.

Chapter Twenty-One

"Well, isn't this . . . cozy," Aunt Flora said as she and the other ladies entered Simeon's studio.

He'd nearly forgotten about the promised meeting, but Aunt Flora had sent a nudging note, and he'd spoken with Myrtle, who'd been as enthusiastic as before about it. Perhaps more, now that their charade was coming to an end, and she'd be looking to start her next adventure, while Simeon . . . while Simeon finished his painting and picked up the pieces of his life.

Which sounded far more morose than he meant it to. It was just that he knew there would be a Myrtle-sized gap in his life, a life that would be bereft of open, earnest honesty, of playful sexuality, of clever brains and sharper thinking.

He'd always be able to keep up with anyone now.

Simeon had spent many hours, along with Mr. Finneas, setting up his quarters to receive visitors. They'd hauled in extra chairs and a long table that Mr. Finneas used to cut fabric for the garments he made. Mr. Finneas had unearthed a piece of material that would do as a tablecloth, a sumptuous silver fabric with gold thread details.

Simeon had put candles on every available surface, and had hung a few of his paintings rather than keeping them leaning on the floor. The overall effect was that of an elegant artist, which was better than the spare garret look he'd had before.

He and Mr. Finneas had then spent the rest of the time prior to the event baking, making simple scones, muffins, and biscuits, while also brewing copious amounts of tea. He didn't have time to do the shopping and ensure the rooms were tidy. He'd also had the foresight to stock some sherry, just in case any of the ladies preferred something stronger.

"Mr. Jones was very kind to offer his home for our meeting," Myrtle said.

"My apartments," Simeon corrected. This wasn't a home, not with only him living there.

"Mr. Jones's apartments, then," she said, looking amused. Myrtle looked as delicious as one of the scones Simeon had just pulled out of the oven—she wore a light green gown with white dots set on the fabric. A green ribbon was threaded through her hair, and she had a necklace with some sort of green gem nestled in the valley between her breasts.

Simeon needed not to get distracted by those breasts. Or the rest of her, to be honest.

"He is very kind," Aunt Flora said, in between organizing all her friends' seating arrangements to her satisfaction. To his surprise, Lady Sandington, the first person Myrtle had practiced lying to, was there, and she looked as eagerly anticipatory as the rest of them.

While he didn't want Myrtle to fail, his heart was sinking a bit when he realized just how ideal what she proposed was, and that she would likely be wildly successful. Of course he wanted success for her, but a tiny part of him also wanted her to decide it wasn't worth her magnificent brain, and perhaps she should spend more time kissing him instead.

But he knew that no matter how adaptable she was, she wouldn't choose him. No matter what other options were there. Because she respected his choices as well as her own, and he'd told her in no uncertain terms what he wanted for his life. Which was not a chaotic encyclopedia constantly telling the truth while keeping him from his work because of her allure.

Damn it.

"You look lovely, my dear," Aunt Flora continued, peering at Myrtle. "Being engaged to such a good man as Mr. Jones is good for you, it seems."

"I would point out," Myrtle said in a serious tone, "that you had no experience of me prior to my engagement. It could be that I was spectacularly beautiful before, and now I am merely lovely. Though I do thank you for the compliment." She held the skirts of her gown out wide. "I think a lot of that has to do with my decimal points."

"Pardon?" Aunt Flora asked in confusion.

Myrtle nodded toward her gown. "The fabric

has decimal points all over it. Very appropriate for someone who is interested in numbers and sums."

"Do you mean the dots on your gown, Myrtle?" Simeon asked gently, since Aunt Flora still looked very confused.

"Ah, yes, I suppose they are also dots as well as decimal points," Myrtle said in a conciliatory tone.

"You two definitely suit one another," Aunt Flora said, then went to take her seat. "I think we are all settled, if you wish to begin."

There were seven ladies in attendance, all of at least forty years, all of whom looked to be reasonably affluent, though Simeon knew full well looks could be deceiving—he doubted anyone knew he had periods where he was subsisting on the bare minimum because someone or another had needed help, and a commission payment had been late.

Myrtle went to stand in front of the ladies, looking as confident in front of a crowd as she had at the mesmerist's. Simeon wondered if there would ever be a situation she couldn't handle with ease, but also never wanted to see that—that would mean somehow her remarkable brain hadn't been able to accommodate the particulars, and that would be difficult for her, and anyone who loved her, to bear.

Because he loved her. Had he allowed himself to admit it yet? Or had it skirted through his mind, a forbidden idea he couldn't let take root.

But it had. It had made itself at home nearly as much as she had. When he woke in the morning he thought about Myrtle. When he went to bed at night, he thought about Myrtle. He most definitely thought about her when he did things like pay bills (mathematics) or mix paints (chemistry).

He thought of her in his everyday life, not just as something that was a temporary sparkle, a moment in time. He wanted her all the time, both of them doing ordinary things, living and working together.

But that wasn't to be. It couldn't be, not if they were to see their own hopes and dreams to the end.

Myrtle had begun speaking, and he tried to lose himself in her words, but his mind wouldn't let him—while she spoke about money management, he was thinking about Myrtle. In his bed, in his studio, in his life.

In their home.

Not just damn. *Fuck.* Because all of that could never happen.

MYRTLE FELT AS though she'd just eaten the most delicious slice of cake as she solved Polignac's conjecture, all while wearing the most beautiful gown she'd ever seen.

"They listened so well," she said, scooping up a few empty teacups as she spoke. The ladies had left half an hour ago, and she'd had firm commitments to use her financial services from two-thirds of them, which meant she was well on her way to starting her business.

Her odds were most definitely going up.

Simeon began to move some of the chairs

against the wall. He hadn't spoken much since everyone had arrived, though of course there was so much chatter it would have been difficult to get a word in—Aunt Flora and her friends seemed so grateful to be spoken to, and listened to, that the hour or so they'd met had passed in a whirlwind. But still, it was unlike him not to make his presence thoroughly known. He had neither raised a gorgeous eyebrow in silent response nor deliberately arranged his body so as to increase his attractiveness. Very unlike him.

"Are you all right?" she asked, pausing with all the teacups pressed against her chest. "You're quiet. You're not usually quiet."

He turned to regard her, his expression giving nothing away. She envied that; at this moment, for example, her face likely revealed not only that she was worried about him, but that she was excited about what had just happened, and trepidatious about the future.

She had no idea how one face could contain all those elements, but she knew hers did. Somehow.

"I am fine," he said, then turned back to drag another chair.

"You're not," she told his back. "If you were fine, you'd be speaking. More than that, you'd be teasing me about all of what just happened."

He spun back, and her eyes widened at seeing his expression. This was the face of someone in the throes of some great emotion—what that emotion was, she wasn't certain—but it was nearly palpable.

"I am fine, Myrtle," he said, and she could see a muscle twitch in his jaw. "I am tired of all the chatter, and I just want to go have a glass of ale." He spread his arms out to indicate the room. "But first I have to return this room to being a workspace, not a gathering spot for talkative ladies." He exhaled, and then ran his hand over his face. When he spoke again, his tone was much lower. "I'm sorry. It's not anything you've done, or did, or anything like that." He uttered a rueful snort. "It's something I've done. Something completely idiotic."

She advanced then, placing the dirty cups back down on one of the small tables. "Let me help. You've done so much for me, and—" She grasped his arm then, and she was shocked by how quickly he shook it away.

"I'm fine. Let's just finish up here, and then you can return home. I imagine you and Lilah have a party tonight or something to attend."

She hesitated, her hand still hovering in the air where she'd tried to touch him. What was happening? It all felt so strange, so unlike him, and she didn't know what to do. For once, she couldn't just . . . adjust. Because this was Simeon, and there was something wrong, and she had no idea what it was. Just that it was wrong.

This is what it will be like later, her mind reminded her. *Only instead of him being here and distant, he won't be here and just as distant. He'll be gone from your life.*

She wished she could barrel into him, embrace

him, and tell him how she truly felt. But that would jeopardize everything: her future, his future, and would incur Richard's anger, which would mean financial insolvency, at least until she got her own business going. And she hadn't calculated the odds on that success yet, but it wasn't even close to fifty percent.

It would adversely affect his success as an artist also—nobody would want to admire the work of a bastard who'd managed to steal the heart of a lady. Who'd irrevocably altered, for the worse, her reputation and her livelihood.

She'd have to practice lying earlier than she thought.

"I'll be off, then," she said, using as bright a tone as she could muster. "You're correct. I do have an event this evening." Not that she recalled what it was, just that there was likely . . . something. Because there was always something, until there was nothing. Until Lilah got engaged, or the Season ended. Whichever came first.

And then she would be advising ladies on how to manage their funds, and she and Woof would live together somewhere, alone, perhaps with an occasional visit from Aunt Flora or Lilah, if she and her as-yet-undecided husband lived in London.

They wouldn't have cause to meet again.

SIMEON FELT TERRIBLE as soon as he heard the front door close behind her. Not that he hadn't felt terrible before—he had, hence his abruptness in speaking to her—but this was a different kind of terrible.

This was a permanently terrible kind of feeling.

For a moment, he considered going after her, telling her how he felt, but that wouldn't be the right thing to do. It would be selfish, for both of them. It would put on her an obligation she had explicitly said she never wanted, and it would be an admission on his part that something was more important than his art, his talent, which would betray his mother's legacy.

He heard the door open, and his heart lifted; had she returned? Could he find some way to fix this?

But then Theo and Bram appeared in his studio, and he felt a moment of regret before being flooded with happiness at seeing two of his best friends.

Bram and his wife traveled in very different circles than Simeon, now more than ever, and it had been difficult to find a time to meet up. Theo had recently married also, and he and his wife had had a baby girl, and had been understandably busy.

"I didn't expect the two of you," Simeon said. He glanced around at the studio, which indicated a party had recently left. "Let me just . . ." And he picked up glassware and plates hastily, bringing an armload into his kitchen area.

"What's been happening while we were away?" Theo asked, looking around with interest. He strode toward the covered painting

Simeon had been working on, the one Myrtle had been posing for.

Theo had been adopted by a single gentleman, a wealthy merchant. Theo had taken his father's business and increased its profits considerably, meaning he had enough money to overcome the stigma of his birth.

"Don't touch that," Simeon barked, holding a warning hand up toward his friend. "It's not ready."

Theo ignored him, as Simeon knew he would, and flung the cloth up and over to reveal the painting.

All three men stopped to look at it, silent, until Simeon couldn't stand it anymore.

"Well? What do you think?"

Bram turned a startled face toward Simeon. "It's your best work. By far," he said.

Theo nodded, still not speaking.

"I-it's," Simeon stammered. "It's Artemisia."

And it was.

"Who's that?" Theo said abruptly, ruining the moment.

"She was a famous warrior queen. She fought alongside Xerxes—"

"Another person I don't know," Theo commented.

"And got Xerxes's sons—illegitimate, I might add—to safety."

"Ah," Theo said, approaching the canvas more closely. "She is fond of bastards. I see why you might have wanted to paint her." He accompanied his words with a wink toward Simeon, who rolled his eyes in response. Theo was now within six inches of the painting, and Simeon itched to yank him away, but he knew that would just end up in a physical brawl, since he and Theo were the most alike and often came to blows.

"Who's the model?" Theo continued, and now Simeon really wanted to hit him.

"I think I've seen her," Bram answered, joining Theo to stand in front of the painting. "Perhaps she's one of Wilhelmina's friends?" Wilhelmina was Bram's wife, an amateur astronomer who preferred science over Society.

"I don't think so," Simeon said, keeping his temper in check, "though I imagine they would get along." *She only has one friend,* he thought, *and it's me. And Woof.*

He should have thought to introduce Myrtle and Wilhelmina before. They both shared a passion for knowledge, scientific and mathematical, and both would rather talk about their passions than gossip. But he liked being her only friend in town. He liked being the one she depended on, whether for lying practice or for the other part of her kissing experiment.

"Why are the two of you here anyway?" Simeon asked. He pulled out two chairs and gave them each significant looks indicating they should sit.

And stop standing directly in front of his painting.

"I almost forgot!" Theo said, taking his seat. Bram followed, and Simeon was able to breathe again. They weren't paying attention to Myrtle.

"What is it?" Simeon said, not really interested in the answer. His mind was too focused on his own troubles—thank goodness Theo was distracted, or he would have figured it out as soon as he arrived. Out of the Bastard Five, they were the two most likely to be distraught in love. And since Theo had found his forever love, and married her, that left Simeon.

"We have a commission for you."

"Another portrait?" Simeon said, his tone dismissive.

"No, you idiot. Listen," Theo said. He sounded much more serious than usual, and Simeon pried part of his brain away from Myrtle to actually pay attention.

"What?"

"I'm closing the Garden of Hedon," Theo explained. The Garden was a notorious pleasure house, one where Theo had met his wife in an anonymous tryst. Though that was another story. "And I am going to reopen it as an exhibition hall—one for artists of all kinds to show their talents. I want you to do a mural for the main area."

"A mural?" Simeon said.

"Yes. I will use the rooms during the day for business meetings. It's far too dull and too crowded to gather everyone into an office."

"We're planning to host meetings between various government offices and merchants there," Bram explained. "Benedict is enthusiastic about the idea. The change of venue to a much livelier one will make these meetings much more productive. You'll make your name there, for certain."

"No more Garden?" While Simeon hadn't visited quite as often as Theo, he did like to go for occasional satiety of his needs.

Though he couldn't fathom going there now. He couldn't fathom doing any of those things to anybody but Myrtle now.

"I'm reopening the Garden in another, more discreet building," Theo said with a sly smile. "You'll be satisfied, I promise."

"Ah," Simeon said. "And you want me to—"

"Yes. I had hoped to present the idea to you earlier, but then you hied off into the country for something, and I've been too busy with Alexandra and Theodora"—Theo's daughter—"to come by. I wanted to get the work started before this, but now that you know, I'd want you to start immediately."

If Theo had managed to reach him before he went to the country . . . he wouldn't have had the unfortunate encounter with the viscountess. He wouldn't have had to leave in the dead of night, and he would never have met Myrtle.

What would his attitude toward things be then? Would he have changed as profoundly as it felt that he'd changed?

He doubted it. And it was all because of her.

You'll make your name there, for certain.

"I—"

"You're not leaping up and accepting," Bram observed.

"Can't put one past you, Lord Justice," Theo said dryly. He turned his attention to Simeon. "What is it?" Theo leaned back in his chair, squinting at Simeon. "There's something off about you."

Simeon exhaled, knowing it was useless to try to lie to these people, at least. Everyone else he could fool, but not them.

So he told them.

Chapter Twenty-Two

Are you certain you can't come?" Lilah said.

Myrtle nodded, then shook her head. "No, I mean yes, I am certain I cannot come. I just—" She made a vague gesture toward her room, and her books, and Woof. Hoping Lilah would not ask for specifics, since Myrtle still wasn't all that confident in her prevarication skills.

"I wish you could," Lilah said, sounding pleading but also resigned. "But Father said he would escort me."

The reason Myrtle knew it would be fine if she missed this evening—Richard had announced at dinner that he would make a rare appearance, no doubt to secure some business deal or another, and that was when Myrtle had made her decision.

It was exhausting going out every single evening. Spending time looking longingly at the door, or waiting anxiously for gentlemen to—hopefully—pass you by when choosing dance partners.

Simeon couldn't accompany them every night. It wouldn't be fair to him, though Myrtle would love it. But people kept asking them when they would have their wedding, what with their being engaged and all, and Myrtle was exhausted from lying to them, too.

It was just all exhausting.

"Well, I must go change, then," Lilah said, giving a disparaging glance toward her perfectly lovely evening gown. "Mr. Hopper said his favorite color is blue, and this is *pink*." Spoken as though the color pink had mortally offended her family.

"You will look lovely," Myrtle assured her, then exhaled in relief as Lilah made her departure. *Mr. Hopper*, she thought to herself. Perhaps she would be relieved of her chaperoning duties sooner than she'd anticipated. Then she could turn her full attention to her own venture.

"I just cannot this evening," she explained to Woof, when the door had shut. She'd been running things over in her mind, every interaction with Simeon that day, from when she arrived to help him set up the room for the meeting to after, when he'd been so abrupt.

She didn't know just what had occurred during that time, but there had to be some reason he had become so distant.

"I'll just send him a note," she said, rushing to her dressing table. She withdrew a piece of paper, one with only a few numbers written on it already, and scribbled a few lines, then sealed it.

"I might be doing the wrong thing," she said, though Woof had no opinion on the matter. "I'll send this after Lilah and Richard have left."

Myrtle spent a few frustrating hours trying to concentrate on something—anything—but all she could do was listen for any sound at the door. She'd sent the note as soon as her relatives had left, and been impatiently waiting ever since.

She was halfway down the stairs by the time the knocking had finished, and had flung the door open before the startled footman could do so.

He stood there. There, on her doorstep. And suddenly she wasn't certain what she should do, or say. Just that—

Her mouth was dry, and she made a gesture for him to come in.

Not that she'd forgotten in the few hours since she'd seen him, but goodness, he was handsome. All that languorous elegance in his lean, muscular body. His sharp blade of a nose with those full, luscious lips just below, a remarkable juxtaposition that caught her—and everybody else's—attention.

His dark hair, rakishly tousled, even though that was likely just the result of his pushing his fingers through it in thought.

"I'll escort Mr. Jones to the library, you needn't bother," she said, addressing the footman, even though her eyes remained on Simeon.

The footman bowed, then left, and she took Simeon's arm, guiding him up the stairs to her bedroom.

Was it shocking? Yes. Would it be cataclysmic if anyone saw them? Also yes.

But she didn't care. She needed to speak with

him, alone, and it was far too problematic for her to venture out alone at this time of night—during the day she could get away with it, but Richard had taken the coach, and she hadn't the faintest idea how to hail a hackney cab, and she knew it would be ridiculous to walk there.

Her bedroom it was.

"What?" he said, then stopped speaking as she slammed the door behind them, shoving him against it, and trapping him with her arms.

The mirror image of what he had done to her in the narrow hallway connecting the kitchen to the main floor.

She stared at him for a moment, now not at all certain what she should say. What she should do. Just that they were here together, that she wanted to know what was happening with him, but she didn't feel as though she had the right to ask him.

"What do you want from me, Myrtle?" he asked again, this time in a softer tone.

She lifted her face to his, swallowing hard against the emotion.

"I want you."

HER WORDS—JUST three words—made his whole body react. He'd fought against the urge to storm over to the town house, demand she listen to him as he told her everything.

But he already knew he couldn't. It wouldn't be right.

He could show her, though.

Myrtle's gaze was clear and direct, and he knew

she meant what she said. Not just because it was Myrtle, and Myrtle didn't lie—at least not to him—but because every one of her emotions was written on her face.

She wanted him. And right now, that was all that mattered.

But he had to make certain she knew what she was saying.

"You want me," he replied, and she nodded, still staring into his eyes. Her hands were on either side of his body, theoretically imprisoning him, though of course he could break the hold whenever he wished.

But he didn't wish.

"How do you want me, Myrtle?" he said, willing his heart not to race. But it wasn't behaving—he felt as though he'd been lit up from the inside, her words, her self, her Myrtle-ness, burning a hot flame through him.

She jerked her chin toward him, a knowing smile on her lips. "You know how. I want to conclude the experiment. It is the logical resolution, is it not?" She wrinkled her brow in thought. "We are six days into it, we should make sure our interactions are as complete as they can be."

"You mean . . ." He needed to be absolutely clear on what she wanted. He would not do anything that she wasn't expecting. Her consent, her approval, was vital.

"Mmm," she murmured. "Do you want me to say it?" she said, tilting her head, an intent expression on her face.

"Yes," he said, his voice ragged. "Yes, I need you to say it."

She inhaled, then bit her lip and glanced away. He put his fingers to her chin and turned her back to him.

"I want you to look at me when you say it," he said in a low tone. A tone that to his ears contained all of his love, his desperation. His need.

"I want you to—to fuck me," she said at last, the words dropping like individual bits of flame into his soul.

For a moment, neither of them moved. Just looked at one another; her still pressing the door with her palms, him with his back against the door, his hands against the wood, gripping hard so he wouldn't touch her.

And then he shifted so suddenly she gasped, ducking down to hoist her onto his shoulders, her delicious, bitable arse under his hand, holding her steady, her legs dangling against his thighs. He strode to her bed, flinging her onto it so she bounced, her face shining with delight as he joined her, crawling on all fours to reach her.

Pushing her against the mattress with one strong hand, his palm on her upper chest. She lay still under him, her eyes wide with interest, with passion, and her breath coming more rapidly than before.

This was the face of a woman who was eager for what was next. Who was here to enjoy every moment of it, and he felt assured of her complete and utter participation.

He lowered his mouth to her ear, exhaling as he spoke, making her writhe against the bed.

"I will fuck you, Myrtle. And you will fuck me." He smiled, and he knew she could hear that, too. "We will fuck each other."

WE WILL FUCK each other.

Myrtle hadn't considered that mutual aspect before; she'd assumed that gentlemen did things to women, not that the other way around was possible. But of course an equal trade in pleasure was the desired goal, was it not? For both people in the pair to feel just as empowered as the other? It made sense, once she thought about it.

And then she was annoyed she hadn't thought about it before—thought about how pleasure was not just bestowed on one hand, received on the other. But that was the point of this, wasn't it? Education, exploration, conclusion?

"How do we start?" she asked, sounding nearly perky. Odd. She never sounded perky.

He snorted in laughter, then jerked his chin toward her. "Where do you think we should start? We could try removing our clothing first, or we could just start doing what feels good."

She pondered that. "I think a mixture of both would be best," she replied, as gravely as if she was weighing in on a mathematical formula.

He smiled, showing his strong, white teeth, and she had a sudden urge for him to bite her. Where had that come from? Was that something people did?

Then again, it didn't matter if people did it—if she wanted to, then it was fine. That was what his words implied. How they were here together, enjoying one another. Perhaps for the last time. Or no, not the last; tomorrow was the actual final day of their experiment, so today was the penultimate day.

She mentally shook herself for having such pedantic thoughts when she was lying on her actual bed with an actual handsome man, the actual handsome man she loved, atop her. Truly, if she had ever wondered if her brain would ever stop working, now she had her answer. No. No, it would not.

"I thought you would say that," he said, easing off her to sit on the bed. She was about to protest when he yanked his boots off, sending them flying into the corner of her room.

"Shh!" she said, her eyes wide.

"What?" he replied. "Won't they just think you're tromping around in search of an answer to a thorny problem?"

"Oh," Myrtle said. "I hadn't thought of that." She grinned at him. "You really do keep up, Mr. Jones."

"Oh, I do," he said, waggling his eyebrows in a salacious way.

"I suppose that means something sexual," she said. "I do hope you are going to refer to it later on, so I understand better."

His mouth widened into a broad smile, and he met her gaze. What she saw there—the admiration, the desire, the interest—made her breath hitch. He truly liked her, and seemed to be fascinated by her. She'd never spurred that reaction in anybody before.

And it wasn't because her person was adjacent to a large fortune. He could never have her fortune, they both knew that. He was here, with her, because of her alone.

That made it feel extra precious.

"I will explain everything to you, my desirable mathematician," he said, pulling his shirt up and over his head.

Ah. At last she could see his chest. And it was far, far better than her imagination.

His shoulders were broad, and she could see the delineation of muscle on his chest. His pectorals were well-defined, with a dusting of black hairs in the middle, narrowing to a thin line that ran vertically down and disappeared into his trousers. His abdominal muscles were equally well-defined, and her fingers itched to explore, to touch every indent, to discover his body as if it were a topographic table.

"And you?" he said, nodding toward her. "If this is an equal exchange, surely I should get to see more of you?" His expression was one of avid interest, and she felt herself get heated.

"You'll have to help," she said, twisting over onto her back.

He let out a soft growl, then quickly undid the buttons of her gown, sliding his warm palm over her bare skin.

It felt delicious and sensual and it was just a hand on her back, neither of which were reported to be erogenous zones. She'd read about the zones in some book she wasn't supposed to know about, tucked deep within her brother's library, brought back from India by some distant relative.

He slid the fabric over her shoulders and down her arms, and she flipped back, sitting halfway up to tug the gown off her upper body.

She wore a chemise, but hadn't bothered with a corset or anything else because she was just dining at home, and not going out that evening.

Her chemise was old, and thin, and she knew he could see through the fabric. Not just because she knew the chemise was old, but because of how he was looking at her.

As if he was drinking her in, cataloguing every bit of information in his artist's brain.

"May I?" he asked, his hand hovering about her chest.

"Please do," she said, not at all surprised to hear she sounded breathless.

His palm came down on her breast, and he made a noise of pleasure as he ran his hand over and around it. She usually was fine with the size of her breasts—they were larger than most ladies', and she appreciated that low-cut gowns made them look like two soft pillows, but she'd never actually realized that their area—her pi times the radius squared—would increase the total amount of her own erogenous zones.

She nearly shared her revelation, but she wasn't sure she could speak.

Because now he'd bent his head and was licking her nipple through her chemise, the soft wetness of his tongue doing incredible things to her entire body.

She grabbed his arm and held on, pulling him more on top of her, anticipating when he'd put his hand there, there where she ached. For something.

And she knew what that something was, given that it was making its presence known against her hip.

"Doesn't that hurt?" she blurted out, wiggling where their bodies made contact.

He chuckled against her skin, then raised his head and met her gaze. "Only in the most intoxicating way," he said.

"I think we need to move this along," Myrtle said, sitting up on the bed to immediately shove the rest of her gown down, then to find the hem of her chemise and raise that.

He watched, his gaze intent on her body, his hand going down to there, stroking it in a rhythmic motion.

Like she had, before.

"Do you do that to yourself?" she asked interestedly.

"Yes," he said, his voice hoarse.

"Ah, no wonder you knew what you wanted when I touched you," she said, and he shivered.

She nodded toward him. "You should take your

trousers off." And then she could see him—all of him—here, in her bedroom. It would be an image she would hold in her mind for the rest of her life, she knew. Because what other time would she be able to see the most beautiful man in the world naked and eager for her?

Never, she knew that well enough.

The life she was planning would have no beautiful men. Or ugly ones, for that matter. Not that beauty was anything but subjective, but still.

No men at all. Just women who needed help because of men.

Meanwhile, he was obeying her directive, shoving his trousers down his legs and kicking them off to land in a pile on the carpet.

"Oh my," she breathed, when she saw all of him.

His body looked as if it was molded by a sculptor. A sculptor who appreciated the naked form, she amended; not the kind of sculptor who immortalized famous people in stone, people one would most definitely not want to see naked.

"What do you think?" he said, turning in a slow circle.

Every part of him was stunning.

"You are just—" She waved her hands in the air to indicate the enormity of her admiration.

"You are just also," he said, getting back on the bed with her.

She was nude now, too, her chemise lying at the foot of her bed. In normal circumstances she'd be cold, but with his gaze heating her skin she felt as though she was on fire from the inside out.

"My God, Myrtle," he said, his voice a low, reverent whisper. "You are beautiful. I wish I had asked to paint you like this."

"Richard would never have agreed," she said, then laughed as she realized what she'd said. "I mean, it wouldn't even be a question one would ask."

He reached to touch her skin, trailing his fingers from her shoulder down her arm, to just under her breast, then lower, until they'd skimmed her belly and were now just there, at her entrance.

She knew she was wet there. For him. For them, for what they were doing together.

And she needed it all, and now, and she grabbed him, pulling him onto her, sliding her palms down his back, over his arse, to as much of his upper leg as she could reach, then back again.

His penis throbbed against her, and there was a palpable ache for him there.

"Please," she said, and shifted under him. "Please."

"Please what, Myrtle?" he said, his mouth against her ear.

"Please fuck me. Please."

Chapter Twenty-Three

Simeon had never been with a woman so open, so expressive, so transparent about what she wanted. Even the most experienced ladies generally demurred at stating everything they wanted, but not Myrtle.

She was just . . . her. She wanted something, she asked for it, and she took it when offered.

He reveled in that, in her frank delight in everything they were doing together.

And he knew it would mean as much to him as to her when she climaxed during their most intimate moment.

He had to make it good for her. He knew it would be good for him—it was already good for him. Just being with her was incredible.

Please fuck me. Please.

He reached down to spread her legs wider, shift his body so he lay between them. She obliged, making small noises of agreement, and he slipped his hand between them, sliding it down to her pussy. She was wet, and his finger stroked her clitoris for just a moment, making her nearly leap off the bed.

"Good?" he said, a humorous tone in his voice.

"Mmm-hmm. You know it is," she said crossly. "Why do you ask questions to which you already know the answer?"

He smothered a laugh. He hadn't expected sex with Myrtle to be so joyous.

"Because I like to have my theories proven beyond a reasonable doubt," he said smoothly.

"Humph," she said, but her grumble turned into a moan when he slid his fingers inside her, pressing his thumb against her clit as he stroked his fingers in and out of her.

"Oh, is that . . . ? I mean, is that . . . ?"

"Where my cock will go?" he said, predicting her question.

"Yes. That."

"Say it, Myrtle," he urged. "Say it."

"Is that where your cock will go?" she said, her tone breathy.

"Now tell me," he demanded.

"That is where I want your cock to go," she said, sounding like her usual peremptory self.

"God, Myrtle," he said, taking himself in hand and rubbing the tip of his penis against her, getting her juices on him to make the way in easier.

"What about . . . ?" She sounded anxious, and he paused for a moment.

"I'll withdraw before anything can happen," he promised.

"Oh. Yes, of course. Proceed, then," she replied in a relieved tone of voice.

He did, biting his lip to keep himself from just pushing all the way in. His body wanted him to—God, did it want him to—but that would not be as good for her, and he wanted to make this an amazing experience for her.

Instead, he slid in a bit, then withdrew, then slid in, and then withdrew, each time going in just a bit deeper, until she had clamped her hands on his shoulders and was begging him.

"Please, now, I want all of it now. I want you inside of me. Your cock, I want it." He heard the aching want in her voice, and he took a breath before pushing all the way in.

She gasped, and he felt something ease his way, and then she had wrapped her legs around his body, pinning him in place inside her.

He stilled for a moment to get both of them accustomed to the feeling, and then he began to move, slowly at first, then a bit faster as he found his rhythm.

"It feels so strange," she observed. "So strange and so wonderful. I feel so full, like you're stretching me."

"Mmm," he replied, not able to concentrate on a conversation at the moment. What with being so close to the edge and all.

He rose up to rest on his forearms so he could see her—her beautiful breasts swaying with each movement, her face alight with curiosity and desire, her lips red and damp from where she'd licked them.

She was stunning.

"I need—" she said, then shook her head in frustration.

"Soon, Myrtle," he promised, then moved even faster, pushing in and out of her until he felt the inevitable start to build, and he withdrew, wrapping his hand around his fist and pumping until he came. Spilling over her lush body, marking her.

And then he shuddered a deep breath as he collapsed on top of her.

She idly stroked his hair as he recovered.

"That was fun," she said, and he brought his head up to look at her.

"Not as much fun as it will be," he said. "Did you think we are done?" He shook his head. "We've just barely begun, my love."

WHEN SIMEON HAD said *we've just barely begun*, she had thought it mere hyperbole.

But no, their interlude lasted for hours—he brought her to pleasure with his fingers, his mouth, and then a combination of both, so she felt as though her bones had dissolved and she were a pile of well-pleasured jelly.

It was nearing midnight when it seemed everything was done. The two of them lay in her bed, her lying as she usually did, him draped horizontally over her. Both of them naked, her bedsheets and comforter a tangled mess.

She'd lit a few candles as the night got darker, and they cast warm shadows over their bodies. She hadn't thought it possible for him to look more appealing, but the candlelight enhanced all of his interesting grooves and indents, and she could not look away.

Not that she wanted to.

She wanted to look at him forever.

Even though that wasn't possible.

"What are you thinking about?" he said, idly stroking a circle on her hipbone.

"How did you know I was thinking about something?" she asked.

He turned his head to regard her. "Because you are always thinking about something. If there's one thing I know about Miss Myrtle Allen, it is that her brain does not stop."

She gave a rueful laugh, and his eyebrows creased into a frown.

"What is it?" he asked, now in a more serious tone.

She took a breath. "I—this has been wonderful. But tomorrow is the seventh day, and then we have the other testing period. I think Lilah might be close to getting an offer, and then all of this is over. I will miss it, you know. I will miss you."

She spoke as close to the truth as she dared.

He pressed his lips to her skin.

"I will miss you as well," he replied.

"Is there—can I ask for another thing?" she said.

He offered her a wry smile. "I think I am all tapped out for tonight, love," he said.

She flicked his shoulder with her finger. "Not that. I am quite well satisfied, as you know."

"It was tremendous, wasn't it?" he said, sounding smug.

She rolled her eyes in response.

"What is it?" he continued.

"I—before all of this ends, I would very much like to attend one of your book club meetings. I would like the opportunity to see people, see friends, discuss things that are important to them. With each other." She wished she didn't sound so wistful, but it wasn't as though she could disguise her feelings. Not now, at least. And most definitely not with him

"I would be glad to have you meet my friends." She heard the sincerity in his tone, and smiled in relief. "Though I am not certain Fenton will be there. I think he is still abroad. But I've actually seen Bram and Theo, both are in town, and Benedict is always in town. I'll write them to arrange a meeting—we are overdue anyway, we were just hoping Fenton would return."

"Do you know where he is? He's the one whose carriage you borrowed?"

"No, and yes. We think he's in France, but we're not certain. He's not very good at communicating." He snorted. "In person and by post."

"Thank you," she said, shifting so she was no longer under his body. "And I think Richard and Lilah should be home soon, so you should get going. Much as I'd love to have you stay here forever." She winced internally as she uttered the words, because they were the truth. She hoped he would view them as merely an idle response to so much pleasure.

He got up as well, easing off the bed as gracefully as a naked, physically spent man could, picking up his clothing from where it had landed around the room.

Soon he was dressed, and she had put on her night rail and dressing gown just in case Lilah stopped by to tell her about her evening after she returned.

It was easy to give him instructions on how to slip out of the house without notice; she'd done it enough when going to his studio.

And then he was gone.

She located Woof, who was lying in front of the fireplace in the library, and brought him back upstairs with her, tucking him into bed as she tried to rearrange the untidy bedding.

"It will be just us," she told the dog, who made a snuffling noise as he placed his head on his paws. "Just us, forever and ever."

But she had the memory of tonight, and that would sustain her for as long as she drew breath. It would have to be enough.

Chapter Twenty-Four

Simeon walked home in a fog, unaware of his surroundings until he was inside his rooms.

All he knew, all he could think about, was that he was absolutely in love with her. That he couldn't imagine living without her.

"Goddamn it," he growled, stalking to the kitchen to drown his sorrows in a cup of tea.

And yet he also knew that she was determined to live on her own, to follow the guidance his mother had given him—not to neglect a gift of genius because of secondary concerns.

Even though the love he felt for her was any thing but secondary

He'd fallen in love before. And each time he had felt the wrenching loss when it was all over, though it was usually he that had ended it. He wouldn't negate those earlier loves by declaring this one was entirely different.

But it was.

He could actually imagine a future with her— she'd be a partner who understood his obsessions because she had her own obsessions. They would coexist in a world of their respective talents, coming together when their days were over to share ideas and lose themselves in physical pleasure. He would learn how she took her tea, and she would learn how he took his: too much sugar and a squeeze of lemon.

It would be his ideal life. Even though he'd never imagined his ideal life to include another person.

He took a sip of his tea, but it was still too hot to drink. He glared at the liquid as though it was its fault he'd burned his tongue.

But now he knew. Everything he thought before about who he was and what he wanted was wrong. He wanted her, because he knew she would never inhibit his gift. Instead, she would enhance it because he'd want to improve and concentrate for her, to show her just exactly what he was capable of.

It was a terrible realization.

Because it wasn't what she wanted, and the most important thing for him to do for the person he loved was to follow what they wanted. Not what he wanted for them. That would be as arrogant as one of her myriad suitors insisting he was better than she at managing money, when she was the clear mathematical genius.

But he had eight more days with her, at least—one more day of their pleasure experiment, and then a week of no physical contact.

He could use that week to grow accustomed to not touching her. Eventually, he'd have to grow accustomed to not seeing her, because she would be forging her own particular path, and she wouldn't need his help any longer.

He should be proud of her for that—he *was* proud of her for that, but he also wished, in a tiny portion of his mind, that she did need more help.

But it didn't matter what he wished, one way or the other. The fact was that this would all be over soon, and he would have to deal with the worst heartache he could imagine.

Perhaps, he thought with a rueful smile, it would inspire his work. Perhaps he'd finally create the painting that would make it clear to everyone just how talented he was.

Perhaps it would be his painting of her as Artemisia—and wouldn't that be ironic?

It was now one o'clock in the morning, but he couldn't sleep. He didn't want to sleep, for fear he'd have happy dreams where they were together.

Instead, he changed into his work clothes and lit all the candles in his studio, dragging the easel with the Artemisia painting to the center of the room.

He didn't need her to pose any longer—he'd gotten the basic look and feel of her on canvas already. Her fierce determination, her strong, proud gaze, her warmth.

All of it was there in front of him. Now he had to complete the painting, put Myrtle as Artemisia in context for the viewers so they could see just what made her so special. So deserving of love and admiration.

He went to work, his mouth set in a grim line,

as his brain continued to mull over the various scenarios, none of which ended with him being happy ever after.

Life wasn't a fairy tale where everything was all right at the end thanks to true love.

No, like this painting, life was a battle—a battle to do the right thing even though there was loss along the way.

In an actual battle, the loss would be the most profound, the loss of human life. But in a situation like his, the loss would be of a type of life—a life where a person could be living up to their promise in both romance and skill.

His mother was wrong. He knew that now. But that wasn't her fault; it was the fault of her world. That she thought she had to sacrifice one for the other was the result of being a woman in a man's world. A man could have everything he wanted, as long as he had good birth, a reasonable financial start, and most of his teeth.

But if one lacked the right gender, the right type of parents, or the right kind of skill it would require a sacrifice of some sort to succeed.

Now he knew what his sacrifice was: Her. His happiness. His complete and fulfilling future.

Eight more days to hope for something that could not come true.

It was both too long and too short a time for such a monumental consideration.

"SHE'LL BE HERE," Benedict said, not for the first time.

Simeon, Theo, Bram, and Benedict were at the

Orphans' Club; Fenton was still missing, though they'd had word he'd left France for Italy.

"Perhaps she won't come," Theo said, his expression mischievous. "Perhaps she'll meet another, more talented artist on the way and decide he is more worth her time."

"That's impossible," Simeon retorted, "since there are no other artists more talented than I."

Bram clapped him on the back, accompanying the motion with a broad smile. "At least we can be assured you'll still be the most arrogant man, even when you're brokenhearted."

"Very amusing," Simeon said through gritted teeth.

"Are you going to tell her anything about how you feel?" Benedict asked.

Simeon was opening his mouth to reply when there was a knock at the door.

"Your guest, gentlemen," the footman said, gesturing for the visitor to enter.

Myrtle had disguised herself well, donning an enormous caped cloak that covered all her curves and a hideously shaped hat atop her head.

The Club knew, of course, that females were sometimes within, but the effort had to be made to preserve the rules.

Simeon made certain the door was shut before helping her off with her cloak and hat. The latter took some wrangling because she'd shoved all her hair up inside, and some of her hair was stuck to the hatband.

Simeon was acutely aware of his friends

watching, and no doubt laughing, though they were polite enough to be discreet about it.

He made the introductions when she was finally disgorged from her clothing.

"Miss Allen, may I present my friends? This is Mr. Benedict Quintrell, Mr. Bram Townsend, and Mr. Theo Osborne."

She nodded toward them, saying, "The Bastard Five, I believe. Even though I only count four of you."

"I'd heard you were a whiz at mathematics," Theo said, stepping forward to take her arm and guide her to a seat. Simeon resisted the impulse to shove Theo aside and help Myrtle himself.

This was an opportunity for them to know her as well as vice versa. And besides, Theo was besotted with his wife, who'd just borne their daughter. Simeon shouldn't be jealous.

Even though he was.

"Thank you, Mr.—"

"Osborne," Theo said with a bow.

"Mr. Osborne." Myrtle's interested gaze darted around the room. "This is a very pleasant meeting spot," she said. "You've got a good fire going, the room is well-furnished, and there are snacks." The last bit she said with even greater interest, and Simeon sprang into action.

"Can I fetch you a plate?" he said, going to the table where the refreshments were laid out.

"Please."

"Miss Allen, what types of books do you enjoy?" Benedict asked as Simeon debated whether to add a third biscuit to the already full plate.

He decided yes, because he wanted her to have the best possible experience here, and it was far better for her to decide she didn't want a third biscuit rather than have him decide for her.

"I like all types," she answered, taking the plate from Simeon. "I mostly read mathematical tomes, but I like to escape with works of fiction as well." She took a piece of cheese and regarded it with such avid hunger Simeon felt jealous all over again.

Of a piece of Brie.

He was ridiculous.

"Have you read the book we're discussing tonight?" Benedict continued. "Margaret Tyler's *The Mirrour*—"

"*The Mirrour of Princely Deedes and Knighthood*?" Myrtle finished. "I have. One of the reasons I asked Mr. Jones—"

"You can call him Simeon here, you know," Theo interjected.

"Why I asked *Simeon*," she said, "if I could come to your meeting is that I have never had the opportunity to speak with anybody about the books I read."

"Well, then, Miss Allen," Benedict began.

"Please call me Myrtle," she replied, a warm smile on her face.

"Myrtle, if you would like to start off by sharing your thoughts?"

BEFORE SHE COULD even ask herself, she knew the answer. No, nobody had ever asked for her opinion on a book before. Actually, very few people had asked her for an opinion in general— Lilah just wanted to be reassured she looked beautiful, which wasn't an opinion so much as corroboration, and Richard steadfastly avoided asking her anything for fear, she presumed, he or his employees would be revealed to be wrong about something.

Simeon had asked her opinion on things before, though.

And now here his friends were doing the same.

Was this because she had so few friends? Or did she have such few friends because these people were rare to find, and she hadn't found her own Bastard Five yet?

"I admire what Tyler has done here," Myrtle said slowly. Taking time to be thoughtful rather than just blurting everything all at once, as was her wont. "She's created a romantic atmosphere but also made it about more than just the romance."

All the men regarded her with varying expressions of interest on their faces.

So unusual, to be the focus of men's attention when none of them had designs on her dowry. When they were just . . . listening to her.

"I know she has translated the original work, but her preface shows she has real passion for the book, and it is clear she has used her own opinion in her choice of words." She gave a wry smile. "I suppose it is similar to when I solve mathematics problems—not that there are a variety of solutions, generally there is only the one, but the way each solver chooses to approach the problem is unique."

"Like when Simeon here does one of his paintings," Simeon's friend Mr. Osborne said. Myrtle didn't notice the way he waved his hand, as though "one of his paintings" was just a minor event, not something crucially important to the artist.

Simeon, however, just looked over at his friend and raised a disdainful eyebrow. Myrtle had the impression that these exchanges were common for the two of them.

"So is it your opinion, then, Miss Allen, that there can be a variety of solutions—of translations, say—for a particular problem?"

Mr. Townsend, whom Myrtle thought vaguely was involved with the law, certainly spoke with some sort of legal authority.

"I believe so, though I would not have said so before. I would have said before that Margaret Tyler should stay as close to the original words as possible, to preserve the author's intent. But if she understood that the audience for an English translation was different than the original Spanish, and that British people would relate to different things than what the original author wrote, then I see no reason not to try to make the work the best possible for its audience."

Mr. Townsend gave a satisfied smile, and Myrtle felt as though she'd passed some sort of test, though she had no idea what kind it was.

"But what do you all think of it?"

The next two hours was filled with the sounds of spirited debate, with only a few moments where Myrtle thought someone might be getting seriously angry. The four men were all well-spoken, supporting their opinions in a variety of methods.

Mr. Townsend presented the facts as though he was Socrates presenting an argument; Mr. Quintrell just said things as though they were facts, while Simeon and Mr. Osborne discussed more about how they felt.

She didn't speak much herself during the time; she far preferred to watch them discuss the book, and other things, while she observed. It was so rare for her to be in the same room with people she thought might be nearly as intelligent as she that she had to just be quiet. Who knew when she would have this kind of opportunity again?

"Miss Allen, what do you—"

And then the door swung open, and a fifth man entered.

"Fenton!" the others called, and Myrtle felt a prickle of interest—this was the odd Fenton that Simeon had mentioned.

He didn't look odd so much as bedraggled. She could recognize his clothing as being excellently tailored, but it also seemed as though he'd been wearing them for a few days—his coat was spattered with something, his boots showed signs of hard use, and he wasn't wearing a cravat.

Most importantly, his expression was just as beleaguered. His eyes darted around the room, restless, and his mouth was set in a hard line.

She rose as he dragged a chair to join the others.

"I should be going," she said. She nodded toward the new arrival. "I understand, Mr. Fenton, that you have been away. I am certain your friends will want to speak with you without a stranger present."

Simeon popped up out of his chair, followed more slowly by the other gentlemen. "I'll escort you."

She shook her head. "There's no need. I have my coachman waiting around the corner."

"No," he replied. "I want to."

Mr. Fenton had sat down, though none of the other gentlemen had, since she was standing. Mr. Osborne, she noticed, had his hand on his friend's shoulder and he looked concerned.

"Mr. Fenton, I am Miss Allen. It is a pleasure to meet you. I have heard of you. Though I must be going."

"Not a pleasure at all, I imagine," Mr. Fenton said, then frowned. "It's just Fenton. Not Mr. Fenton."

"Fenton," Myrtle corrected. Startled by his bluntness as well as by his correcting her on his name, making it seem as though they were friends when they had just met. Entirely improper, of course. But since she was a lady at a gentleman's club, and this gentleman wished to be addressed in a particular way, she saw no reason to be rude about it and ignore his thoughts on the matter.

"I'll take Myrtle home," Simeon said. "Fenton, I'll return in a while."

Fenton merely waved in reply as Simeon gathered Myrtle's cloak, helping her get back into her disguise. The other three men clustered around Fenton, shielding him from her view, and she felt relief that he would clearly be taken care of.

"Are you certain?" she whispered as they exited the building. "I can—"

"It's the seventh day," he said. "Or have you forgotten?"

She shook her head. "No, I haven't. You know I haven't. But your friend—"

"My friend, more than anyone, knows the importance of preserving all the elements of a successful experiment," Simeon replied, humor lacing his words. His tone sobered. "Besides, I think I know the cause of his distress. The others can help him now, and I will be there later."

"You're a good friend," she said in a soft voice. A good friend to both her and Fenton—here he was, insisting he escort her, when his close friend was upset, just because he knew it would make her more comfortable. Knowing his other friends could carry the burden until he got back to the club.

They walked around the corner to where her carriage waited.

He helped her inside, then vaulted up behind her, taking a seat beside her.

The seventh day. The final day of their experiment, at least the final day of pleasure. This was it, all of it. This was all that would ever be.

She took a deep breath, scowling at herself as she felt the tears start to gather.

The final day was not the day for crying. That could be for later, when she was truly alone.

"Well, then," she said, twisting to face him, "what should we do for the final day?"

Chapter Twenty-Five

Simeon's heart was in his throat. He couldn't speak for a moment, because speaking might mean saying how he felt, and he could not do that.

Instead, he did what he always did: adopted his rakishly debonair persona and tried to charm his way through it.

At least, he thought ruefully, he would be able to commiserate with Fenton. He knew Fenton had gone to Paris with Theo's step-sister-in-law and stepdaughter, and he imagined Fenton's current state of mind was due to something occurring with his traveling companions. None of them had ever seen Fenton in love, but his expression certainly seemed to indicate some sort of heartache.

But meanwhile, he had his own heartache to anticipate.

"I will leave the choice of the final day up to you," he said, offering her his best smile. "I got to choose last night, and that was quite satisfactory."

He could see her looking at him, that direct Myrtle stare seeming as though it was piercing through all his charm, all his easy diplomacy to the man within. Though that wasn't possible. She couldn't know anything he was actually thinking, because if she did she would toss him out of the carriage for even considering changing the course of her life because of his desires. His love.

"Satisfactory," she echoed, and for once, he couldn't read her tone.

"Yes, I believe you felt the same. Twice? Three times?" he said.

"Three times," she confirmed. Which he'd known when he said it, he just wanted to boast. To lure her into a lighter thread of conversation so he wouldn't be tempted to veer into the serious.

He couldn't allow that.

"I have to be home soon, Lilah is at a party with friends, but Richard waits for her on evenings I am not with her. He'll know how late I am in returning."

Her voice was stilted, as though she, too, was feeling things she couldn't express.

Again, odd.

But if he thought too much about it he'd end up blurting out the questions—*What are you thinking? How do you feel about me? Is there a chance?*—that were flooding his brain, and he couldn't.

"Then we'll have to end this as we began," he said lightly.

"And that is . . . ?"

"A kiss. You should ask me for a kiss, like you did before, when we first arrived."

"I don't even remem—"

"I do," he said, interrupting her. "It was *Do you think you could kiss me?*"

"Oh. I see. I had forgotten."

I cannot forget anything about you, he thought. *You're the only person I've ever met who can match my talent, my passion for work, my adventurous spirit. If you were in my life permanently, you would drive me to be even better than I am.*

The coach hit a bump, and they were jostled together, and he instinctively took her arm to steady her.

"Thank you," she said, nodding at him. "Shall I . . . ?"

"Go ahead."

She cleared her throat. "Do you think you could kiss me?"

"Yes. Yes, I could."

He turned to face her directly, and she did the same. He took her hands in his, uttering a soft chuckle as he met her gaze.

It was dark in the carriage, but there was an occasional flare of a streetlamp, and he could see her clearly. Her expression was thoughtful, almost somber. He knew she would miss the physical part of their experiment—that aspect of it was not in question—and he wondered if she would miss more than that. Like him.

But he couldn't ask.

All he could do was what she'd asked.

He leaned forward, slowly in case the carriage lurched again, and softly, gently, put his mouth on hers.

She uttered a soft sigh and tilted her head up, welcoming the kiss.

For once he didn't want anything to escalate beyond what was happening now—this kiss, this perfect, beautiful kiss—was all he needed. Just two people doing something natural and right and honest.

Because it felt, when he had his lips pressed to hers, that in the kiss he was able to express everything he couldn't say. His love, his desire, his respect. Everything that made it impossible for him to stop loving her, even when they no longer saw one another.

It was the most perfect kiss. A kiss that would live on in his memory forever, even though there would be other kisses. There was no possibility any kiss would top this one. Because he loved her.

For a moment, Myrtle couldn't recall anything. Not her name, her goals, her desires, her interests—nothing.

All she knew was him and her in this dark carriage. Not quiet, since the carriage's wheels were rolling along London streets, but it still felt as though it was just the two of them in their own world.

She recalled what she'd said before, when she was merely attracted to him, not in love with him: *It does feel like we're the only two people in the world right now, doesn't it? As though this is the only thing that exists.*

If only, she thought. If only it was just them,

without the constraints her Society imposed on people like her, who were not allowed to fall in love, much less marry, people like him. Even beyond that, he would not be allowed to fall in love with her because then it would impede his talent, making his and his mother's life goals fall short.

No. This was all there was, and it would have to do.

Eventually, unfortunately, the kiss ended, the carriage slowing as it arrived at the town house.

There were a few moments before one of the footmen would open the door. "Thank you," she said quickly, her voice harsh with all the emotion she couldn't express. "For all of this. For helping me, not just with Lilah's debut but also with furthering my goals. I am so grate—"

And then the carriage door swung open, and the moment was over. She wanted to slam the door shut again, keep the two of them locked in there forever, but of course that wasn't possible.

"You are welcome," he said, his tone equally low and serious. She hadn't heard him be this measured before; likely something to do with his friend Fenton, not their kiss or anything. She knew he had kissed many women in the past, and would kiss many more in the future.

This was a pleasant interlude, to be sure, but it wouldn't leave a scar on him as it would her.

She knew that. But the same woman who had been irked he hadn't recalled meeting her earlier that evening when she had burst into his bedroom was also irked that their physical relationship would mean no more to him than the next one.

The footman waiting at the carriage door cleared his throat, and Myrtle scrambled out, the sharp prick of tears stinging her eyes.

"Good evening," she said, not turning around to look at him. He might see the shine of moisture on her face and realize the idiotic thing she'd done, even though it was the last thing either one of them was supposed to do. "Thank you for the escort, Mr. Jones."

"You're welco—" he said, the last part of the word lost as another footman closed the carriage door.

That was it. They would see one another again, but in public. Not privately, certainly not intimately. Perhaps the next time she saw him would be when she did what Richard had asked—break off the fake engagement by lying as she had never lied before.

His tutoring would come in handy, and she would have to fool the one person who knew she could not lie.

If it wasn't her heart and her whole life at stake, she might actually enjoy the irony.

SIMEON TRIED TO lose himself in his work for the next few days. It was successful, up to a point, but it was also painful, since the work he was so immersed in was a painting of her. "Not really making things any easier," he muttered as he focused on the canvas.

Today he was concentrating on getting the look in her eyes just right—that fierce determination, that confidence that said she knew what she was doing was right, even if everyone else doubted her.

She was as proud and confident in her work as he was in his. He'd never met another artist with the same combination of talent, drive, and ambition as he. Until her.

He knew she would succeed in her ventures. Not just because her ideas were good—though they were—but because she had the elements necessary for success. That she was an aristocrat certainly didn't hurt either. Perhaps she would not even need her vast inheritance, if her own business did well enough. It wasn't as though she was particularly profligate; he knew she liked beautiful clothes and sweets, but she wasn't excessive with either. She would do just fine on whatever she earned.

"And she'll do fine without you," he added with a frown.

The painting was nearly complete, and he'd already made inquiries of the Royal Academy and a few other exhibition spaces about it. Some of his earlier works had gotten notice, but this Artemisia painting was, he knew, his best work so far.

Because he was in love with the subject? Because the image of a woman commanding a fleet of ships during battle was so compelling to begin with? Because he was convinced in the rightness of the composition, and his own fierce determination came through in the work?

Regardless of the reasons, it was a glorious work. One that would make his name, if things went well. And if this painting didn't make his name, then he would allow himself no more chances—if this work wasn't recognized, then there was no point in continuing. He'd find something else to do, something that required less of a sacrifice and resulted in fewer paint-streaked clothes.

"And then what?" he mused aloud. "If you succeed, then what?"

He'd never contemplated that before because he'd never been so close before.

Just thinking about it made his chest tighten. What if—what if this wasn't all worth it? What if talent like his was meant to be put in perspective, alongside other things of value. Things like friendship, comfort, pleasure. Love.

What if this wasn't what he was supposed to be doing, after all?

"Hell of a time to be thinking that," he said to himself in a wry tone. "The only thing you can do is continue as you have. Or you'll never know anything."

He just wished his own words didn't make him feel so hollow.

"AND WE WANT to announce the engagement tomorrow night!" Lilah exclaimed.

She'd returned from her party and immediately rushed to Myrtle's room, forcing her aunt to stop moping about her own future and pay attention to her niece's. A welcome relief, if she was honest.

There wasn't anything she could do about her future, after all, which was causing the moping in the first place. A tautological situation if ever she saw one, though that realization didn't keep her mind from going over and over it again.

Thankfully, Mr. Hopper and his timely proposal made it possible for her to stop the churning cycle of regret.

"Where are we going tomorrow?" Myrtle asked, leaning past Lilah to snatch a biscuit from a plate. She'd asked the kitchen for tea when she'd returned from doing some errands, and the kitchen—who seemed to know her well—also sent along an assortment of biscuits. Myrtle was making her way through the varieties to figure out what kind she preferred.

The mathematical approach to biscuits was an intuitive one, but would also be of use when she next spoke to Cook or any of the other food-related staff. She'd like to return their kind gesture by indicating she'd given thought beyond the delight of having some excellent snacks.

"We're going to—actually, I don't know," Lilah said, waving her hand in clear dismissal. "Just that it's another party and so it is a good opportunity to tell everyone. I cannot wait until it is just me and my dear Charles, though," she said, sounding as though she hadn't just been the debutante determined to appear at every single event held this Season.

"You and your dear Charles," Myrtle replied. "When do you suppose you'll be married?"

Lilah frowned in thought. "I'm not certain—it is so early, and Father wants to write Mama to tell her. I suppose we'll have to decide later on."

"Ah."

"But this is the best part, Aunt Turtle!" Lilah exclaimed. "It means you won't have to worry about taking me around to parties anymore. Mr. Hopper's mother has said she is glad to escort me, and this will give me an opportunity to get to know her a little better as well."

"Oh, yes, wonderful news," Myrtle said in a faint voice.

It was. It was precisely why she was in London, with the chance to receive her money without having to have a husband attached to it. Why she'd agreed to a false engagement, and going out to parties, and generally being more of the center of attention and less focused on her own work. That was all over now. She should be relieved. She could pivot to the life she actually wanted: a small businessperson helping people who didn't understand numbers and finance nearly as well as she did.

But since she was always honest, in general as well as to herself, she had to say she was not relieved.

"WE ARE ALL very pleased at the news," the viscount said.

Simeon clapped along with everyone else, though he could feel the tension in his body. He was happy for Lilah, of course, but that meant the end was near.

"And I have something I would like to say," Myrtle said, stepping up to where her brother stood.

Apparently the end was now.

He swallowed, his throat suddenly dry.

She glanced over at him for a moment, and he tried to read something—anything—in her gaze, but could not.

"As most of you know, Mr. Jones and I became betrothed a month or so ago." Her voice was strong and clear, like when she made her presentation to all the ladies in his apartment. "And I wanted to let you know that the engagement is over."

Most of the people in the room began to whisper furiously, Myrtle staring out at them as she waited for the furor to subside. She truly was Artemisia, only here she wasn't leading men into battle, she was forcing them into silence. The latter, given Society, might be the more formidable task.

"I wish to add that Mr. Jones is a gentleman. He has done nothing wrong, and he is not the reason I am breaking this engagement." More whispering, but lowered, as though the whisperers didn't want to attract Myrtle's attention. "It is because I have always wanted to live my own life, on my own terms. I am too independent and talented to subsume myself into anybody else."

Basically what she'd said when they'd met. His heart sank. If there had been any chance, any chance at all that she might have feelings for him, they were dashed with those words.

"There is nobody, in fact, that I would tolerate

marrying. Marriage, for a woman, means giving control of your life to somebody else, someone who just happens to have the good fortune of being born male." She turned to regard him, gesturing toward him as she spoke. "Mr. Jones has been nothing but kind, generous, and sympathetic." He heard the sincerity in her tone. "If there is anyone to blame, it is me. I do not believe that I am cut out to be a wife."

She took a breath and surveyed the room. "I know this sounds like a trivial matter. It only affects me and Mr. Jones. It's not something that will result in a huge triumph or loss. It's the kind of thing most women struggle with—whether to value themselves above what you expect of us. Usually, we don't have a choice. I am fortunate enough to take my choice. This will be talked about for a few days, perhaps as long as a week, but this decision affects all of the rest of my life."

And with that, she stepped away, back toward her familiar spot at the edge of the room.

There was more whispering, and then Simeon felt his feet move as if of their own volition, and he walked to the spot she'd just occupied.

Making everyone stop talking, making it sound as though they were all communally holding their breath, waiting for what might happen next.

"I have something to say," he began.

Chapter Twenty-Six

Myrtle glared at Simeon's back when he spoke.

She'd done what was necessary, she didn't see the need for him to follow up with—with anything. She had no idea what he might say. Perhaps he was going to speak about something entirely unrelated to her, though she thought that unlikely. Maybe as low as a five percent chance, if she was calculating the odds.

Which she absolutely was not, because her brain felt as though it were on fire.

It was very difficult, as it happened, to lie in front of a vast crowd of people. Though she had followed his lessons and stuck to the truth as much as possible—it was true that she had *always wanted to live my own life, on my own terms*, but while she was busy with social life and fake engagements, her brain had pivoted to imagining a life with him. She'd still live her own life, on her own terms—and one of her terms would be Simeon.

But she'd left that crucial bit of information out.

It had felt real, felt *honest* to admit that her life wasn't important in context. She was just one person out of many, even in her rarified world. But the need to make her own future burned like the most fearsome fire within her, and she wanted—she hoped—some other lady would hear Myrtle's words and reconsider what she'd always accepted.

He started speaking again.

"I have heard what Miss Allen has to say, and I wanted to ask her, in this public setting, to reconsider."

Reconsider. Like she'd just wanted some unknown lady to do if she heard Myrtle's words. But this was very different.

The crowd got very excited at that, some even clapping their hands in glee.

Myrtle couldn't glower at all of them, so she just stared at the floor.

"I have fallen in love with her."

Which made Myrtle's head snap back up, her eyes wide. He had turned, and was facing her, his hand outstretched in a pleading gesture.

"I have fallen in love with her despite knowing she wants to live her own life on her own terms." He paused for dramatic effect, which was when Myrtle realized what he was doing.

She was aghast at his boldness. At his lying so believably.

He was ensuring that their farce was absolutely credible—he was supporting her announcement of wanting to live her own life, thereby breaking the engagement, by asking her to reconsider her truth.

Which wasn't her truth anymore.

It was a brilliant strategy, and she knew he had thought of it himself, since Richard would never be so devious. But Simeon would; he had a talent, he'd admitted, for prevarication, and had used it to his advantage many times before.

Of course he was doing what he always did—lying to prove himself.

"I have fallen in love with her intelligence, her wit, and the courage of her convictions."

"What about her money?" a voice from the crowd heckled.

Simeon gave a thin smile. "I would be happy to forgo her fortune if I could have her. I have enough confidence in Myrtle herself to know that we would be more than fine. And if we were together, we would be happy."

The irony for her was that what he was saying was true. All of it. But it was all a lie because it was coming from his lips at this time.

"I want to marry this bold, beautiful woman," he continued, his voice resonating through the room. "I love her, and I will never love anybody else."

If it was anyone else, she'd say they were speaking the truth. His tone rang with sincerity, and he had everyone in the crowd hanging on his every word, all of them clearly on his side.

He stretched his fingers out to her. "Well, Myrtle? What do you say?"

For a moment, she considered saying yes. *Yes, I will marry you, you charming scoundrel, because I've fallen in love with you, and now you are going to have to follow through on your word because we're in public and you could not survive this scandal.*

Yes, I don't care about my money. I know you and I are both smart enough to figure out some other way to survive.

Yes, because I cannot seem to think about anything else but you, which makes doing sums quite problematic. So to speak.

She thought about it, but just for a moment.

"No, thank you," she said, and the crowd made noises of distress that tore at her soul. "I have to live my own life, and I know you respect that."

He held her gaze, his fingers still reaching out to her, and she felt the sting of tears. *Do not cry, Myrtle,* she told herself. *Then everyone would know your true feelings. Then he would know your true feelings, and you cannot have that. Not if you want to keep your word not to let anything interfere with his goals. His future.*

So she forced herself to take a deep breath, feeling the air shudder through her, and she concentrated on keeping her expression still. Not revealing an iota of the turmoil and pain surging within.

He pressed his lips together, then whirled around and strode out of the ballroom, parting the crowd like Moses and the Red Sea. It was clear Society was on his side, not hers, and if this was what she truly wanted she would be grateful; he had done enough damage to her reputation to make it nearly impossible for anyone to approach her, much less court her.

Thank you, Simeon, she thought sadly. *You've done everything you were supposed to, and more.*

It's just unfortunate my heart doesn't feel the same way.

"WELL, THAT WAS unexpected."

Simeon turned at the sound of the viscount's voice. He donned his medium-intensity smile, which seemed as though it was still too much, since the viscount staggered a little as he approached.

Myrtle still stood by the wall, her expression set. Everything about her was rigidly set, as though she were a statue.

It had only been a short time into the second part of their experiment, and he already knew the results—he couldn't think about anything but her. He found it hard to concentrate even on saying hello to people he knew, much less create.

In time, it would be easier. Though it would also be harder because the distance from when they were intimate would be longer. The memories wouldn't fade; they would hang there, in his mind, reminding him of what had been possible for one exhilarating and wonderful week. That he had been able to share his thoughts and his body with her in equal measure.

"Unexpected but effective," Simeon said at last. He nodded toward the rest of the company, some of whom were still shooting sympathetic glances his way. "I assume your sister will no longer be bothered by mere fortune hunters. They'd have to be quite determined to get past the twin walls of her tattered reputation and your hold on her money."

"Yes, exactly so," the viscount replied. He narrowed his gaze at Simeon. "You weren't telling the truth back there, were you? You haven't gone and fallen in love with her, have you?"

Simeon would not lie. Not now, not about this.

"What do you think?" he retorted.

"Of course not," the viscount replied, sounding smug.

Because Simeon was just that adept at being slippery.

"That was well done."

He started at the sound of her voice. Not quite as firm and clear as when she'd spoken before, but still strong.

"Oh?" he said, aiming for deliberate vagueness. If there was a chance she felt the same way, he wouldn't ruin it by closing down any avenues to happiness.

"Yes, to make it obvious that I am very prickly and independent and you are not at all at fault in this breakup."

They stood together, so more people were glancing at them. Simeon took her by the arm and tugged. "We should leave. We don't want to cause even more of a stir."

"No, of course," she said, but she shrugged his hand away as she spoke.

"I will fetch the carriage," Richard said. "Lilah has invited some of her friends back to the town house for a small celebration."

Myrtle winced, and he wished he could whisk her away to his apartments, where they'd be alone, and she wouldn't have to deal with any more people this evening.

But of course that was the opposite of what would happen.

He would hail a hackney and go back to his rooms, while she would sit in her brother's town house, toasting her niece's engagement while also deflecting any comments on her own broken one.

At least, that's what he imagined.

He wouldn't be there to see it, so he couldn't know.

Which was true for the rest of his life: *He wouldn't be there to see it, so he couldn't know.*

"I'll get your cloak while I'm there, Myrtle," her brother said.

Leaving them alone.

For a moment, he thought about confessing everything: *What I just said, it's the truth. I love you. I will always love you. I want you to be in my life and challenge me to be a better person and a stronger artist.*

But he couldn't. Not after having done and said all that just now, and she just reacted as though he'd read a recipe aloud, or was reciting too much poetry.

He would have been able to tell if she felt anything. She wasn't able to lie, and that included how she responded to what people said. She'd spoken her truth earlier, and then he had spoken his.

Unfortunately, she didn't believe him because of who he was. How he navigated through life. The scheme her brother had concocted that had protected her from gossip, the end of which would bring more gossip onto her head, but would be welcome now.

"I will wait for Richard's return, and then will be heading out. Thank you for taking care of"—*of breaking my heart*—"of breaking our engagement so publicly. I imagine you will be safe now."

"I imagine I will," she said. Her face was still set, unmoving, and he was sorely tempted to do something that would make her react; take her in his arms and kiss her to oblivion, or toss her over his shoulder as he'd done before.

But he wouldn't do anything without her consent, and she didn't want this.

She didn't want him.

LEAVING WITHOUT ADMITTING she was lying was the hardest thing Myrtle had ever done.

But if she was to have done the right thing, she needed to see it all the way through. She needed him to think she spoke the truth so he wouldn't suspect.

"Thank you, Myrtle," Richard said in a low voice when they were safely inside the carriage. "I know that must have been difficult for you, since you don't like being the center of attention."

You have no idea.

"I thought you and Simeon made a lovely couple," Lilah observed. "I wish you would reconsider. He is so handsome and so talented." She accompanied her words with an admiring sigh.

"Not as handsome as my Charles, of course," she added hastily.

Myrtle repressed a snort. She didn't recall what Lilah's Charles looked like, but there was no possibility he was better-looking than Simeon.

Certain Greek gods were not as good-looking as he.

And yes, she was biased, but it was also the truth.

"Well, what is good for you might not be good for me," Myrtle replied, a sick feeling in her stomach. Lying to her family might prove to be even harder than this evening's bout of lying. "You know how I've wanted to live on my own, and now is my opportunity."

"Yes, and I've heard you already have clients, Aunt Turtle," Lilah exclaimed. "I might even use your services myself."

"Your husband might have something to say about that," Richard said.

Myrtle didn't have to see Lilah's face to know her niece was prickly.

"I will be married, Father, not bound to him," she said sharply. "If there's one thing Aunt Turtle has taught me, it is to speak up for myself. For what I want. Isn't that right?"

Myrtle exhaled in relief. If she could affect just one person, especially a person she loved with all her heart, it was all worth it.

"Yes, that is right," she said, ignoring Richard's sniff of disdain.

Though hours later, lying in her bed alone, it

was a lot harder to hold on to that confidence. Had she done the right thing? Would her heart recover?

She ached with missing him. As they were, in his apartments, as she posed for him; she did not miss their interaction tonight, where she had to listen to him tell her the thing she most wanted to hear—and know it was an absolute falsehood, and it could never be true.

That was why she couldn't, and wouldn't, speak her heart. Yes, it would have the information out in the open, that she had fallen in love with him, but it wouldn't make any kind of difference.

All it would do was make him feel sorry for her, and she did not want that.

She could feel enough sorry all for herself, thank you very much.

The tears came then, and she sobbed, holding the covers over her head to muffle the noise. Woof came closer, then licked her face, and she buried her nose in his fur, holding on to his warmth.

She and Woof. At least she had emerged from this adventure with a friend. A canine, nonspeaking friend, but a friend, nonetheless.

It would have to be enough. Because there was nothing else.

Chapter Twenty-Seven

"You can't stay here and mope forever," Theo argued.

Simeon raised one eyebrow at his friend. "Is that a challenge? Because I most certainly can."

It had been a month since that evening, and Simeon hadn't found himself able to resume any of his usual activities beyond painting. Thank goodness he was still able to do that, though it was exquisite torture to work on Artemisia, with her face staring back at him.

"The point is," Theo said exasperatedly, "that either you have to tell her how you feel or you have to move on. You cannot both hold on to it and refuse to say anything."

"Is that your professional opinion? Because I recall you yourself had difficul—"

"Stop arguing, you two," Bram said wearily. "We have to figure out Fenton's situation as well. Let's just decide about Simeon and move on."

Theo and Simeon both swung their heads toward their friend, who lounged on the infamous settee.

"As though you also didn't do the same thing," Theo said in an accusing tone.

Bram flung his hands up in surrender. "Fine! Yes, we're all idiots in love—except for Benedict, thank God—but that doesn't mean we can't offer good advice."

"Even though you don't take it," Simeon murmured.

Bram glowered at him, but didn't reply.

"So you think I should tell her that what I said was true?" Simeon asked, his voice skeptical. "Because I told her the truth, and she didn't say anything."

"You told her in front of a crowd of people after she'd just theoretically broken your heart," Bram pointed out. "The poor woman couldn't just leap into your arms then because how was she to know you were telling the truth?"

"I did say so," Simeon replied.

Both of his friends rolled their eyes.

He held up his hand. "Fine. I understand. But the thing is, she hasn't come to me yet."

Now they both gave him incredulous looks. Theo spoke first. "She hasn't come to you. When she thinks you said what you said to make her retreat from Society even easier. Seriously."

"How many times have you been in love?" Bram asked. "A multitude, we can agree?"

"But this is different," Simeon argued. "This is—I've never felt this way before. I've been in love, but I've never been in Myrtle-love."

"And when the affairs were over, did you have

regrets?" Bram pressed, his legal training show-ing to its best advantage.

"Of course I did," Simeon snapped.

Bram pointed an accusatory finger at him. "Make certain that you have no regrets about this love affair, because this is your chance at having everything you've ever wanted. A home. Love. A family. A career."

It would be entirely possible, Simeon realized. That was, if she was willing to risk the chance he'd end up being a typical husband, smothering her hopes and brains with domestic mundanity. Would she trust he wouldn't be that kind of man?

He knew he would never allow her to put her talent aside if she wanted to use it. But there was no guarantee, at least not for women, that a hus-band would respect his wife's autonomy. Worse, there was no guarantee the husband wouldn't abuse whatever trust the woman had put in him.

If he told her how he felt, how he really felt, he'd have to hope she would believe in him.

Simeon exhaled. "Fine," he repeated. "Can we agree I am an idiot and should go to her imme-diately?"

His friends nodded.

He took a deep breath. He was an idiot. He knew that. He also knew that when he told her— now that he was going to—that her answer would irrevocably change his life. Now there was the chance, albeit a slim one, that there was hope.

Once she understood then whatever she said would be the decision.

He scooped up his hat and coat and ran downstairs, calling for his friends to lock up after him.

Now that he was going, he needed to be there immediately. Yesterday. The day after that night.

He hoped it wasn't too late.

"IT'S TOO LATE," Myrtle said as Woof looked up at her from his spot on the carpet. "I should have said something the day after, when there was a chance. But it's been a month"—a month of heartache and agony, interspersed with great joy when she helped Lilah plan her wedding—"and if he had felt anything at all, wouldn't he have come to see me?"

Woof tilted his head.

"You're probably right," she said. "That is, it is very likely he has no feelings about me at all, and whatever happened between us was just"—and she gave an airy wave—"and I should try to forget it myself, as he likely has."

Only she couldn't forget. She remembered all of it—the discomfort when she'd posed for too long, the way he looked at her, like she was the most magnificent cake. How he'd made certain she was comfortable, or nearly comfortable, in any setting. How he'd touched her, both physically and emotionally.

Their time traveling to London together, so long ago, though it was only a couple of months.

"I'll just—"

She stopped speaking when she heard a knock at the door.

"Enter," she said, expecting a maid to inform her as to this evening's dinner time.

Instead, both Richard and Lilah stood at her doorway, each wearing respective determined expressions.

"Can we come in?" Lilah asked, but Richard just walked in like he owned the place. Which he did, to be fair.

"What is it? Is there something wrong with the wedding planning?" Please don't let Mr. Hopper have called it off or anything—seeing Lilah so happy was the only thing keeping her going, after all.

"No, that is all fine, though I do want to ask your opinion on the flowers," Lilah began.

Richard gave his daughter a sharp look, and she clamped her lips together.

"We want to speak to you about something very important," he began, using his most pompous Richard voice.

Myrtle felt a feeling of dread wash over her.

"Go ahead," she said. "Do you want to sit? I'm not sure I want to, but you could, if you like." She gestured vaguely toward her desk chair, one of two in the room.

Richard nodded, drawing the chair out and indicating Lilah should sit. She shook her head no, and he shrugged, taking the seat himself.

"Well?" Myrtle said.

"The important thing is," Richard began, and Myrtle braced herself for whatever he was going to say.

"The important thing is," he repeated, "that you are miserable." He glanced to Lilah, who gave him an encouraging nod. "And we want to ask you something, and we want to know the truth. That is, we know you can't lie anyway, but we want to hear it from you. Have you—did you—fall in love with Mr. Jones?"

Myrtle's eyes widened, and she froze.

"I knew it!" Lilah exclaimed, sounding gleeful. "Didn't I tell you, Father?"

Richard kept his gaze on his sister, and Myrtle felt the resonance of that stare to her very bones.

"If it is true—and I believe it is—you should do something about it."

"Do something?" Myrtle snapped. "Like fall out of love with him?" She rolled her eyes. "It's not as easy as a subtraction problem, brother."

"I know that. I'm not saying that," he replied, and now it sounded as though his tone was . . . kind. Odd. "I'm saying we want you to be happy, and if Mr. Jones would make you happy, we want you to have him." He knitted his brow. "Though you'd have to go tell him, and—"

"You have to tell him," Lilah urged. "What if he meant what he said that night?"

Myrtle shook her head. "He didn't. He's very good at lying."

"We saw his face." Richard shifted in the chair. "We saw his face, and I know he is good at deception, but he isn't that good. We think he was telling the truth, Myrtle. If it turns out we are wrong, then—then you will know. And we will be here to help you, like a good family should."

"Not try to marry me off to someone who

doesn't know Babbage?" Myrtle couldn't resist the dig.

Richard scowled. "I still have no idea who that is, but I support your ability to—to demand any of your husbands meet your standards."

"Any of my—Never mind," Myrtle said hastily. "You mean now you want me to marry Mr. Jones? Even though he comes from unknown parentage and would have control over my money?"

"Yes." Richard met his daughter's gaze, and she gave him another encouraging nod. "We know you are intelligent enough to make your own decisions, and if you end up making a bad one, we also know you are intelligent enough to strategize a way out."

"Oh."

"Also I want him to come to my wedding," Lilah added. "And it would be awkward if you're casting him longing looks during the ceremony."

"I would no—Never mind." Myrtle stopped speaking when she saw their expressions.

Myrtle didn't know how to respond to this. To any of it—to have her stuffy older brother tell her to follow her heart? To have her niece be thinking about someone other than herself for once?

That was a lot to digest.

"Well?" Richard said, impatient. "Are you going to go see him in that studio of his, or are we going to have to listen to you sighing for the rest of your life?"

"I wasn't sighing," Myrtle said, stung.

Both of them gave her pointed looks, and she

deflated. "Fine. I was sighing." She went to her wardrobe and withdrew one of her hats, clapping it on her head. "I'll go now. But just because I don't want either of you to have to hear my unintelligible noises any longer." She raised her chin.

"Thank God," Richard said in a fervent tone.

Myrtle shot him one last glare, then went down the stairs and out the door.

She did love her family. And they had seen how she felt, and responded. That meant the world to her.

Hopefully they wouldn't ask her if Simeon knew who Babbage was, because she was certain he did not.

As certain as she was that she loved him.

SIMEON BEGAN TO run as soon as he was on the street. The sun was just beginning to make its descent into inevitable darkness, but the London streets were still bustling with merchants, sightseers, carriages, carts, and any number of grubby children.

He dodged most of them, though he had a near run-in with a child carrying an errant balloon.

He almost missed seeing her.

She was walking toward him, her usual determined Myrtle expression on her face. She was moving swiftly, and he saw her weave expertly within the crowd. She had learned a few things while in London, at least.

He stopped, for a moment just watching her, until she spotted him and also stopped dead in her tracks.

The two of them stared at one another as the current of London streamed around them.

After a few moments, or possibly a lifetime, Simeon began to move again, making his way purposefully toward her.

She moved also, and then they were together, and he was looking down at her beautiful face, feeling as though his heart was too big for his chest.

"Hello," he said.

"Hello."

Another moment of silence.

"I wanted—"

"I was coming—"

"No, you first," she said.

"Can we—can I escort you to my apartments?" He glanced around. "This doesn't seem like the place to have a conversation."

She nodded, looking as though she was going to say something, but stayed silent. He held his arm out, and she took it, wrapping her arm through his. Even this minor contact felt as though he'd been infused with an electrical current, as though he'd been lying dormant until she touched him.

Dear God, he hoped—well, he hoped. That was all he could articulate, even in his own mind.

"Have you been well?" she said in a strained voice.

"I ha—" he began, then stopped, shaking his head in frustration. "No, I am only going to tell the truth. I have not. I have been terrible. And you?"

"So should I lie, then, I wonder?" she replied.

"If so, I have been wonderful. I have not spent a moment thinking about you, or the time we spent together in your studio, or at parties, or how you taught me how to lie." She turned her face to his. "How am I doing, actually?"

"Excellent."

She frowned. "Is that a lie, or are you speaking the truth?"

"The truth, Myrtle. Always. For always."

"Oh," she said, sounding as though she'd heard some sort of revelation. He hoped she had—he hoped she understood what he was about to say, or—or it wouldn't bear thinking about, but at least he'd have plenty of material for his work: *Artist Pining Away*, or *Hopeless Man Losing More Hope*. That sort of thing.

So there was a bright side to heartache.

They walked the rest of the way in silence, which only meant he could hear the pounding of his heart that much clearer.

They walked up to his rooms, and he took her cloak, then gestured for her to sit. "Do you want to go first, or should I?" he asked.

"You go first," Myrtle said. She felt breathless, as though she'd climbed a mountain, when all she'd done was walk to his home.

When all she'd done was walk arm in arm with the man she loved with her whole heart, unsure if there was a future for them, not certain how she could pivot if this turned out to have a disappointing ending.

So perhaps her breathlessness made sense.

She was perched on the edge of the settee, her hands folded in her lap, though she couldn't keep herself from clasping and unclasping them.

He began to pace in front of her, and for a moment his lithe grace distracted her from the potential for doom—but only for a moment.

"I said earlier I would only speak the truth," he said at last. He twisted his head to meet her gaze. "I am only speaking the truth. I know at the very least we count one another as friends. Can you trust me?"

She considered that. "Yes," she said, inclining her head.

"I was telling the truth that last night also, Myrtle." He'd stopped pacing and now stood directly in front of her, his hands behind his back, his whole body tense and still. "The most important thing to me is your happiness—but I also know I need to speak my heart. My truth."

She had never seen him look so vulnerable before. She imagined his expression was mirrored on her face.

"I know it is not what either one of us wants—wanted—but I have fallen in love with you."

With each word, she felt her eyes widening more and more.

He held his hand out. "Don't say anything just yet. Just—just hear me out."

"Go on," she managed. Though her voice was strained.

"When we met, we spoke about the importance

of cherishing and prizing our talent," he began.
"And I do, I still do, but I have learned from you,
Myrtle. You've taught me the value of reassessing.
Of not accepting that what is now is always what
has to be. You've taught me it's important to re-
consider one's goals, one's life, along the journey."

He knelt in front of her, his beautiful face lifted
to hers. "I love you, Myrtle. The most wonderful
thing about loving you, though, is that I believe
we could have everything. We could have our
life together and we could utilize our innate gifts
to their maximum. I don't think you would ever
stifle my creativity—in fact, I think you'd enhance
it—and I would never do the same to you."

He exhaled, then set his expression. "Would
you do me the honor of loving me, Myrtle?" He
shook his head in frustration. "That love can be
however you want it. I know your natural antipa-
thy to being trapped in marriage. I would never
trap you. I would like to marry you, however, and
more than that, I'd like you to marry me."

She felt as though her heart was going to burst
out of her chest. Like sunlight was streaming out
from her body, only her body was too small to
contain it all.

He moved as though he was going to take her
hand, but stopped himself. "I've spoken nothing
but the truth, Myrtle. I love you. And I trust you
to know what is best for you. So tell me, Myrtle—
what do you want?"

Chapter Twenty-Eight

She didn't speak for a few moments, and Simeon held his breath. Waiting. He would wait forever, if she wished. Though he would have to breathe sometime.

"I want you," she said simply.

He went to rise, but she stayed him with her hand on his shoulder. "I have more to say also. You will have to listen to me as patiently as I listened to you." His imperious Myrtle.

"I have learned a lot from you as well," she said, a slight smile on her lips. "I know how to lie so well that the most deceptive man I know—that is you, by the way—cannot tell I am lying. I was lying that night, Simeon."

She wrinkled her brow in thought. Making her even more adorable than usual. "That is, I told the truth, but I allowed it to be interpreted in a misleading way. I said I have always wanted to live my own life, on my own terms. I am too independent and talented to subsume myself into anybody else. That is true. All of it is true, and I know you feel the same. Any reasonable person should. But what is not true is that I believe I can only achieve that on my own."

She lifted her chin and met his gaze. "In fact, I think I would be better able to do all of it with you at my side." She took a deep breath. "With you as my husband."

She didn't stop him this time when he leapt up, grabbing her in his arms and taking her mouth in a kiss. She wrapped her arms around him and made an enthusiastic noise, deep in her throat, as she kissed him back with as much alacrity as he might want.

Eventually, they broke apart, gasping.

"You really love me? Even though I don't know who Babbage is, much less what his relevance might be?"

Her lips twisted into a smirk. "I can teach you about Babbage. Because you are curious, and open-minded, and will consider my opinion and my thoughts." She smiled wider. "Because I love you. I trust you. And I want you."

Simeon didn't know who started it, but an hour or so later they were both naked, lying tangled on the settee, with clothing flung everywhere. It felt as though he was on the precipice of a new kind of life, one where he could be in love and not lose an iota of his promise. In fact, it felt as though his promise was enhanced because she would be by his side.

"And now," she said, breaking through his haze of bliss, "let me tell you about Mr. Babbage."

Epilogue

Six Months Later

"His work is stupendous," Aunt Flora enthused.

Myrtle smiled at the other woman, who'd arrived with many other of Myrtle's clients. Once the Season was over, and Lilah was married off with great ceremony—and several slices of delicious cake—Myrtle had focused most of her attention on setting up her new enterprise. Business was going well, and while she now had access to all her money—as promised, Richard had released it once she and Simeon were married—they actually didn't need it. That meant that her softhearted husband was able to fully fund every single request that came to him, and it was wonderful to see his pleasure at doing so much good for so many others with her money. He and Phoebe had been corresponding regularly, and he'd adapted to his older brother role quite well.

In addition, he had held a series of private viewings for several art experts in London, and it had become a heated battle for which gallery would exhibit his painting, *Artemisia Leads Her Men into Battle*.

Today was the first day of the exhibition, and the gallery was overflowing with attendees, and several of Simeon's paintings on exhibition had already been sold.

"How are you, wife?" Simeon asked, sliding his arm around her waist.

Myrtle looked up at him, still amazed that this beautiful man was hers. They'd gotten married in a quiet ceremony two months earlier, and every day since then had been a delight. Simeon was as proud of her work as she was of his, and they spent their days working in their own rooms in their new house, which was situated very close to Mr. Finneas's Fine Establishment where Simeon had had his rooms.

They spent their nights together, sometimes entertaining one or more of the Bastard Five, other times just by themselves. Woof was their constant companion, and everything just felt . . . right.

"I am excellent," Myrtle replied. She indicated the crowd. "And it seems you are excellent as well, husband."

He smiled at her, and for a moment it felt as though they truly were the only two people in the world, as she'd said when they'd traveled to London together so many months ago.

"If we were the only two people in the world," he murmured, accurately reading her thoughts, "we would have nobody to admire our brilliance."

She laughed, and he leaned down to give her a quick kiss, causing Aunt Flora and the other ladies to make cooing noises.

"I love you," she said in a low voice.

"I love you," he replied.

EXPLORE MEGAN FRAMPTON'S TITLES

— SCHOOL FOR SCOUNDRELS SERIES —

— HAZARDS OF DUKES SERIES —

THE DUKE'S DAUGHTERS SERIES —